The Undergrounders
&
the Deception of the Dead

C T Frankcom

First edition November 2019

Front cover design by Sam Waters.

Graphics from www.pexels.com, www.Brusheezy.com

Inside cover illustration by C.T. Frankcom

Special thanks to T.Frankcom, T & J Shardlow and M & J Frankcom.

Other titles in this series:

The Undergrounders & the Flight of the
Falcon

The Undergrounders & the Malice of the
Moth

For Tim x

Anonymous

From: Anonymous
To: J21
Re: Bird of Prey {Encrypted}

I see that the bird you had been so carefully monitoring has slipped through your poorly constructed net and not only released his flock but escaped with some precious cargo.

I handed him to you on a plate, yet a thirteen-year old boy could see things more clearly than your whole unit. Your entire operation is a disgrace.

Here's a piece of hard-earned advice: you need to look more closely at your own flock. You need to decide who you can trust and who you cannot.

I will be in touch. You are not the only one who would quite happily see the bird of prey caged for good.

End.

From: J21
To: Anonymous
Re: Bird of Prey {Encrypted}

Who are you?
How did you get this comms address?

End.

From: Anonymous
To: J21
Re: Bird of Prey {Encrypted}

It doesn't matter who I am – what matters is that I know where you can find her.
Await my instructions.

End.

Chapter 1: Tormented

The fine, icy spray swept across George's face. He could feel it stinging his eyes and burning his open cuts. He was flat on his back – every limb felt broken. The water slapped at his feet and then rolled towards his head as the ground beneath him seemed to sway and rock. His ears were submerged again, and the screaming and groaning returned. He could hear her voice – calling for help, "George!"

I must save her.

The water rose with every new wave.

She will drown.

He shivered and tried to open his eyes, but the salty water forced them closed again. In a flicker, he could see them circling above – the birds. With greedy eyes and razor talons, they were waiting to take their prey as soon as it was weak enough.

George strained against the weight of his sodden clothes, dug in his heels and pushed hard at the debris at his feet. He turned. There, protruding from the shallow, sandy grave, was a thin fragile arm. Her head was turned towards him, and her fine hair was plastered to her damp face.

"Gran!"

As he heaved himself up, his legs felt like jelly; his feet sank into the soft, flowing sand. He dragged one foot and then the next, but fell to his knees – she felt no closer. However hard he tried, she remained just beyond his reach. He screamed her name again, and her eyes peered up at him – her soft, warm eyes.

A shadow descended, covering the bay in darkness. George looked up. They were coming: giant falcons, swooping down, talons bared, coming to take her away.

No! Leave her! Leave her alone!

George raised his arms. The gun was clamped in his trembling fist. He wanted to drop it, but his fingers were frozen rigid. It felt heavy and the metal seared his skin.

No, I won't! I won't do it!

He tried to shake the weapon from his grip, but she was screaming again, louder and louder.

"George! George! George…"

"George! George, wake up!"

George woke. Sweat trickled down his forehead. The bed felt like it was still swaying. He steadied himself and looked into his dad's puffy eyes.

"You fell asleep," his dad whispered, his voice hoarse. "It's gone midday."

George and Sam had barely slept since she'd been taken. It had been five days that had merged into one long nightmare. Five days of people George didn't know coming and going from the house. Five days of fear, false hopes and grasping at fitful sleep. Five days with barely any news.

Sam's mood was the darkest George had ever seen: his eyes sunken, his untrimmed beard burying his tense jaw and his temper at its most explosive. And yet, he had spent more time with George in those five days than at any other time in George's memory.

Sam sank down onto the end of George's bed.

"Have you heard anything?" George asked, sitting up and rubbing the crust from his eyes.

He was still in his clothes. His hair was beyond help, and his head still ached from the blow he'd taken while being held hostage by the same gang that now had his gran. The pain was a constant reminder to him of what Victor Sokolov and his crew were capable of, and he knew that as every day slipped past, Gran was likely to be in more and more danger.

"Nothing, George. I'm sorry," Sam said, his head in his hands. "The last report we had was yesterday's. We haven't managed to pick up the trail since we had to drop it at Dover. We have to believe he won't hurt her if we don't try to follow them."

"But, Dad, if he's taken her over the Channel, we'll never know where she is … We need to … You must keep following."

"We have to trust the team. They know what they're doing."

MI5 had brought in a specialist team to try to track Victor's movements. It had proven almost impossible, as Victor's crew had split up. No one really knew where Gran was, and George could feel her slipping further and further away from him. He swung his legs over the side of the bed and sat beside his dad.

"What about Philippe and Mr Jefferson?" George asked. "They must know something."

"Freddie is pushing them as hard as he can, but they're not talking," Sam replied, his head still buried in his hands.

George looked at his dad. He'd never seen him this dejected. He could see a shadow of how he must have been when George's mum had died. Gran had once told George that his dad hadn't come out of his shed for almost three weeks after they announced her death.

George knew that Sam was blaming himself for Gran being taken, but he couldn't understand why he wasn't out there searching for her.

"Dad, *you* should interrogate them," George said, hoping that he could nudge him into action.

"I can't," Sam replied, finally looking up. "They won't let me. It's too … personal."

"There must be something they can do to force them to talk."

George was frustrated. He was sure that Philippe and his old form tutor, Mr Jefferson, must know where the agreed rendezvous point was. He couldn't stop picturing Gran tied up, frightened and somewhere far away from Chiddingham.

With that, Marshall peered around the corner of George's bedroom door. He looked more bedraggled than ever and had lost weight. George had forgotten to feed him for the first three days, until he'd found the cat tearing at the cupboard door that held his kibble.

Marshall slunk over to George's bed and wound his way through George and Sam's ankles. George lifted him onto the pillow and smoothed his scruffy fur. He didn't have much affection for the cat, but somehow he felt closer to Gran when Marshall was around. Sam must have felt it too, because he suddenly stood up.

"I can't sit here any longer doing nothing," he said, striding from the room.

"What are you going to do?" George asked, jumping up and following him out onto the landing.

"I'm going into the office. We need to take you in for your debrief, anyway. I'll go and see Freddie and the chief."

"Great!" cried George, bounding down the stairs behind him.

"You're right, George. We need to put more pressure on Philippe and Jefferson. I'll camp outside the interrogation room if I have to."

Sam made his way down the corridor, but George stopped at the bottom of the stairs and stared at the small pinprick on the back of the front door where the note from Victor had been left. He could see the tip of the yellow tape that had barred them from the house while forensics had scoured the place. The dusted fingerprints still remained on the glossy paintwork. The lock had been changed, but the wood was still splintered, and standing behind the door, George could almost feel the fear that Gran must have felt as someone forced their way into her home.

Sam had come back down the corridor. He placed his hands on George's shoulders. "Are you OK?"

"We need to sort out the door," George said.

He could feel the tears coming again, but he tried to shake them off.

"We need to leave it all as it is," Sam said. "There could still be clues here – clues as to who took her."

"It was Victor!" George spat. "He barged into our home and–"

"Wait! That's it!" Sam said, staring at the door. "Victor didn't come back here!"

"What?"

"Of course! How did I not see it? Victor wasn't here – none of them were here!"

"But how…"

"He must have sent someone else … there's someone else, George!" Sam yelled, charging back down the hallway towards the kitchen. "They wouldn't have risked coming here and getting caught, especially once they'd got away with the weapon. There must be someone else!"

With that, Sam disappeared through the back door and out towards his shed.

"Get washed and dressed," he called back over his shoulder. "You smell!"

George didn't need asking twice. He hosed himself down, combed his hair and put on fresh clothes. He dumped the tracksuit bottoms and t-shirt, that he'd been wearing for two days straight, into the laundry basket. It was almost full. Gran would usually keep on top of all that kind of stuff. George looked away. He couldn't imagine them coping without her. He grabbed his hoodie from the back of his chair and dashed back downstairs.

When he entered the kitchen, Sam was sitting at the breakfast bar hunched over a small handheld device, just larger than a phone. He was swigging black coffee.

"I've put toast and beans on," he said, not looking up. "We need to eat."

George agreed. They'd survived on minimal snacks to stave off the hunger pangs but hadn't eaten a real meal in five days.

George stirred the beans and buttered the toast. He rummaged in the fridge and found a carton of long-life orange juice. The milk had gone bad. He poured two glasses of juice, served the beans and sat next to his dad and ate.

George peered over his dad's shoulder at the device in his hand, but the screen was blank.

"Er, Dad, are you OK?" he asked, worried that his dad had gone mad.

"Huh?"

"It's just, you've been staring at that blank screen for more than five minutes and—"

Sam chuckled. "It's not blank, George, see."

Sam turned the device towards him. When looking at it straight on, you could see a dim black and green screen. George looked puzzled.

"It's a surveillance tablet," Sam said. "To anyone else it looks like a normal smartphone, but you can only view the data from a certain angle. Stops people being nosey and reading over your shoulder," he explained, raising an eyebrow in George's direction.

"Oh, sorry, I just…"

"It's OK. I'm just looking through a list of Victor's associates and their last known locations. I think there must be someone else involved. Someone that Victor thinks we wouldn't suspect. Someone who could have easily come into Chiddingham without raising any suspicions."

"Right, makes sense," George said. "Got any leads?" Sam raised an eyebrow again, and George sighed. "Of course – you can't tell me, right?"

"Afraid not."

"Maybe I could help. Maybe I saw someone when we were in London."

"Well, that's what today's debrief should help us find out. Are you ready?"

"Yes, definitely," George said, sliding off his stool and dumping his empty plate in the sink.

George left some water and snacks out for Marshall who seemed grateful enough. He grabbed his newly cut keys and made his way to the front door. Sam was heaving on his heavy boots and had pulled his faded blue cap on. They both glanced at Gran's well-worn armchair as they passed the lounge door. Without saying another word, they left the cottage behind them and clambered into Sam's van.

As they pulled out of the village, George realised that he had no idea where his dad's office was.

"Are we going to London?" he asked.

"No, I don't spend much time at HQ. I have a … regional office," Sam said carefully. "But it's not a publicly known location, so I can't take you there, I'm afraid."

"So, where has Freddie got Jefferson and Philippe?"

"Ah, I can't tell you that either."

"But I thought we were going to—"

"I said I'd take you in for your debrief and then I'll go and see Freddie. I've arranged for you to meet a colleague of mine, Officer Knowles, at the Pendleton police station."

"Right – of course." George said, sliding down in his seat.

Now that he knew about his dad's job at MI5, he hated being left out. He had barely paid any interest when he thought his dad was a self-employed plumber. Sam was never around, and their relationship had been fragile at best. Now that he knew, he felt much closer to him, but there seemed to be even more secrets, and George hated it. He felt like he could never fully be part of his dad's life.

"I'm sorry," Sam said, noticing George's mood change. "I do trust you, you know that, right?"

"I know, Dad. Just promise me you'll do everything you can to find her. I can't bear another day not knowing where she is."

"Me too, George."

They drove the rest of the way in silence, and before long, they pulled up to the security barrier outside the small police station. It was manned by a female security guard who was slumped on a rather uncomfortable looking chair with her feet propped up on the window ledge of her small hut. Sam had to honk the horn to get her attention.

She held up her hand to acknowledge them but continued to read her book. Sam honked his horn again. She finally lifted her head, put down her book and strolled over to Sam's van.

"Can I help you?" she said, leaning in through the window and peering around the cab.

"About time," Sam grumbled. "Are we disturbing you?"

George cringed. His dad's patience was at its thinnest, but the guard had obviously heard it all before.

"Do you want to be let in?" she asked, frostily.

Sam's nostrils flared. "We're here for an appointment with Officer Cate Knowles."

"Right, one minute," she said, sauntering back to her hut.

She rifled through a pile of paperwork on her desk. Sam tutted and shook his head. George was pretty sure she would have heard, but she chose to ignore him. Finally, she found what she was looking for and made her way back over.

"Name?" she said, peering down at her crumpled piece of paper.

"Jenkins," Sam said, curtly.

"Yes, here you are. Go through and park anywhere on the left. Not the red spaces!"

Sam closed the window and put his foot down, almost taking out the slowly rising barrier.

"You OK, Dad?" George asked, as they parked up.

"Yes, just can't abide time-wasters," he grumbled. "Let's get you inside."

They were buzzed into a small lobby filled with plastic chairs. A friendly old man at the front desk signed them in and called Officer Knowles.

George suddenly realised that he was actually quite anxious about his interview. He hadn't thought about it, or much about what had happened in London, since Gran had disappeared – maybe because he didn't want to. Now he was going to have to go through it all step by step.

"Will you come in with me?" he asked Sam.

"If you want me to," Sam said, as they perched on the plastic seats. "But there's nothing to be worried about. You're not being interrogated. Cate's job is to document everything that you can remember about what happened. That's all."

Just then, a set of internal doors swung open and a young woman in a smart, navy suit stepped out. She made her way towards them, smiling.

"I don't need you to stay," George said, suddenly standing up and striding towards Officer Knowles.

"Are you sure?" Sam called after him.

"Yes, I want you to go and nail Philippe and Jefferson!"

From: J21
To: Anonymous
Re: Bird of Prey {Encrypted}

Why haven't I heard from you?
You said you knew where she was.
If you are serious about helping us, I need to know what
intel you have.

End.

Chapter 2: Adrift

George sat with Officer Knowles for over four hours, only stopping once for a loo break and a small snack. The room was cold (which she apologised for several times), so he kept his coat on. She said he could call her Cate and spoke gently, letting him do most of the talking. Another lady sat in the room with them but said nothing. She was introduced to him, but he'd forgotten her name. All he remembered was that she was some kind of chaperone.

George struggled to keep his mind focused. He tried to recall everything that had happened from the day he had delivered the paper to (the now deceased) Mrs Hodge, through to his dad entering the cave and saving him from Victor. It was amazing how quickly some of the details had blurred in his head.

"It's OK, George. Take your time. It's alright if you can't remember everything," Cate said, as he glazed over again. "Do you need another break?"

"Huh? No, no – I'm fine."

In truth, he wasn't even thinking about that day. He was thinking about whether his dad had managed to get to Philippe and Jefferson.

"Shall we talk about what happened after you got home?" Cate asked, her expression soft.

"Why?" George said, a little more abruptly than he'd intended.

She sat back in her chair and closed her folder.

"I know it's painful, George, but maybe there's something about the house, the scene when you came home, that might give us a clue as to who entered your home and took…"

"Does it really matter?" he said. "It was Victor. It was all Victor. Even if it wasn't him in the house, it was his idea!"

"I think that's enough for today," the other woman said, rising from her seat.

Cate nodded.

"You've done brilliantly, George. You've given us so much," she said, smiling. "I can't imagine how hard this is for you."

"I'm sorry," he said, sighing. "If I think of anything else, I'll…"

"You can call me, anytime. Your dad has my number. I'll call him now and let him know that we're done."

They shook hands, and George followed the other woman back out of the double doors and into the lobby. She deposited him in the entrance hall and left him with some leaflets on witness support. He didn't look at them. He wanted to call his dad. Instinctively, he shoved his hand into his jacket pocket to grab his mobile but quickly remembered that Mr Jefferson had taken it, and it was now sitting in an evidence bag somewhere within the confines of MI5.

Bored, restless and impatient to hear news, he got up and stared out of the window. He was about to ask the old guy behind the reception desk to borrow the phone, when the front doors opened and Felix bounded in.

"Felix!" George exclaimed.

"George! Where have you been? You've gone radio silent on me," Felix said, grabbing him and nearly knocking him over with his embrace.

George had been so lost in his own world that he'd barely thought of anyone else. Felix didn't even know about Gran.

"Man … I … how are you?"

He wasn't sure what he could tell Felix. Felix was the only one who had been there when Victor and his gang had escaped and the only one who knew that Sam worked for MI5. But he didn't know about the stolen weapon or about anything that had happened since.

"I'm good – you know – got my bandages off," Felix said, raising his hands up to show George. "Your face still looks pretty smashed up."

George grimaced. "Yeah, guess so." That was the least of his worries.

"At least that makes me the better looking one now," Felix grinned.

George grinned back. "It's really good to see you. What are you here for?"

"I thought of some stuff I'd forgotten to mention to Officer Knowles. You?"

"Like what?" George asked, intrigued.

"Stuff I saw in the woods after I left you in the tunnels."

"Really?"

"Yeah, I got lost on my way back to school and now remember seeing a burnt-out fire. I thought it was weird because I figured: who'd be down there doing a fire?"

"What, like a bonfire?"

"I didn't stop to check it out, but it looked like burnt paper – not wood."

"Mr Patterson?" Cate had returned. "I can see you now."

"Gotta' go," Felix said, slapping George on the back.

"Yeah, of course. Call me later," George said, as he watched Felix disappearing through the double doors.

"Sure thing," Felix called back. "You've gotta' answer the phone though, mate."

George and Sam's phone had been redirected via a secure line to tap any incoming calls. All calls were being screened by MI5. They had left a daily log with Sam, but neither of them had looked at it. Poor Felix must have thought he'd been ignoring him.

The doors flew open again, and Sam stormed in. He looked like he'd had a bad day.

"Dad," George said, "what happened at–"

"Let's go," Sam said, making his way back out of the doors.

George had to run to catch up with him. He barely managed to pull himself into the cab of the van before Sam pulled off. He was struggling to get his seatbelt on as they exited the car park and careered around a corner. He nearly ended up on Sam's lap.

"Dad, slow down," George said. "What happened?"

"Nothing!" Sam shouted. "Precisely nothing!"

"Did you see Philippe and–"

"Eventually, after a lot of begging."

"Well, what did they say?"

"Ten minutes I got with them each. Liars – both of them, bare-faced liars!"

Sam nearly took out the back of a bus. He swerved, throwing George's head against the window.

"Ow!"

Sam slammed on the brakes – red light. He looked over at George who was rubbing his temple.

"Oh God, sorry, George … I'm so sorry … I…"

He was trembling.

"It's OK, Dad. I understand. I feel the same way."

With that, Sam's eyes filled with tears.

"I've let you down. I've let everyone down. I've let Gran down…"

George had never seen his dad cry. His face was in his hands. George could feel his own eyes welling up. Seeing his dad break down was too much.

Sam's phone buzzed. He lifted his head, wiped his face with his sleeve and looked down at it. His eyes widened as they scanned back and forth over the message. He threw the phone down, yanked the van into reverse and did a full U-turn in the middle of the junction. Several cars had to skid to a halt as Sam's beaten up van veered across the oncoming traffic. They must have looked like convicts on the run.

"Dad, what's going on?" George asked, gripping tightly to the cab's side handle as they weaved between the traffic at top speed. "Dad!"

"I know where she is!"

George's heart skipped a beat. "How? How do you know?"

"A tip off – hold on tight."

They raced back through town and out onto the motorway. Sam broke every traffic law, making several fellow drivers throw curses and hand gestures at them as they passed. Sam didn't say another thing until they eventually pulled up to the entrance of the Dungeness National Nature Reserve.

George peered out of the window. It was late and there wasn't another soul for as far as the eye could see. The flat, sparse marshland extended all the way to the sea. The barren landscape was littered with crumbling outhouses and abandoned rowing boats, and a rusting train line swept across the shingled bay. The horizon was only interrupted by a couple of lighthouses and the imposing outline of the

Dungeness Nuclear Power Station. George wasn't sure what made it special enough to be a nature reserve.

"Here? Is she here?" George whispered, barely able to breathe. "There's no one here, Dad."

Sam was looking down at his phone again. "Yes, at least – let's hope so."

"Are you sure?"

"I need you to stay in the van," Sam suddenly said, looking up.

"No, I want to come with you."

"No, please, George, stay here. I don't know what I'll find."

Sam opened the door and leapt out. George twisted and watched him disappear to the back of the van. He could hear him rummaging around in the back before the rear doors slammed shut again and he re-appeared at George's window.

"Take the keys and this spare phone," he said. "If I'm not back in fifteen minutes, call Freddie. His number is in the contacts under C38."

"What? But–"

"Lock the doors and stay here."

George watched his dad as he ran across the flat scrubland, past a cluster of crumbling sheds and off towards the waterline.

Ten, fifteen minutes passed. He peered out of the front windscreen – no sign of his dad, no movement at the water's edge. Heavy clouds raced across the fading skyline. George's brain whirred. He fidgeted.

Where is he? Is she there? Is she alive?

Giving in to his anxiety, he picked up the phone, but just as he was about to dial, lights appeared down at the water's edge. He could make out someone's silhouette and a boat. A boat was steaming across the water towards the dark figure. Unable to contain his fear any longer, he burst from the van and raced out across the flats, hurdling over large areas of scrub and skipping around a couple of old fishing boats, not once letting his eyes stray from the source of light.

As he got closer, he could make out two figures, and the boat had hit land. He ran harder, his ankles turning as his footing slid in the deep shingle. Twenty metres to go – he could now see the Coast Guard's flag hanging from the back of the boat and Sam – he could see Sam and a small dinghy – a black, rubber boat. It had been thrown up onto a ridge of stones.

George slowed. An arm hung over the side of the dinghy – a small, frail arm. He couldn't move. His breathing sharp and broken, he could feel the tears and the panic rising in him. He tried to call out to his dad.

"Is she alive?"

But his words were lost in the wind as the air above blasted him like a tornado. He ducked, just as a helicopter swooped overhead. It turned a full 180 degrees and descended further up the beach, its searchlight casting a glaring arch across the bay and its rotors whipping up stones and grass. George covered his eyes.

The wind dropped as the rotors stilled, and George stared at the scene ahead of him. Bodies surrounded the dinghy. Someone had climbed in beside her. George's eyes stayed firmly fixed on her fingers. He prayed for any sign of movement, but there was none. Someone moved into his line of sight. He edged forwards – one step and then another until he could see her. So pale and small, her tiny frame was engulfed by a large, silver blanket. Only her face was now exposed. It was ghostly white, and the shadow of a bruise swamped her left cheek.

George's chest was shuddering. He dared not believe that she was dead even though every fibre of his body feared it to be true. He stood paralysed, a useless by-stander, as the medics and coast guard hooked her up to mobile monitors and wrapped another blanket around her. He could feel himself floating inside his own head. He felt dizzy.

"George!" It was Sam. "George, look at me."

George looked up. "Dad, is she…"

"She's in a bad way – hyperthermia at the very least – but she's with us now."

"Will she be OK?"

"We'll get her the best care. We won't let anything bad happen, George, I promise," Sam said, engulfing him in a hug.

George couldn't fight back the tears any longer – relief and fear. He buried his face and stifled a scream. All he could picture was her tiny, limp body and the anger seared inside him. He looked up as they lifted her onto the stretcher. As he closed his eyes again, Victor's face floated into his vision – his dark, soulless eyes – his rough, scarred hands – the menacing falcon tattoo that covered half of his shaven head. In that moment, George silently swore to himself that he would stop at nothing to make Victor pay.

From: J21
To: Anonymous
Re: Bird of Prey {Encrypted}

Thank you.

End.

From: Anonymous
To: J21
Re: Bird of Prey {Encrypted}

This is only just the beginning.
We have a bird to catch.

End.

Chapter 3: Time to Heal

George came to. He was too hot and the air smelt of bandages and disinfectant. He tried to shift his position but was buried beneath a thick woollen blanket and wedged into a battered, old, leather chair. The room was dark, but he could make out the outline of Gran's features silhouetted against the glare from her monitors.

He had slept deep and long, but he ached from being crammed into the confines of the chair. One leg was hanging over the armrest and had gone dead – he couldn't feel his toes. He tried to lift it, but it was as if all the muscles and bones had melted away, leaving him with a jelly-like stump that refused to move.

He tried to wiggle his toes. Slowly, he could feel a tiny tingling in his foot. It stung and prickled like a thousand needles, but he continued to urge it back to life. The sensation crept up his shin until, finally, he could swing it back over the armrest and onto the floor.

"Gran," he whispered. "Gran, are you awake?"

She didn't stir. He glanced over at the monitors. Everything looked normal, as far as he could tell.

They had been camped out at the Fort Monckton Military base for two days. Sam had insisted that she was taken there. It was a Secret Service training centre, and he wanted her under 24/7 protection. The hospital wing was tiny and basic, but the staff had treated her like royalty.

George had barely left her side since they'd let him in to see her. The previous five days had been the worst in his life. It was the longest time he'd been without her. With the exception of the odd night out with her friends, she was always there: pottering around the kitchen, tidying his room, snoozing on the sofa with Marshall curled up in her lap.

She had come to take care of a six-year-old George when his mother had died, and she'd lived with them ever since. However, George didn't know any different as he'd been brought up by his gran from day one. His mum had gone back to work soon after he was born, and all his young memories were of him and Gran. Going to the park, learning to read, trips to the zoo; it was all with Gran.

George was about to get up from his seat when he heard his dad's voice outside the door.

"She's stable, but it was touch and go," Sam said under his breath.

"Has she said much?" a woman asked.

George recognised her soft voice. It was Cate Knowles.

"Not much. She came to last night but was disorientated. The nurses just wanted to keep her calm and comfortable."

"Makes sense. There's no rush. As soon as she's ready, I'm more than happy to sit with her."

"Any other progress?" Sam asked. "Did we get anything at all from George and his friends?"

"We got lots of detailed insights, and they all pretty much married up. With that, and the snippets of CCTV from the vault, Scotland Yard and the hub, we can pretty much pull together the whole timeline."

"What about the abduction? Do we have anything on who broke into my house?"

"Your hidden cameras were taken out. Whoever entered had done their homework. They disabled all your surveillance."

"Who the hell?"

George could hear the frustration in his dad's voice.

"Sam, listen. Felix Patterson, George's friend, he told us about a fire."

"Right."

"We found it, in the grounds of the school, not far from where the tyre tracks were."

"And?" Sam pressed.

"We've gathered up all of the burnt debris. Forensics are piecing it together as best they can. It's gonna' take a while, but from what we can see it's letters, documents and the remnants of a red bag," Cate whispered. "Does that mean anything to you?"

George could barely make out what Cate was saying. He leaned over the armrest, towards the door. With that, an alarm sounded and George toppled clean out of the chair. Just as he was picking himself up from the floor, a nurse dashed in and flicked the lights on, quickly followed by Cate and Sam.

"What's going on?" cried Sam.

George peered around the nurse. Gran was sat bolt upright in bed.

"Well," the nurse said, "your mother has removed her cardio monitor."

"Gran!" George was by her side in a heartbeat.

"Good morning, my gorgeous boy," she said, smiling so broadly that her whole face creased up like a soft, overly-ripe peach.

"Take it easy," the nurse said, reattaching her to the monitor. "I think we should keep this on for a bit."

"I'm perfectly fine thank you, young lady," Gran insisted. "There's no need to fuss over me."

"Just take it easy," Sam said, moving around to the other side of the bed.

"I must have done something special to have both my boys at my bedside," she said, as the nurse propped her up with pillows.

George smiled but glanced at his dad. He was worried that she had no memory of what had happened.

"I'm not sure 'special' is the word I'd use," Sam said. "How are you feeling?"

"Wonderful," she said, beaming at him.

"Do you know why you're here?"

"Well, I assume it has something to do with this," she said, holding up her bandaged wrists.

George glanced at his dad again. Sam was looking uneasy.

"Mum, I think that – I'm sorry but–"

"Let's give your mum some space," Cate said, stepping forwards. "There's plenty of time to talk once she's got used to her surroundings. We'll go grab some breakfast. I'm sure the nurses need some time with her right now."

Sam nodded. As Cate ushered George and Sam out of the warm room, George looked back over his shoulder and couldn't help smiling as Gran turned and winked at him.

"Do you think she remembers anything?" Sam asked, as they wandered down to the canteen.

"It's early days," Cate said. "She'll be confused and in shock. It may be a blessing if she doesn't remember everything."

They grabbed a coffee and some bacon sandwiches. The officers' mess was busy with trainees. George stood out like a sore thumb. Several quizzical stares were being thrown his way.

"But she's the only witness," Sam said, as they sat down with their trays. "With Philippe and Jefferson refusing to talk, it's our only other lead. If we can find out who broke in that night, then we might be able to track them down and–"

"Sam, leave it to me. I think it's best if I conduct the de-brief."

George couldn't help noticing that Cate had placed her hand on Sam's and his dad's shoulders had visibly eased at her touch.

"Thanks, Cate," Sam said. "I just want her to feel safe. We mustn't let her know that the threat is still out there."

"It's OK. We'll stick to the story. She doesn't need to know more than absolutely necessary."

Sam squeezed Cate's hand. "I know you'll look after her."

"A-hum!" George coughed. "What story?"

He felt invisible and slightly awkward at the chemistry between his dad and Cate.

"We'll find out what Gran knows first, and then we'll tell her it was a case of mistaken identity – a drug vendetta gone wrong," Sam said.

George frowned. "Will she fall for that?"

"I can't exactly tell her she was kidnapped as a personal revenge attack on her own son. How would I explain that one?" Sam said.

"I guess," George said, but he was sure Gran would have her suspicions. She always saw straight through him whenever he tried to lie his way out of trouble.

It was another twenty-four hours before they were allowed to bring Gran home. Her memory was slowly returning, and Cate had sat with her for a good part of her last day in the hospital, but Cate had updated Sam in private, much to George's frustration.

As the unmarked ambulance pulled up behind them, outside their cottage, George looked over at his dad.

"Will she be OK?" he asked, worried that going back home would trigger more unpleasant memories. "We should have cleaned up the door."

"I got it done," Sam said, climbing out of the van. "I've had all new locks, cameras, alarm and a new door put in. There's no evidence left to remind her."

"Good," George said.

He was keen for everything to go back to normal but knew that things would never really be the same.

It didn't take long to get Gran settled back in. She acted as if nothing had happened. George kept asking her if she was OK to which she always replied, 'Right as rain, my boy.'

Marshall had been fed by one of Sam's colleagues that had been fixing up the house and looked like he'd put on a few pounds. He struggled to leap up onto Gran's armchair but quickly retook his place on her lap, purring loudly.

After a few days, Sam told George that he was planning on going back to work. "Now remember, you must text me if you need to go out. I don't want her left here on her own for too long."

"We'll be fine, Dad, honestly. I'll look after her." George reassured him. "Are you allowed near Philippe and Jefferson now?"

"Maybe," Sam whispered.

He was eager for Gran not to overhear them talking about the case, but George figured she couldn't hear a thing with the TV up so loud.

Gran had given a pretty good account of the night she was kidnapped, but the attacker had managed to creep into the kitchen, knock her out and smother her in a hood. There was little chance of getting a positive ID from her statement, so they were back to pressing Philippe and Jefferson for leads.

George had been thinking about what he had heard in the hospital. Something had been nagging at him.

"Dad, I wondered whether we should look into that post van? You know, the one that nearly ran us off the road that night," he said, tentatively.

"Hmm, I looked into it already, but it wasn't linked to a person of interest."

"But maybe the stuff that Felix saw – burnt letters and a red bag and–"

"You been earwigging?" Sam said, frowning.

"Er, I just overheard you and Cate…"

"George, I appreciate your input, but really, you need to focus on getting ready to go back to school."

"But, Dad–"

"I mean it, George. You've done more than enough to help."

That was the end of the conversation. Sam made his way out to his shed. With Sam back at work and school restarting, George knew that their time together would go back to how it was before – intermittent, at best.

It was Monday morning, and George had one more day to get himself sorted before school restarted on Tuesday, including buying new uniform and shoes. The burnt-out east wing of the school had been cordoned off, and Mrs

Hamilton, the Headmistress, had managed to arrange to borrow a few pre-fab buildings to be trucked in to make up for the lost space. Letters had been sent out to all parents informing them of all the new safety measures that had been put in place to stop anything like this from happening again. Plenty of rumours had circulated about what had caused the fire – none of them true.

George opened one eye and nearly leapt out of his skin. Gran was sitting at the end of his bed staring at him.

"Sorry, gorgeous boy," she whispered, "didn't want to wake you. You looked so peaceful."

"What time is it?"

"Gone ten, Georgie. You've got errands to run."

"Er, yeah. I've gotta' go and get my new school stuff," he said, dragging himself from under his bed sheets.

"You want me to come with you?" she asked, standing up and straightening out his duvet.

"No, it's fine, Gran. I'm meeting Felix. You'll be alright here for a bit – on your own?"

"I won't be alone. I've got Marshall," she giggled, leaning down to pick up the clothes that he'd dumped on the floor.

It felt so good to have her there, safe, back home and fussing over him. But as she straightened up, George's eyes fell to the scars on her ankles, and the anger rose up in him. He bit his lip.

"Leave that, Gran, I'll do it," he said, rising to his feet.

She beamed at him. "Well, why don't you get yourself ready, and I'll pop on some porridge."

"You should be resting."

"Oh – no need to fuss over your old gran. I'm absolutely fine."

"But, Gran, the doctor said–"

"He knows nothing," she said, tutting.

"But what you've been through – please, Gran, just take it easy."

"I'm much tougher than I look," she said, bundling up his laundry.

As she shuffled from the room, she stopped and turned to look at him. "You know, George, scars fade – even the ones on the inside."

But George wasn't sure that that was true.

"Breakfast's ready!" Gran called, ten minutes later. "Get it while it's hot."

George stumbled out of his room and was surprised to see his dad on the landing.

"Dad! Why are you still here?"

"Good morning to you too," Sam said, pulling his faded blue cap from his back pocket and shoving it on his head.

He looked like he'd hardly slept.

"I just thought you'd be in the office already."

"Shh! Quiet, George. Gran's up."

"But I thought you were interrogating Mr Jefferson today," George whispered, "and I just–"

"That's enough!"

With that, he pulled his cap down lower and disappeared down the stairs.

Sulking, George lumbered down the stairs after him and almost tripped over Marshall, who was loitering in the hall. He was slowly returning to his normal, obnoxious self, now that Gran was home. George scooped him up and carried him towards the kitchen.

Sam was trying to eat his steaming porridge while fumbling with his phone. He almost dropped it into his bowl. Gran shook her head as she passed him and winked at George.

"You never were any good at doing two things at once, Samuel," she said, handing George his breakfast.

"I've got to go," Sam said, ditching his bowl.

"Of course, taps and boilers can't wait," Gran chirped.

George smiled and watched his dad leave, his face still buried in his phone, his frown as bevelled as always.

After breakfast, George went upstairs to change. Felix was due to meet him in Pendleton at midday. He was just combing his hair when he heard a knock at the front door. He froze. He could hear Gran's voice. He dropped the comb and raced to the top of the stairs. She was standing outside. Someone was there. George could see their shadow on the hallway wall. He bombed down the stairs and reached the bottom just as she turned and stepped back inside.

"Who was that?" George said, trying to peer around the door.

"Just the postman, Georgie," she said. "No need for alarm."

"The postman?"

"Yes, you know, the man that delivers the post."

"Why did he knock at the door?"

"He had a parcel, I think."

"What parcel?"

"Wrong address," she said, shuffling back down the hallway.

George re-opened the door and peered out into the street. In the distance he could make out the back end of a small red van. He slammed the door and went back into the kitchen.

"Gran, you really mustn't open the door to strangers."

"It was the postman," Gran repeated, bending down to stuff the laundry into the washing machine.

"You can't trust anyone! You never know if–"

"If what?" Gran said, straightening up and looking straight at George. "If Victor comes back to get me?"

"What?"

"He's not coming back, boy. He was far too intent on leaving the country." George stood gob-smacked. "They all think I'm a daft old bat. That Officer Knowles in particular with her story about 'mistaken identity'. Nothing gets past old Cerys Jenkins – I'll tell you that."

"But Gran – you need to tell them – if you know more than you're saying, you must tell them."

"I've told them what they need to hear," she said, bending down again to finish with the washing.

George came closer. "Gran, we need to catch him. He needs to pay for what he did … to you, to everyone he hurt."

"He didn't hurt me. I'm as tough as old boots," she said, lifting a basket loaded with wet clothes. "Ouch." She flinched and grabbed at her ribs.

"He did hurt you, and I'm going to make him pay," George said, taking the basket from her.

"No, George. You leave that to your father."

From: Chief
To: C38
Re: Bird of Prey {Encrypted}

Update 26.1

Officer C38, I have authorised Officer J21 to rejoin the investigation into the whereabouts of the bird of prey.

He has been cleared by the psych team, but I fear his mental state to be fragile.
I do not want him to have access to the subjects being questioned without you present.

He is your senior, but I instruct you to keep a close eye on all his dealings.
He has refused to reveal the details of the Dungeness tip-off.
He insists on protecting his source.
You are closest to him – make sure he stays within protocol.

End.

From: C38
To: Chief
Re: Bird of Prey {Encrypted}

Response to Update 26.1

Orders received.

End.

Chapter 4: False Allegations

George had been right all along – nothing got past Gran. She knew far more than Sam realised, and George was sure she knew even more than she was letting on to him. It turned out that she had suspected Sam's job for a while and had chosen to act ignorant. She had also kept her wits about her when she was kidnapped by Victor's crew, picking up enough snippets of conversation to know that these criminals were using her as a way of escaping the country – a hostage always guarantees an easy exit.

George was careful not to push her too hard, but soon deduced that she knew nothing of the weapon. She couldn't identify the person who had entered the house, but from what George could tell, she had been in Victor's company as they headed towards the coast.

What worried George the most was that Gran seemed to think that the danger had sailed off into the sunset.

"Gran, we still don't know who came here and broke in," George said. "The person could still be out there, maybe right here in Chiddingham. Victor may still want to hold some kind of power over the investigation – over Dad. You need to be careful."

"I appreciate your concern, boy," she said, holding his chin in her hand. "But the same goes for you. You need to leave the investigation to your father and focus on getting back into school life."

"You need to tell Dad what–"

"I think it's best we leave your father to focus on his job. If he wants me to think it was all a big mix up, then I'm happy to go along with that. He doesn't need anything more to worry about. You leave it be, Georgie."

"But–"

"Please, George, do this for me."

On that note, she trotted off up the stairs to get dressed. "You're going to be late for Felix," she called over the bannister.

George had promised Felix that he'd cycle into town as Felix had got a new bike for his birthday and wanted to use it. George would rather have got the bus. He ventured out of the back door and unlocked the squat storage shed where the bikes were kept. He hadn't used it in months. The tyres were half deflated, and a rather nasty looking spider had built a home in the handlebars. He evicted the intruder by prodding it with the bicycle pump before dealing with the tyres. By the time he was ready to go, it was already approaching midday.

He checked in on Gran once more before he left and reminded her that he had a new mobile number.

"Yes, yes, dear," she mumbled idly from behind her bedroom door.

The ride into town was hard going. George's legs screamed out for a break half way up the steep hill that divided the village from town. He put his head down and pushed harder. If nothing else, the exertion would warm him up. The autumn temperatures had been unseasonably low, and his fingers felt like they were turning into icicles.

As he finally free-wheeled into Pendleton High Street, it was busy with lunchtime traffic. He slowed down, hopped off his bike and pushed it down the cobbles towards the old uniform shop. He couldn't help noticing that the Library and Museum were still shut. Its curator, Wilbur Cook, had survived his run in with Philippe and Jefferson but hadn't had the strength to come back to work. A small hand written 'temporarily closed' sign was taped to the window. George sighed. Victor may have vanished across the English Channel, but there were plenty of reminders of the devastation he had caused still etched throughout George's everyday life.

"You're late!" Felix had appeared from inside the school shop.

"Sorry," George said, "I had to resurrect my bike."

"Chain it up next to mine," Felix said, proudly pointing at his shiny new road bike.

"Nice!"

Felix grinned.

"Close the door, please, unless you want to pay the heating bill!" The stern old lady who ran the school shop was bellowing at them from inside.

A warm blast of air hit George in the face as he crossed the threshold. It was like entering a different era: soft lighting; fuzzy, mustard carpet tiles; a window display full of headless manikins and rickety, wooden shelves that reached all the way to the sloping ceiling.

"Can I help you, boys?" the rather large lady asked them, as she made her way, rather precariously, down the ladder that leaned up against the towering shelves.

"Yes, please," said George. "I need a new blazer and a pair of trousers for Oakfield Manor."

"Size?" she called out, as she swung the old step ladder around 180 degrees and mounted them again.

"Er … age thirteen, maybe fourteen," he said, shrugging.

She grabbed several sizes and heaved her way back down to the ground.

"Changing room's at the back. Only one person at a time."

George nodded. He wasn't sure what made her think that you could squeeze more than one body into the tiny cubicle. It was almost impossible to get your trousers on without sticking your bum out of the wayward curtain. There was definitely no way that two people could change in it while keeping their dignity. Felix perched on a little step stool while George changed.

"Hey, George," Felix whispered through the gap in the curtain, "has your dad made any progress – you know, on catching Victor?"

"Shh," George hushed, peaking his face through the gap, "keep your voice down."

"The old battle-axe can't hear me. She's half-buried in the window display."

George stepped out. His blazer sleeves were halfway up his forearms, and his trousers were swinging around his ankles.

"Hmm, not sure that's right," sniggered Felix. "You look like Mr Jefferson."

George laughed. "*I don't want to see this again, Patterson! Do as you're told or I'll ... I'll ... lock you in a cell and leave you for dead!*"

Felix giggled. "*I'm warning you, Jenkins! One more broken rule and I'll…*"

"Once a loser, always a loser," a voice proclaimed from behind them.

Felix frowned, and George swivelled around to find himself face to face with Liam Richardson and Connor O'Grady. The last time George and Felix had seen Liam they were heaving his unconscious body from a burning schoolhouse. They had pretty much saved his life.

They stood staring at each other. George didn't know what to say. He waited to see if Liam would at least thank them, but it was wishful thinking. Liam was far too proud for that. He looked George up and down, and George became very conscious of his exposed ankles.

"Where are your underpants?" Liam grunted.

"What?" George said.

"You're missing your underpants, superhero. They should be on the outside of those ridiculous trousers," Liam said, smirking.

"Yeah!" Connor grinned, exposing his tiny teeth. "What shall we call you now? Captain Cockroach?"

The two boys burst out laughing.

"You should be thanking him!" Felix blurted out, half-hiding behind George.

"What d'you say?" Liam snorted, moving a step closer.

"We saved your life," Felix said, his voice high and quivering.

"That's bull!" Liam growled. "It was you clowns that caused the chaos. You set off the fire alarm. How'd you know there was gonna' be a fire, huh?"

"Yeah, you the arsonist the police are after, cockroach?" Connor sneered.

"What?" George was confused.

"You were the only one who seemed to know there was gonna' be a fire. Wouldn't put it past you to pull a stunt like that – trying to make yourself seem like some kind of hero."

"Shut up!" George shouted.

"What's going on here?" The shopkeeper had appeared behind them. "I'll have no nonsense in my shop. You hear me?" She turned to Liam and Connor. "What do you two want?"

"New uniform, please, Madam," Liam said in his politest tone. "But don't make me look like him."

"That's enough of that." She wagged her finger at him. "Follow me. And young man, I suggest you take the next size up – in both."

George rapidly changed, grabbed the bigger blazer and trousers and made his way to the till. They waited while the lady saw to Liam, then quickly paid and left.

"What the hell was that all about?" George said, as they peddled through the back alleys.

"Well, he wasn't exactly grateful, was he?"

"He thought I'd started the fire!" George was steaming. Surely, no one else believed that.

"It's just Liam. He can't say anything nice to anyone."

They skirted around the pedestrianised square and ducked down one of the narrow cut-throughs, nearly crashing into two bodies that were huddled in the shadows. George squeezed his brakes and almost toppled off his bike.

"Jenkins! Watch it!" It was Josh, with Francesca in his arms.

"What are you two doing hiding down here?" Felix asked.

George saw that Francesca had turned a slight shade of red, so nudged Felix in the ribs.

"Man, it's good to see you … alive," George joked, trying to change the subject. "How's your arm?"

"Not bad, considering," Josh said, looking down at his sling. "I had to have it cleaned up and stitched, but it could have been a lot worse, I guess."

"I'm not sure there's much worse than a gun shot wound," Felix said.

"True," Josh replied, looking pretty proud of himself.

"How are you, George?" Francesca asked, sliding out from behind Josh.

"Not bad." He really wanted to tell them everything that had happened since he last saw them, but he knew he couldn't.

"We're going to the coffee house. Would you like to join us?" Francesca asked.

"Sure," George replied, without conferring with Felix.

The coffee house was pretty empty. Most people were at work or school. A troupe of mums and gurgling babies took up one corner, so George and the others decided to occupy the opposite corner by the window.

"We just ran into Liam," George said, picking up his hot chocolate and stuffing his change in his pocket.

"What did he have to say for himself?" Francesca asked, balancing her cookie on top of her teacup.

"He blamed George for the fire!" Felix exclaimed, as they slumped down into the squashy sofas.

"What?" Josh said.

"Yeah, he reckons I started it. I mean – it was a massive explosion. What on earth makes him think I'd do that?"

"He reckoned it was arson," Felix added.

"Ah," Francesca said, snatching a copy of the Chiddingham News from the table next to them, "it may have something to do with this."

George grabbed the paper. The front page had a photo of their school engulfed in flames. The headline read: 'Arsonists to blame for Oakfield Inferno.'

"What?" George shouted, a little too loudly. A couple of the mums scowled in his direction. "Where did they get that rubbish from?"

"It's what the police said in their statement," Francesca explained. "Haven't you been reading about it online?"

George shook his head. He had been busy with his own dramas. "But why?"

"Think about it, George. They can't exactly say that the school was blown up by some Russian gangster," Felix said, giving George a knowing look.

"Right, of course."

"Yeah, I mean you guys had your debrief." Josh said. "We've all been asked to stick to the same story, right?"

The others all nodded.

"No, what story?" Officer Knowles hadn't mentioned anything to George. He'd just been told to keep all the details to himself. The others looked puzzled.

"We got this whole lecture about the fact that we were accidentally caught up in a crime that was nothing to do with us and that the fire at the school was meaningless arson and there was no proof that there was a link between the two." Josh explained.

"But it was Victor!" George said, infuriated. "I told Mrs Hamilton that and Officer Knowles."

"To be fair, George," Felix said, lowering his voice, "there is no evidence that Victor planted those explosives, and even if we did tell anyone at school about Victor and his crew, do you think they'd really believe us?"

"Mrs Hamilton said she believed me."

"Yes, I'm sure she does, but she's got the school's reputation to think of," Francesca said. "You only have to look at how my mother responded. No parent wants to think that the school was the target of major criminals. It's easier to say it was a random attack by reckless vandals."

George grumbled to himself.

"Where do you think they are now, Victor and his gang?" Josh asked, stuffing a sugar cube in his mouth. "And what did they want in that tunnel?"

"What about Philippe and Jefferson?" Francesca added.

"I hope they're being roughed up!" Josh said.

Felix glanced at George, but George didn't want to get drawn into a conversation about it. He buried his face in his mug. He was just glugging down the dregs of his hot chocolate when he nearly choked because Gran was trotting past the window. She was wrapped up in a large purple shawl and seemed to have something buried beneath it.

"What do you think, George?" Francesca asked. "George?"

But he was already springing from his seat. "Um – I've gotta' go – sorry. Promised my gran I'd do something."

"Me too," Felix said, jumping up and rocking the table with his knees.

They both dashed towards the door, leaving Josh and Francesca looking perplexed.

"Where are we going?" Felix asked, as they unlocked their bikes.

"To follow my gran."

"What? Why?"

George was scanning the road ahead for any sign of her. She couldn't have gone far. He peered over the traffic and spotted her little white bun bobbing along past the pub.

"What is she up to?" he said under his breath.

"Why on earth are we spying on your gran?" Felix panted, as they peddled up the hill.

"She's supposed to be resting. I want to know why she's out."

"George, I'm sure your gran can look after herself. She's heading towards the post office. I'm sure she's just posting a letter or something."

"Wait!" George screeched to a halt. She had stopped by the back of the post office and was fumbling around under her shawl. She looked up and down the street.

George decided to cross. He was just waiting for a break in the traffic when a red post office van pulled up to the pavement and blocked his view. He couldn't see her. His pulse rocketed. He ducked out into the road almost colliding with an oncoming moped. The rider beeped his horn and waved his fist at him.

"What the hell are you doing?" shouted Felix. "You're gonna' get yourself killed!"

"He's gonna' take her!" George screamed back.

He dumped his bike and dived between the cars, skipping around the bumpers. Tyres squealed and horns blasted. Felix was hot on his heels. As he rounded the back of the post van, Gran was nowhere to be seen. He lunged for the driver's door, just as it slammed shut, and yanked on the handle. The door flew back open, and George tumbled to the ground, his head bouncing off the kerb. As he picked himself up, the dark, stubbly face of a young man peered down at him.

"Are you crazy?" the man asked, in a Spanish accent.

"Where is she?" George gabbled, grabbing the man by his jumper and making him stumble forwards.

"Mate, you're mad!" Felix had caught up with him.

"She's gone!" George shouted.

"You need to settle down," the Spanish guy said, trying to pull away.

"Where is she?" George screamed.

"Georgie, I'm right here."

George let go of the postman and spun around to see Gran standing at the door of the post office, her arms folded and a quizzical frown on her face. He immediately flushed red. He had just assaulted a postman and nearly caused a pile up, and all for nothing.

"Er … I thought…" he mumbled.

"I don't think you were thinking at all," Gran said. "Now, apologise to this young man."

"No hay problema," the postman said, glancing at Gran and climbing back into his van. "It's OK."

Gran spoke to him through his window before he pulled off. She turned back to George with a look on her face that reminded him of the many times he'd been told off as a child for teasing Marshall.

"Enough is enough, George. I told you, there is no need for you to worry about me."

"But I thought –"

"Felix, my dear, would you take him home, and make sure he doesn't do anything more to risk his life or anyone else's for that matter. There's been enough of that behaviour recently."

"Of course, Mrs Jenkins."

George couldn't get his helmet over the lump on his head without it hurting, so they pushed their bikes to the bus stop.

"So, you wanna' tell me what that was all about?" Felix asked, as they sat down on the bench.

George sighed and rubbed the lump on his head. At least it wasn't his face again. "I'm not sure if I can tell you."

"George, you can trust me. I know about your dad's job, what could be a bigger secret than that?"

The bus pulled up and they dumped their bikes and bags in the luggage area and wandered to the back. It was deserted apart from two old ladies nattering away to the driver at the front.

"Victor kidnapped Gran," George whispered.

"What?" Felix was stunned. "How? When? I mean, why didn't you tell me?"

"Oh God, Felix. It was awful. That same day, we got home and she'd gone. It was Victor's way of making sure Dad didn't tail him. We found her half dead in a washed up dinghy on Dungeness bay, over five days later."

"George, I'm so sorry. You must have been doing your nut!"

"Yeah, well, now I guess I'm paranoid that he'll do it again."

"But he's gone. He's left the country, surely."

"Yes, but Dad reckons the person who actually broke in and snatched her wasn't one of the gang we saw. He thinks there's someone else, and I think that whoever it is was disguised as a postman."

"What?" said Felix, not quite convinced.

"Listen, we saw a red van that night, speeding away from Chiddingham, and the fire you saw in the woods – it was letters and a red bag – what if it was a Royal Mail bag?"

"Why would they burn a bag full of post?"

"I don't know, but it's all a bit suspicious, don't you think?"

"Mate, I get that losing your gran was pretty messed up, but I think you may be over thinking it. I think she's right. You need to chill out a bit. And anyway, there's like a hundred postmen and women in the Pendleton area alone."

George realised that he sounded crazy and paranoid, but he wasn't going to stop until he found some way of tracking Victor down.

From: Anonymous
To: J21
Re: Bird of Prey {Encrypted}

I see that you are making little or no progress with your interrogations. We need to know what the bird plans to do with that weapon.

Word has spread fast of the release of his flock. He has made a significant impression, and there is chatter amongst key players.

His network is rebuilding; allies are emerging from the shadows. He will soon have the funding and support he needs to mobilise his plans.

You need to push the prisoners harder.

A useful bit of knowledge: Jefferson has a son.
Find his weak spot and exploit it.

Keep me posted.

End.

From: J21
To: Anonymous
Re: Bird of Prey {Encrypted}

Chief has me on a short lead.
It is impossible to get time alone with the prisoners. I will struggle to get around the usual interrogation protocol, but

From: Anonymous
To: J21
Re: Bird of Prey {Encrypted}

Why would your chief want to watch you so closely?
And why won't he let you push them harder?
Do you trust him?

End.

Chapter 5: Cloud Nine

Tuesday morning arrived in a blur. George had dreamt about mud-wrestling a giant of a man who was dressed in a bird costume. It was completely surreal and quite disturbing, but the part that nagged at him the most was that he had been bare foot and couldn't get any grip as he slid about in the thick, slippery mud.

When he got downstairs, he suddenly realised that he had forgotten to pick up new school shoes. His old ones had practically fallen to bits after their journey through the depths of hidden London and were beyond repair. He had no option but to wear his beaten-up, old trainers to school.

Nice one, George!

Gran had somehow managed to get back on top of all the housework, laundry and shopping in the few days since her return to health and had prepared the first decent breakfast that George had seen in far too long. He relished every mouthful.

"You'll take it easy today, won't you?" he asked her, as he pulled on his new blazer. It was like wearing a straight-jacket – the sleeves hardly bent. It was so new, stiff and itchy.

"I'll be fine," she replied. "Your father has given me this." She held up a white plastic disc that was attached to a string necklace. She scrunched up her nose. "Apparently it goes directly through to his phone. He expects me to wear it all day."

George couldn't help smiling. He knew that the panic button made sense, but he also knew that she was very unlikely to wear it.

"Maybe just keep it nearby," George suggested, before turning to leave.

George was filled with a different type of anxiety as he made his way to the bus stop. He was excited to see his friends but wasn't sure what reception he would get from the rest of his year, or the rest of the school. He stood at the bus stop alone and wondered how many people believed Liam's story. Would they all be blaming him? Would he be a laughing stock? He had silently hoped that the whole thing would have given him some miniscule dash of credibility – popularity even, but he knew in his heart that, however hard he tried, he would always be the brunt of Liam and Connor's jokes.

He slumped down onto the wooden bench and stared at his lame, stinky trainers. He could hear the grind of the bus' engine and the hiss of its brakes as it pulled up to the stop, but he didn't dare lift his head. If he could clamber onto the bus unseen, maybe he could get through the short journey without drawing any attention.

As he mounted the steps, he heard the silence descend. He reluctantly lifted his eyes to see every young face peering down at him.

"George Jenkins," Mr Steckler loudly announced, "welcome back!"

George cringed. He could have done without the introduction, but to his complete and utter surprise, the bus was suddenly filled with the sound of rapturous applause. Kids from all years were on their feet. Even the rugby boys on the back row were standing on their seats and whooping.

"Go, George!" someone hollered.

George stood frozen still. It felt like one of his weird dreams. His eyes scanned across the sea of faces, and he couldn't believe it when he saw Lauren, his secret crush, cheering his name. His knees went weak, and although he desperately tried to resist, a huge grin spread across his face.

"Come on, mate." It was Josh. "Come up the back and sit with us."

George looked up at Mr Steckler who winked and grinned his toothless grin. "Find yourself a seat, young Jenkins."

George shuffled down the aisle; people slapping him on the back as he went. As they reached the back row, several of Joshua's teammates moved aside to make space for him. George felt like a champion, and he didn't want the feeling to ever end.

"So, Josh told us what you did," one of the rugby guys said as the bus pulled off. "Pretty ballsy."

George smiled. "Er … thanks."

It turned out that Josh had told all his friends that George had spotted the fire burning in the lab and had tried to fight it himself, but when he realised that it was out of control, he'd hit the alarm and managed to evacuate the whole school before the Bunsen burners' gas supply had caught alight, causing a huge explosion. However, the story had been retold several times and somehow morphed into a tale where George had disturbed the arsonists, scared them off, battled the fire, spotted the threat from the gas leak and saved the entire school, as well as carrying an unconscious Liam on his shoulders through a wall of flames.

By the time they got off the bus at school, George was more embarrassed than flattered.

"Josh, I really appreciate you telling everyone that I saved the school and all that, but the story is a bit … inflated," he said, as they wandered up the drive.

"So," said Josh, shrugging. "It's miles better than the story Liam's gonna' try and spin, and let's face it, you did save everyone. You deserve the credit."

George tried not to blush. "Thanks."

Everything about school felt different. Not just because George had been bestowed with a new found fame, but several things had changed. The east wing was covered in scaffolding and plastic sheeting, four new prefab huts stood on the lawns (one of which was George's new form room) and a brand new fence was being constructed on the boundary. Mrs Hamilton wasn't going to risk losing students again.

The school hall had been deemed unsafe, so assemblies were suspended until further notice. Instead, Mrs Hamilton stood waiting for year nine as they approached the new form rooms. They were all ushered into one of the huts. It was a squash, but they managed to get both classes jammed in. George stood next to Felix and was whispering to him about what had happened on the bus when he became aware that Lauren was loitering to his right. He willed himself to have the courage to turn and say hello but found his neck stubbornly locked in the forward position. The only problem was that he was now staring straight at Liam and his friends who were all giving him a death stare.

"Jenkins," someone whispered from behind.

George was forced to turn around. "Will! Jess!"

He hadn't heard from them since the day of the fire, and it felt great to see their beaming faces.

"How are you?" Jess said, giving him a hug.

It took him by surprise, and he flushed red again. He could feel Lauren's eyes on him. The day had already been filled with feelings that George couldn't quite get his head around.

"I'm good," he replied. "You?"

"Squeeze up!" Mrs Hamilton called from the front of the room. "Make space for the stragglers."

George turned to face front, and Lauren shuffled up next to him, her arm brushing against his. He side-glanced at her and half smiled. The temperature in the room was definitely rising, and his blazer felt even thicker and stiffer than before.

"Right," Mrs Hamilton said. "Can everyone hear me?" There were a few shouts of 'yes'. "Welcome back year nine. It has been a difficult couple of weeks, and we have all had to come to terms with what happened to our dear school, but we are all here and all safe." Her eyes rested on George for a split second. "In response to what happened, we have installed new CCTV, security and alarm systems which are already up and running. The police have reassured me, and the Board of Governors, that we aren't in any danger of seeing a repeat of this type of careless and spiteful vandalism. I hope that we can all now get back to learning and growing."

A few people clapped, but George fumed. She had not only completely disregarded everything George had told her that day but had also added credibility to Liam's twisted theory by eluding to the fire as being an act of vandalism. He felt betrayed but knew that there was little he could do about it. He had promised his dad that he would keep quiet. Will could obviously sense his frustration and lay his hand on his shoulder.

"We all know what really happened," he whispered in George's ear.

"I would like to make one more announcement," Mrs Hamilton continued. "We have been in deep discussions with the board and the parent reps about the upcoming year nine Paris trip, and although there was much talk of cancelling, we have agreed that the trip will go ahead as planned."

Several people cheered. George had totally forgotten. They were due to go to Paris next week. It was a year nine tradition – the highlight of the year. His heart sank. It wasn't going to be easy to convince his dad to let him go, now.

"Ooh, Paris. It's so beautiful and so romantic," Lauren cooed in his ear.

George gulped.

Is she talking to me?

He didn't want to ignore her and appear rude. He slowly turned his head and found himself inches from her bright green eyes.

"Have you ever been to Paris, George?" she asked, her cheeks flushing and her hands nervously fiddling with the button on her blazer.

"Er … no," was all he could say.

"It's beautiful," she went on. "I can't wait. It will be so much fun."

"Er … yes." He smiled a stupid wooden smile.

You idiot, George.

"Woohoo, Paris!" Francesca had shimmied her way over to see the others. "Oh, the shopping!" she squealed with excitement.

"We won't be shopping," said Jess. "It's an Art and History trip."

"We'll be expected to speak French all day, I guess," said Will, grimacing.

"Formidable!" Francesca cheered.

"Calm down, please," Mrs Hamilton shouted above the commotion. "I'm glad you are all so excited, but I'm afraid we will need you to get re-confirmation from your parents that they are happy for you to go. Letters will go home with you this afternoon. They need to be returned as soon as possible if you wish to join the trip – tomorrow ideally."

The room was still buzzing as Mrs Hamilton left, but George felt dazed and immune to the excitement. So much had happened in so little time. A concoction of feelings and thoughts were churning around in his brain. Gran, Victor, the mysterious intruder, arson, Paris, Lauren … it was all too much. He slipped through the crowd and burst out into the fresh air.

"Bit hot in there, wasn't it?" a voice said from the bottom of the steps.

George looked down. It was Miss O'Donnell. She was one of the youngest teachers at the school. She was small and slim with delicate eyes that were framed by a splattering of freckles. Her cheerful Irish voice always put George at ease.

"Um, yeah," George said, "a bit … claustrophobic."

"I'm not surprised," she said, trotting up the steps to join him. "Been a tough couple of weeks, huh?" George nodded. "I'm here if you need to talk, George. You know I'm the school councillor, and I'm going to be your new form tutor now that Mr Jefferson has … been dismissed." She smiled and pushed open the door. "Shall we go inside and calm this lot down?"

George nodded again. "Thanks."

He floated through the morning. Even Liam couldn't burst his popularity bubble. Liam got more and more visibly frustrated, as every time he tried to get near George, he was bundled out of the way by various groups of students who wanted to ask George about his heroics. He even managed to get detention at first break for swinging a punch at some eager year seven who asked him if George had resuscitated him after he saved him from the fire. His temper and humiliation had reached a crescendo by lunchtime. George secretly knew that he'd ultimately pay the price for it at some point, but for now, he enjoyed seeing Liam suffer.

The afternoon seemed to race past, and George and Felix were just packing up their stuff to go home when Hayley Fox sidled up beside them.

"Lauren wants to see you behind the prefab," she said, giggling.

"Me?" George said, glancing at Felix.

"Yeah, got yourself a girlfriend, Captain Cockroach," she said, before skipping off.

Felix laughed.

"What's so funny?" George said, slightly embarrassed.

"Well, I mean, girls eh? They're so … weird. One minute they're ignoring you and the next they're all over you like a rash."

"Right – like you know all about that," George teased.

Felix scowled. "Well, are you going?"

"No – I mean, I…"

"Man, are you serious?"

"Huh?"

"You can't not go – you've fancied her for like *ever,* and now she's finally noticed you. This may be your only chance. You know what girls are like. They sulk big time if you ignore them."

"Oh, right. I s'pose I'll go check it out then – you know – wouldn't want her to get upset."

He gathered himself together, checked his breath, tried to flatten his hair and sauntered outside, his stomach alive with butterflies. The back of the block of prefabs was tight up against the new fence. He slid his way down behind the first hut. The smell of freshly cut wood and pine filled his nostrils. The trees overhung the fence, casting gloomy shadows onto the passageway. He could make out someone leaning against the fence as he edged closer.

"A-hum," he coughed, but she didn't turn around. "Lauren?" He stepped closer still. He could feel his mouth going dry, and his tie felt too tight around his neck. "Hi, Lauren." His voice had disintegrated into a croaky whisper.

She turned, but it wasn't Lauren. It was Hayley's twin, Annie. Before he had time to realise what was happening, Liam and his imposing fellow prop, Jake Mullhouse, leapt out from between the two huts. He spun around, but Connor and Hayley were behind him. Panic! His back was against the fence. There was no way out. He tried to shout, but all that came out was a dry squeak.

"Not such a big hero now, are you, cockroach?" Liam said, as Jake grabbed George by the tie.

"Get off me!" George yelped; his voice pinned by the noose of his tie as Jake slowly lifted him off the ground.

"Jake will let you go as soon as you swear to stop lying. Quit telling people that you saved my life, and start admitting that you're just one big attention-seeking freak."

George could hardly breathe. He snatched at Jake's fists, trying to loosen his grip, but it was like prying open the jaws of a shark. He could hear the twins sniggering as Jake lifted him higher, leaving his feet dangling in mid-air.

Do something, George!

In a flash of anger, he took an almighty swing and landed his kneecap right between Jake's legs, who collapsed like a landslide into the dirt.

"I won't!" George screamed, as he found his feet. "I won't lie just because you're too embarrassed to admit that I saved your neck. I should've left you to burn!"

Liam's face was puce; his fists clenched likes boulders. He flew at George, sending Annie flying into the fence. George saw the knuckles coming and swerved just in time, causing Liam to swipe over his shoulder and barrel into Connor. George turned to face Liam as he came at him again, but this time Liam threw a dummy punch to the face with his left fist while jabbing his right deep into George's gut. George felt his intestines rise up, and the air from his lungs fly out of his nostrils. His head spun, but he managed to stay on his feet. He wasn't sure how many more of those he could take. He was just re-adjusting his stance when he felt a crack to his lower back. Jake had got back to his feet and rugby tackled him from behind. Next thing he knew, he was face down in the dirt with a mouth full of pine needles.

Jake was the mass of a small elephant. George felt like his bones might crack under the weight of him. He could hear screaming and shouting, and then suddenly he was free – someone was pulling him to his feet. He braced himself for another attack but opened his eyes to see Jess beaming down at him.

"Get away from him!" Will was at her side, yelling at Liam.

George gathered himself together and looked around. Jake was somehow back on the floor, grasping at his face, and the twins were backing away with Connor not far behind.

"You better watch it, Carter," Liam said, facing up to Will. "You may have taken us by surprise, but it's five against three – or should I say two and a half."

"Bring it on," said Will. "Just leave George out of it. He deserves your respect."

They were now nose to nose.

"What are you, his new boyfriend?" Liam said, shoving Will backwards.

"Rather his, than yours," Will said, jabbing his finger into Liam's chest. "Now back off!"

Liam's head whipped forwards crunching into Will's nose. George flinched at the sound of it. Liam tried it again, but Will wasn't going to let him hit the target twice. He dodged and threw a short, sharp punch into Liam's stomach, knocking the wind right out of him. Liam stumbled backwards just as Jake was heaving himself back onto his feet. George saw him coming at Will from behind and shoulder barged him into the fence. All hell was about to break loose.

"Hey!" Josh had appeared at one end of the fence line with half the rugby team, while Francesca, Felix, Lauren and several others had appeared at the other end, stopping Connor and the twins from escaping.

Liam had Will by the collar, and Jake had George pinned to the fence.

"I wouldn't get involved if I were you," Liam snarled in Josh's direction.

"I am involved, in fact, we all are," Josh said. "You as much as look at George the wrong way and you'll have us *all* to answer to! Let them go!"

Liam scanned the battlefield. He was outnumbered and surrounded by advancing enemies. "You're playing for the wrong team, Palmer," he growled, releasing his grip on Will. "You're an embarrassment of a captain."

Josh laughed. "You know what's embarrassing? This."

Josh held up what looked like a hand written letter.

"Where d'you get that?" Liam said, suddenly flustered. He shoved George out of the way and stormed towards Josh.

"I found it," Josh said, smugly. "Did Mummy make you write it? Shall I read it out? It's a very heartfelt thank you. It seems you are grateful to George, after all."

"Get out of my way!" Liam roared at his teammates, as he hurtled towards Josh, but they stood shoulder to shoulder; an impenetrable wall. Liam was steaming. "You'll pay for this, Palmer. You all will!" he screamed, before grabbing Jake and the others and quickly disappearing through the gap between the huts.

George looked around at the gathered faces. Blood was trickling from Will's nose. "Will, man, your nose. You really didn't have to—"

Will started laughing. "Seriously, it's just a nose bleed. I get them every week at boxing. And anyway, I wouldn't have missed that show for anything."

"Yeah, did you see Liam's face?" Jess said, handing Will a tissue.

"He actually looked scared of us," Francesca giggled.

"He's had it coming," Felix said.

"Yeah, him and those awful twins," Lauren said, brushing the pine needles from George's blazer.

"Thanks, guys," George said. "How did you know I was here?"

"I saw Lauren out by the bus stop and realised you'd been duped," Felix said, wrapping his arm around George's shoulders.

"We all came as soon as we heard," Josh said. "You OK?"

"Yeah, thanks to you guys."

He looked around at his friends. He couldn't believe how much his life had changed in just a few short weeks. Maybe, just maybe, Victor had weirdly done him a favour.

From: Chief
To: J21
Cc: C38
Re: Bird of Prey {Encrypted}

Update 26.2

Officer J21, I am removing you from the investigation with immediate effect.

You have overstepped your authority and broken interrogation protocol. We have a strict policy against threatening relatives of suspects.

The investigation will now be headed up by Officer C38, and you will be re-deployed.

You are suspended from duty until further notice.

End.

From: J21
To: Anonymous
Re: Bird of Prey {Encrypted}

I pushed too hard and have been removed from the investigation. I can no longer help you from this end.

You need to consider breaking your anonymity and liaising with my colleagues if you want to help catch the bird.

End.

From: Anonymous
To: J21
Re: Bird of Prey {Encrypted}

Your hands may be tied but mine aren't.
The investigation was going nowhere, anyway. The two
subjects are obviously being protected.

You need to focus on the bird's wider network.
I have a source who has eyes on some of the bird's allies.
They are converging on a Spanish site.

We must stay in contact and continue to trade intel. I have
heard rumours of a public test of the weapon's capability.
Our priority is to find out the target for that test. If we can
find the target, we will catch our bird.

I will only liaise with you – I do not trust your chief.

I will be in touch.

End.

Chapter 6: The Autopsy

George skipped off the bus outside the newsagent, feeling ten feet tall. There'd been a break in the chilly weather, and the sun was out. He decided to duck into the shops and pick up a bag of Gran's favourite sweets before heading home.

Moments later, he was trotting back out onto the pavement, arms laden with treats, when something stopped him dead in his tracks. Dozens of mourners were streaming out of the village hall. Head to toe in black, of all ages, they flooded out into the car park and headed around to the back of the church. George knew immediately *who* they were mourning. He drifted across the road and followed the procession.

As they turned into the church grounds, George could see the mountain of flowers. A young woman in a long, black overcoat stood shaking hands and thanking those who had come to pay their respects. A shiver raced down George's spine. The only funeral he had ever attended was that of his own mother. He remembered very little but could picture his father, hunched over and broken, shaking hands in the very same way.

"Muy triste," a voice said from behind him. It was the postman. He sidled up beside George, pushing a bike. "You OK, mi amigo?"

"Er, yeah … good thanks," George mumbled, surprised that the man he practically assaulted wanted to make small talk with him.

"They are burying her so soon," the postman said.

"What?" George asked.

"A murder autopsy usually takes an age," he said, looking at George and smiling.

George just smiled back and then watched him as he peddled away. He wore heavily scuffed DM boots and grey shorts, exposing his tanned legs. There was something about him that didn't add up.

What does he know about autopsies?

"Georgie!" It was Gran. She was wearing a long, floaty charcoal dress, a dark beret and carrying a large handbag that was floppy and empty. She looked like she'd raided the fancy dress cupboard.

"Gran, what are you wearing?"

"I'm paying my respects, my boy."

"You knew Mrs Hodge?"

"Everyone around here knew her," she said, hooking her arm through his. "Come on, you can walk me home."

George went straight upstairs and collapsed onto his bed. He lay there rolling a cricket ball around in his hands. He couldn't get the image of Mrs Hodge's decaying body out of his head. It grated at him. People would move on and forget about her. George thought about her niece. He thought about his dead mother. He thought about Victor. He thought about his dad and whether he was any closer to tracking Victor down.

With that, the familiar sound of his dad's engine drifted in through the thin windows. George sat up and looked at the clock. It was barely five o'clock.

Maybe he has news.

He raced down the stairs, desperate to catch him before he got into the kitchen.

"Dad," he called, as he caught sight of him kicking off his boots in the hall.

"What?"

George hesitated. He could tell that the news wasn't positive from his dad's frosty response. He slowly descended the last few steps.

"How did today go … any news?"

"Just drop it, George. I've told you not to talk about it."

"I know, but I just–"

"It's out of my hands."

"What? What do you mean?"

"Just drop it!" he snapped, storming into the kitchen.

George loitered in the hall. He was sure that his dad would go out to his shed as usual, but he didn't hear the back door go. He thought about retreating back upstairs but decided that moping around, waiting for Victor to be caught, was getting him nowhere.

He was trying to decide what to do, when Marshall slunk past him and nudged open the kitchen door, releasing the mouth watering smell of Gran's chocolate fudge cake. George couldn't resist. He pushed the door wide open and strode into the kitchen. Deciding to ignore his dad's outburst, he plonked himself down next to him at the breakfast bar.

"Hmm – what's the matter with you two?" Gran asked, waving her wooden spoon at them. "It's like having two moody teenagers in the house."

"I am a moody teenager," George said, trying to break the tension. He glanced at his dad who was blowing the steam from the top of his teacup before turning back to Gran. "Any chance of that cake while it's still warm?"

"Absolutely!" Gran beamed. "That's when it's at its best."

She served them both up a slice, and they ate in silence. For a full minute, all of George's worries melted away as he immersed his taste buds in the warm, gooey goodness. But when he put down his fork, he remembered that he needed to ask his dad about the Paris trip.

Now's as good a time as any, he thought to himself.

"Dad, it's the trip to Paris next week, and I need you to–"

"You can't possibly go!" Sam said, dropping his fork onto his empty plate.

"What? But you already said I could and paid and–"

"Absolutely not!" Sam said, glaring at him.

"Samuel, don't raise your voice. I think George is trying to explain," Gran said.

"I know what he's *trying* to do, but the answer is 'no'. End of story."

"But, Dad, everyone else is going. I'll be the only one."

Sam growled. "I don't give a damn about everyone else!"

"Samuel, control your temper," Gran said.

Sam breathed deeply and lowered his voice. "George, with everything that has *happened*, I would rather you didn't go." He attempted a strained smile.

George knew what his dad was trying to say and that he didn't want to say it in front of Gran. But George also knew that *Gran* knew what he was trying to say too.

"Dad, I can take care of myself. I'll be fine. It's just a day trip and–"

"What, like your day trip to London? That turned out well for you, didn't it?"

"That was totally different!" Now George was shouting. "I went looking for…"

"Trouble," Sam said, frowning.

"Yeah – well, maybe if people treated me like an adult and actually listened to me!"

"That's enough!" Gran said, whipping her tea towel against the kitchen counter, making them both jump and Marshall scurry under George's stool. With that, Sam was up and heading out of the back door.

"That's right!" George shouted after him. "Go hide in your stupid shed like you always do!"

The back door slammed, and that was the last George saw of his dad for several days.

The week flew by, and slowly George's heroics became old news. By the time Friday arrived, George was starting to feel that things might just return to some kind of normal – a new and different normal.

He had resigned himself to the fact that he wouldn't be going to Paris. It was all everyone could talk about, and it was starting to irritate him. A bunch of his new friends were going into town after school, but he chose to hang out with Felix, instead. They got fish and chips and sheltered from the wind on the veranda of the cricket pavilion while throwing left over chips at the pigeons until it was so dark that even the pigeons went to find shelter.

"You around this weekend?" George asked Felix, as they reached the edge of the green.

"Sorry, mate. Got to go see my grandparents."

"Right, so see you Tuesday then – after the Paris trip."

"Yeah – Tuesday."

George trudged home. It was dark, but the wind was biting at him, so he decided to skip through the alleyway. Halfway down the alley, he became aware of footsteps behind him. He glanced over his shoulder. Someone was running down the path towards him – slim, strong, head down and hood up. George backed up, turned and started running. Swinging about on his back, his bag almost knocked him off course. He looked back. They were gaining on him. With only a few metres to go, he sprinted. Bursting out opposite the village hall, the runner almost tripped over him and looked up in shock. George staggered backwards. It was a woman.

"Sorry," she panted, raising her hand in apology as she continued jogging past, her headphone wires dangling from under her hood.

Jeez, George – you're a total headcase.

As he looked up, he could see someone else shuffling down the pavement towards him, carrying what looked like a tool bag. It was dark and the figure wore a cap. George backed up into the shadow of the old oak and waited for them to pass, but when they came into the glow of the streetlight, he recognised the boots, the cap and the beard.

"Dad!"

"George!" Sam jumped. "What are you doing lurking about in the dark?"

"I've been with Felix. What are *you* doing?"

Sam looked over his shoulder. "I'm … out for a walk."

"Really? Since when did you take up walking anywhere … with your tools?"

George looked down at his dad's boots. They were caked in mud. Sam caught him looking and scratched at his beard.

"Let me guess – you can't tell me," George huffed.

"Actually, you may be able to help."

"Really?"

"Keep walking," Sam said, slinging his tool bag over his shoulder. "The night when you delivered the paper to Mrs Hodge, remind me of what you saw."

"Why?"

"Something isn't quite right about it."

"What do you mean?"

"When you went to deliver the paper, you said it was as if the house was empty, right?"

"Yes – totally – no lights – no dogs barking."

"And you thought you saw someone?"

"Uh, I don't know, Dad. I mean, it was so dark – the street lights were out, and I was freaking out a bit."

"Did anything look … disturbed?"

"Not really."

"Hmm, no, that's what I thought, so I went to check out her house again. The police did the original forensics report, but it was sketchy. I wanted to check it out for myself."

"That's where you've been … tonight?" George asked, glancing at the tool bag again. "Did you break in?"

"No! Well, maybe, but that's not the point."

"Dad, you're MI5, surely you can get a warrant and stuff like that."

Sam looked on edge again. "It's not that straight forward, and anyway, I don't want to raise any suspicions."

"Why?"

"It doesn't matter. The point is: we all assumed that Philippe or Jefferson, or whoever came to the village, kidnapped Mrs Hodge. We assumed that they questioned her for information about the hub and the tunnels and then killed her."

"Yeah, why else would they want to kidnap her?"

"The thing is, George. I knew her, and I'm pretty sure she wouldn't have given that information up easily."

"I don't know, Dad. Surely, Victor could have made her talk."

"Listen, she was not only the local MP but also ex-military. She would have been trained to resist interrogation."

"Military? Mrs Hodge?" George said, astounded.

"Yes, that's how we managed to negotiate directly with her to get control of the tunnels and install the hub in her constituency."

"Right, I see. So, what did you find at the house?" George whispered.

"Very little – the place was undisturbed. The only sign of a break in was a splintered front door lock."

"The same as when they took Gran!"

"Yes, but there was no sign of a struggle."

"So, what does that mean?" George asked, unsure of where his dad's thoughts were leading.

"Hmm, I think it means that whoever broke in managed to take her with relative ease."

"Maybe she didn't put up a fight," George said, shrugging. "She was pretty old."

"I'm not convinced about that, and I'm definitely not convinced that she'd have given Victor that information without a fight – I need to get a look at the autopsy."

"The autopsy!" George said. "The postman!"

"What?"

"Dad, the day of her funeral, the postman was there."

"What postman?"

"Some Spanish guy. He said it – he said that he was surprised that there'd been enough time for a full murder autopsy."

They weren't far from home. Sam slowed and turned to look at George. "What are you talking about?"

"There's this Spanish postman. I saw him in Pendleton and then again outside her funeral. I mean, he seems nice enough, but there is definitely something odd about him. Anyway, he was rabbiting on about the autopsy."

"But how would he know anything about–"

"Exactly!"

Sam rubbed his temples. "Why didn't you mention this earlier?"

"Well, I just thought that I was being … paranoid. Do you think he knows something?"

"Impossible to tell," Sam said, stopping at the front gate.

"So what's our next move?" George asked, looking up at his dad.

Sam smiled. "OK, side-kick. First we get a detailed description of this postman. He may be of interest. I can run a search, and I have a few people I need to contact."

"I told you that the post van we saw was suspicious," George said, grinning at his dad as he sidled through the gate. "See, you should have listened to me."

"Hmm, let's not jump to conclusions, George. We haven't proved anything yet," Sam said, poking George in the ribs as he passed. "A good detective never lets his judgement get obscured by assumptions."

"We'll see."

George buzzed. Finally someone was taking him seriously – his *dad* was taking him seriously. Maybe they were a step closer to finding out who had taken Mrs Hodge and maybe even Gran, and that meant a step closer to closing in on Victor.

From: J21
To: K07
Re: Bird of Prey {Encrypted}

I know Chief has taken me off the case, but I need you to send me a copy of the Hodge autopsy – strictly between you and me.

End.

From: K07
To: J21
Re: Bird of Prey {Encrypted}

Whatever you need.

End.

Chapter 7: The Mole

Gran was snoozing in her armchair when they finally entered the house; Marshall snoring in her lap and her teacup precariously teetering on the edge of her armrest.

"Shall I wake her?" George asked his dad.

"No, she looks comfy. Just grab that cup. We can leave her to rest while we pop up to the shed."

George stared at his dad. He'd never been allowed inside the shed. It was strictly off limits. 'Your dad's oasis', Gran called it. George had never really cared. He knew it was his dad's retreat whenever he was stressed, frustrated or just plain busy, but he never disturbed him – it had been like that for as long as George could remember.

"Come on, before it gets too late," Sam said, creeping up the hallway.

George snuck into the lounge, plucked the teacup from its perch and backed out of the door. As he stepped back into the hall, a floorboard creaked under his weight, and Marshall's good eye sprang open. George froze. The cat scowled at him and turned over, snuggling into the creases of Gran's apron. Within seconds, he was purring again.

George flung the cup down into the sink and raced out of the back door to follow his dad up the narrow garden path.

"Don't touch anything," Sam said, as he yanked open the shed door and pulled George inside. They stood inside a dimly lit anteroom – a small lobby. George's mouth hung open. The front door looked like any other bog-standard garden shed – rough wooden slats, a small latch and padlock, but the inner door was much heavier and bolted with a chunky combination lock. Sam punched in some numbers and pushed the door open.

When George stepped in behind his dad, he could feel warm dry air and hear the buzz of a fan. As Sam stepped aside, George could see a large metal desk, a wall lined with locked cabinets and three large computer screens. Sam was shuffling through something on the desk as George stood and took it all in.

"George, we haven't got long. I need to make some calls," Sam said, jerking him out of his trance. "Sit at the computer and type out your description. Keep it as accurate as you can and to the point. I'll send it straight off to Freddie and see if he can cross-reference it with the database we have on Victor's case file."

"Freddie will be working this late?" George asked.

"I thought you would have noticed by now – we're always working. And, yes, he's working. Hmm … as is Cate, it seems."

Sam was peering down at his tablet, but no light shone up from its screen. George had a sudden and vivid flashback – the man by the alleyway, that Friday night outside the village hall.

"Dad!"

"Yes," Sam mumbled, still distracted by whatever he was reading.

"Your tablet – he had one just like it."

"What?" Sam's head jerked up.

"The guy by the alleyway, that night. I remember. He had one of those. I thought it was a phone, but the screen gave off no light."

"Are you sure?" Sam whispered.

"Absolutely!"

Sam stopped what he was doing. "Get outside!"

"What? Why?"

Sam dragged George back out into the garden, nervously scanning his eyes around the fence line.

"Dad, what is it?"

"George, if what you tell me is true, then we have a completely different situation on our hands." Sam was whispering so quietly that George had to hold his breath to hear.

"I don't get it."

"If the man watching you that night had MI5 issued equipment, then that confirms a link. Someone gave Victor information, classified information. And that someone could be *inside* MI5."

"A mole!" George said.

"Yes, someone who has been aiding Victor this whole time."

"Really?"

"Yes, of course, now it makes complete sense," Sam said, slapping himself on the forehead.

"What do you mean?"

"I just got the Hodge autopsy back from Cate."

"And?"

"No gun shot wound, no trauma of any kind – barely a scratch. The report said she died of natural causes, George – a heart attack!"

"But how? I mean – what does that prove?"

"She wasn't tortured for information, George. In fact, the reason they had no trouble taking her out of the house is that she was possibly already dead! The time of death on the autopsy report was estimated at earlier that day – the day that you delivered the paper."

"But if she was already dead, why would they take her at all?"

"As a red herring! Whoever is feeding Victor information, wants to keep their cover. They wanted us to *think* that Mrs Hodge gave Victor the information. But I knew something didn't add up – too much leaked. The whereabouts of the vault, the hub, the fact that we'd set a dummy trap. Victor knew it all."

"But who would do that?" George asked, his brain struggling to keep up.

"I don't know, but we need to find out," Sam said.

"So, does that mean it wasn't the postman?" George asked, confused.

"What did I say, George? Never make assumptions. Let's get back inside the shed. You type up that description, and we'll see what the search throws up. If we can get the postman's identity, we can check any connections with Victor or within MI5 and go from there. In the meantime, I need to message a contact of mine. We need to work out who the mole is and fast."

"Great," George said, bounding back up the path.

"Wait," Sam said, "there's one more thing. If someone from MI5 is involved, then we need to be extra careful. Victor knew where we lived, where you went to school and my hidden cameras were taken out here at the house when Gran was kidnapped. Someone has been watching us and there's a chance that they still are, even now. Do not say anything – just type. I will do the rest. Once you've finished, I want you to go inside and go to bed. Do not speak about the investigation in the house or the shed. In order for me to track down the person who has been feeding Victor intel, I need them to believe that no one is on to them. Are you OK with that?"

George just nodded, re-entered the shed and typed like his life depended on it.

Saturday morning arrived in a haze of drizzle and fog. 'Frozzle,' Gran called it. George had slept in late after a sleepless night consumed with wondering what his dad had uncovered. Sam had been out working all night, and George could barely contain himself when he finally walked in through the front door at lunchtime.

"Where have you been?" he whispered to Sam.

"Working, Son," Sam said loudly. "Had a few emergencies to attend to – leaking taps and broken pipes." He winked at George, but George just rolled his eyes.

"Seriously?"

"I can smell toasted sandwiches," he said, steering George towards the kitchen.

They sat and ate lunch, making small talk like some weird estranged couple. Sam was prattling on about Mrs So-and-so's flooded basement while George nodded along like a wooden puppet. He wasn't sure whether Sam's show was for the hidden listening devices he was convinced were in the house or for Gran's benefit, but either way it was totally bizarre. By the time Sam disappeared upstairs to get some rest, even Gran was struggling to contain her amusement.

"He seemed … chipper," she said, smiling. "Maybe he's had a productive few days."

"Who'd know," George said, shrugging.

"Let's hope so, for all our sakes."

"Gran?" George wanted to ask her about the postman again but then remembered that he wasn't supposed to talk about it in the house.

"Yes, dear."

"Um … any chance of another sandwich?"

"Of, course."

The afternoon dragged and George was restless. He decided to take a trip into town to pick up the new school shoes that Gran had ordered for him. After locating his festering trainers and hunting down the order receipt, he finally pulled open the front door and came face to face with Cate Knowles. He wasn't sure who was more startled, him or the officer, but she quickly composed herself.

"Afternoon, George. How are you?" she said, standing up tall and holding out her hand.

"Um … good, thanks," he said, shaking it.

"Is Sam – I mean your dad, there?"

"Yeah, he's upstairs resting."

"Who's that, Georgie?" Gran had come out into the hall, and she was wielding her wooden spoon again. "Oh, it's you. What do you want?"

George had never heard his Gran be frosty towards anyone before. He looked back at Cate who suddenly looked less chirpy.

"Mrs Jenkins, how are you fairing?"

"I'm perfectly fine, thank you. What can we do for you?"

"I was keen to speak to Sam if he's available."

"No, he's sleeping–"

"I'm here." Sam had appeared at the top of the stairs.

Gran huffed and disappeared back into the kitchen. George watched her go.

What's got into her?

"We need to talk," Cate said, stepping over the threshold.

"Sure – let's go out into the garden. Mum always has the radio up so loud. It'll be quieter outside." Sam glanced at George as he ushered Cate through to the kitchen.

George wasn't sure how much his dad trusted Cate, but he was obviously still keen to keep all discussions out of eavesdropping distance – from George, Gran or the MI5 mole.

They seemed to be outside for an age. George lingered in the kitchen, peering out of the back window as often as he could without being too obvious. Gran was less subtle. She marched in and out several times, apparently desperate to hang out the washing.

"What are they talking about?" George asked Gran after her second trip to the drying line.

"Not easy to tell, boy," she replied, joining him at the window. They must have looked like a pair of nosey neighbours, peeking over the windowsill. "That Officer Knowles is a sly one. She's got your father around her dainty little finger. I don't trust her, Georgie."

"I noticed," George said. "I wonder if she's…"

"If she's what?" Gran asked, looking over at George. He hadn't meant to say it out loud.

"Well – do you think she's on Dad's side?"

"I think she's after something, that's for sure. Your dad seems to be blinkered by her youthful charm. I haven't figured her out yet, but mark my words, it'll end in tears," she said, folding up another one of Sam's dried dustsheets.

"Gran, why do you insist on washing and drying his dustsheets when you know he doesn't even use them?"

"It keeps him happy, boy. He needs to focus, more now than ever. He can't afford to get thrown off track – there's too much at stake." She was staring out at her son with a solemn affection – worry clouding her usually bright eyes. "Everything comes down to this – the last seven years will have been for nothing if he plays this part wrong."

"What's that supposed to mean?" George said, disturbing Gran from her trance.

"Oh, look at me, getting all sentimental," she said, flapping the last sheet out again. "You grab the other end, Georgie."

"Gran," George said, snatching the corners of the sheet, "what do you know that you're not telling me?"

With that Sam and Cate were making their way back inside.

"Oh, the muffins!" Gran cried, dumping the sheet and scuttling over to the oven.

"Did you want to stop for tea and cake?" Sam said to Cate, pulling out one of the bar stools. "Mum's baking is the best."

"Oh, they do smell lovely, Mrs Jenkins," she said, looking sheepish. Gran didn't look up, but George could see her shoulders tighten. "However, I think I should be getting back to the office."

"OK, goodbye," Gran suddenly said, shuffling over to the kitchen door and holding it open. "Have a lovely afternoon."

"Mum!" Sam said.

Gran huffed, scooped up Marshall and disappeared into the lounge. Within seconds the TV was on and blaring out at top volume.

"I'm so sorry," Sam said. "She's normally very welcoming."

"It's perfectly fine. Please don't apologise. She probably finds seeing me quite stressful – I may remind her of her time in the hospital."

Sam nodded. "That's quite possible." But George knew differently. "We need to head out, George," Sam whispered, as he pulled on his jacket. "Cate has something to show me at the office. I'm not sure what time I'll be back."

"Anything to do with … you know what?" George said, prying.

Sam frowned and followed Cate down the corridor and out of the front door.

Sam hadn't returned by the time George got back from picking up his new shoes, and Gran was out playing cards, so he sat and watched an old movie before deciding to get an early night. Not that he had much need for it because he wouldn't be up at the crack of dawn like the rest of year nine.

From: J21
To: Anonymous
Re: Bird of Prey {Encrypted}

I have uncovered some evidence to suggest that we may have a mole on the inside – someone within MI5 who has been aiding Victor.

I originally assumed that Victor had got his information from the asset he had killed on the south coast and the hostages he had taken.

I now believe that this was all a cover to protect an inside source. He or she may still be in play, so I will not raise the alarm until I have proof and a positive ID.

If I can identify this mole, we may find our link to the bird.

I will do all I can from this end, which will mean leaning on a few friends, as my resources are limited while suspended.

End.

From: Anonymous
To: J21
Re: Bird of Prey {Encrypted}

I told you to be careful about who you could trust.
Do not share this with anyone inside your organisation, especially your chief.
You will have to act alone.

I have ears to the ground in Spain. Details of an attack are emerging.

I will be in touch once we have more information.

End.

From: Chief
To: J21
Cc: C38
Re: Security Summit {Encrypted}

Update 1.0

Officer J21, I am reassigning you to security detail at the European Security Summit in Paris, this coming week.

This is a high profile meeting between the Heads of National Security of several European countries.

Your brief is in your inbox.

End.

Chapter 8: A Turn of Events

George fell into the kind of deep sleep that seems to pass by in an instant without you even remembering when you closed your eyes. The next thing he became aware of was that someone was in his room. He opened one eye and could see their outline silhouetted against the pale light that was creeping in from the landing. His brain wasn't quite engaged, and he wasn't sure if he was dreaming or not. He opened the other eye. The figure was rummaging through his drawers. As he slowly dragged himself out of his dozy haze, he realised it was his dad.

"What's going on?" he groaned.

"You need to get up," Sam said, throwing something onto the end of the bed. "We're going to Paris."

"What? What d'you mean 'we'?"

"I've found your passport. We're leaving in twenty minutes – and try not to wake Gran."

With that, Sam slipped back out of the door, leaving George half dazed and completely baffled.

Ten minutes later, George was dressed, downstairs and necking a glass of milk. His eyes were still adjusting to the glaring kitchen lights as Sam emerged from the bathroom.

"What the hell are we doing creeping around the house at four am?" he asked, squinting at his dad.

"We need to get you on that coach, and I have a flight to catch."

"A flight?"

"Yes, Chief is off to Paris, and I'm going with him. I figured, if I'm there then what's the worst that can happen? So, I'm letting you go on the trip."

"Seriously? I mean, Dad, it's a bit last minute. Miss O'Donnell won't even know I'm–"

"I managed to contact the school yesterday. They know to expect you."

"And you didn't think to tell me?" George said, exasperated.

"You were out."

"I do have a phone."

"Yeah – well – I'm telling you now. You want to go or not?"

"Of course."

"Then the rules are as follows–"

"Rules?"

"Yes, quit whinging and listen. Harry Steckler is driving you guys to Ashford to catch the Eurostar. He will be travelling with you as volunteer chaperone."

"Chaperone? Dad, really, I don't need a babysitter."

"He's making up the teacher numbers. It's not just about you. He's there to keep an eye on *all* of you."

George huffed, but Sam chose to ignore it.

"You are to stick with the group at all times, no wandering off, no lapses in concentration."

"I get it!" George insisted.

"Keep your voice down. I don't want to alert Gran."

"She might, just maybe, notice we've both gone."

"I've left a note telling her that I've changed my mind and have let you go on the trip and that I'm out working all day."

"Right. Plumbing – I know."

Sam glared at George. "Listen, I will be on this number all day." He handed George a folded piece of paper. "Put it into your speed dial."

"Roger that."

"Is there any particular reason why you're being so gobby?"

"You gonna' tell me why you're suddenly racing off to Paris? You onto someone?" George said, under his breath.

Sam glared at him again and zipped his finger across his lips. "Brush your teeth. I'll meet you in the van."

Sam dropped George at the school gates just as the dawn light was seeping across the night's indigo canvas. George stared up at the stars and watched his breath float up to meet them.

"George!" Sam had climbed out of the van. "Stop daydreaming and come here." He grabbed George and guided him out into the open. "Right, listen. Remember to keep your wits about you. Don't let your guard down."

"I won't, I promise."

"I'll be at La Défense. It's in the west part of the city."

"Why there?"

"Chief has asked me to head up security at a conference he's attending."

"But what about finding Victor?"

"Freddie is heading up the investigation now. He's in charge."

"Why?"

"Chief's decision. It's probably for the best."

"But we were making progress. What about the postman?"

"Yes, on that point," Sam said, pulling George closer. "I checked with a friend of mine at Royal Mail. There's no record of anyone by that description working in our area – in fact, no delivery guys of Spanish descent at all. He's definitely suspicious, George. You see him again, you keep well away."

George nodded. "You know, I knew he was dodgy – and that van we saw that night, I bet it was him."

"George, mate!" It was Felix, trudging up the hill in the dark with a torch. "I didn't think you were – oh, Mr Jenkins."

"Hi, Felix," Sam said, looking at his watch. "I've got to go. Remember what I said, George. Don't make me regret my decision."

"I won't," George said, rolling his eyes.

Sam's van disappeared from view, and Felix and George wandered up the path together. Several cars passed them on the drive, lighting their way with their headlamps.

"How come you walked up?" George asked.

"Dad's old Morris Minor struggled to get up the hill," Felix chuckled. "Engine was too cold, apparently. How come your old man had a change of heart?"

"Between you and me, he's gonna' be in Paris as well, and old Steckler. He reckons that makes me safe."

"What's he doing in Paris? Is Victor there?" Felix gasped, shining his torch in George's face like he was interrogating him.

"No, it's some security thing." George shrugged, pushing the torch away.

"Huh! No progress on Victor then?" Felix seemed as disappointed as George.

"No, not really."

The watery dawn light and misty air made the school look haunted. Year nine students and parents stood huddled in ghostly clusters. Felix and George weaved between the groups until they found the others.

"You sneak out of the house?" Will said, nudging George with his elbow.

"Do we need to smuggle you over the channel?" Josh asked, grinning.

"Er ... I just..."

"His old man decided to let him go, after all," Felix said, saving George from having to search for an explanation.

"Did you have to promise to stick to all sorts of rules?" Will asked. "I know, I did."

"Yeah, like not chasing a bunch of blood-thirsty crims' across the city," Josh chuckled.

"Yeah, something like that," George replied.

"Wouldn't have been the same without you," Francesca said, smiling. "If it's any consolation, my mum was completely against me coming until my dad suggested she could spend the day in Paris, shopping."

"Your mum's coming with us!" Josh said, looking horrified.

"Relax," Francesca said, "she's being chauffeured to the station, has booked herself into first class and she won't be going anywhere near anything vaguely historic or educational – we won't even get a whiff of her overly pungent perfume!"

Jess snorted. "So, she's going to Paris to keep an eye on her daughter, then?"

"Precisely!" Francesca giggled.

They bundled onto the coach and managed to commandeer the back seats. Mr Steckler made the most of the deserted roads, and they were at Ashford International Station in no time at all.

Once they'd all cleared passport control, they were corralled together and given a briefing on what to expect from the day and what was expected from them. Miss O'Donnell, ancient Mr Walters, Mrs Stone and Mr Steckler hovered on the outskirts as a tall, pallid-looking French lady introduced herself as Madame Dupont, their tour guide. She reminded George of a French baguette: long, thin and pale. Dressed in high-waisted tan trousers, a billowing cream blouse and beige parka, George couldn't tell where her clothes ended and her skin began. Even her neatly plaited hair was the colour of under-baked bread.

"We will be seeing some of Paris' most spectacular sights," she said, raising her voice above the station clatter. "After we arrive at Gare du Nord, we will make our way into the heart of the city. You will have the privilege of visiting the famous art museum, Le Louvre, followed by a boat trip up the historic Seine to the imposing and strikingly gothic Cathédral Notre-Dame and then back down the river to the Eiffel Tower."

"Definitely no time for shopping, then," Francesca grumbled under her breath.

"Told you," Jess said.

George and Felix were distracted by the smell of freshly baked pastries that was wafting in their direction from the station café. The early start had left their stomachs unusually empty. They snuck off from the back of the huddle to grab a croissant but immediately found Mr Steckler on their tail.

Most people would take one look at old Mr Steckler and assume he wasn't fit to look after a goldfish, let alone protect a group of teenagers. But George had seen what the ex-secret service officer was capable of and knew that he'd be a better chaperone than any of the younger and more agile teachers.

"You two vigilantes need to stick with the group – none of your sneaking off. Far too adventurous for your own good," he said, with a mischievous grin. "You remind me of a younger … well … me! Did I tell you about the time that I canoed up the Amazon, George?"

"Er, yes, I believe you did, Mr Steckler," George replied politely.

"Call me Harry, boys. But just when the others are outta' earshot. Or Officer S47 – that's me' old call sign. You know, I got my finger chewed off while on duty in the Amazon."

"I thought my dad shot it off?" George asked, perplexed.

"Who told you that?"

"You."

"Right, of course I did. Well, we need to be on high alert," he whispered. "Your dad reckons there's an attack afoot. Need to be on our guard."

"An attack?" Felix said. "Where?"

"No idea," said Mr Steckler. "No one tells me anything any more. Nevertheless, I'm in the mood for catching me some scallywag. Don't wanna' miss out on the action. You tell me if you see anything odd, won't you?"

George was starting to re-evaluate his assessment of the usefulness of his allocated chaperone. He wasn't sure if he was having them on or losing his marbles. Maybe his years undercover had hindered his ability to tell fact from fiction, truth from bluff. Either way, George didn't think he should rely on the old bus driver if anything life threatening were to occur. He glanced at Felix and could tell from his poorly-suppressed grimace that he felt the same way.

Before they had time to grab their breakfast, Mrs Stone's whistle blew and they were all loaded onto the train. They had a whole carriage to themselves, and it was quickly filling up. George and Felix scrambled on board, keen to get the pick of the seats. They quickly found Will and Jess and grabbed two window seats across the aisle from them.

It wasn't long until the carriage was packed. Francesca and Lauren were the last to board; little patisserie bags swinging from their arms. They squeezed their way over to where George sat. There were only two seats left, and one of them was next to George.

"Is this seat taken?" Lauren said, smiling down at him. "We have cake."

Francesca waved the bag of patisseries in front of George's nose.

"Um – no! I mean – yes – no!"

"I think what George is *trying* to say is that it's not taken," Francesca said, saving him from his own stupidity.

"Exactly – it's not taken," George said, trying to regain some composure.

"And we're starving!" Felix added.

The train pulled off and George settled back in his seat. It was warm and comfy, and he sat amongst friends, sharing snacks and excitedly chatting about the day ahead. George felt at peace as the countryside flitted past.

What can possibly go wrong?

There were no stops before the tunnel, and they would be in Paris in under two hours. George had never been on the Eurostar before and was keen to take a look around.

"Hey, Felix," he whispered, "did you see where old Steckler went?"

"No, why?"

"I fancied a nose around the train and didn't need him on my case for 'wandering off'."

"Fair point."

Lauren and Francesca had gone to the toilet, so George shuffled over and peered down the aisle. He couldn't see

Mr Steckler, but he could see a couple of the teachers standing by the toilets. He turned to look the other way and locked eyes with Madame Dupont. She was staring right at him. She didn't flinch or smile or even acknowledge his existence. He slid his head back behind the seat.

"Teachers are blocking that way," Felix said.

"Yeah, and the freaky-looking tour guide is sitting right there."

"You think she'll stop us from stretching our legs?"

George stuck his head back out, expecting to see her steely eyes still pinned on him, but she had vanished.

"She's gone. Now's our chance," he said to Felix.

The two boys slid out of their seats.

"Where are you off to?" Jess said from across the aisle.

"To find some more food," George whispered, before dashing towards the door.

The train was brimming with passengers, but George and Felix managed to navigate their way through two packed carriages and into the buffet car. They both bought an energy drink and a large packet of crisps before heading back.

"I need to pee," George announced, as they passed another toilet. He yanked open the door and regretted it immediately.

"Urgh, you can do that alone," Felix said, holding his nose. "That's rough. I'm outta' here."

George took a deep breath and dived into the cubicle. By the time he had figured out how to flush the loo and use the tap, he was desperate to escape, but just as he was reaching for the door lock, he thought he heard a familiar voice outside.

"Don't be a fool. Leave it to me." It was a French accent, and it sounded very much like Madame Dupont.

George pressed his ear up to the door.

"There's no need to worry. No one will question why I'm here," a Spanish voice replied.

George couldn't believe his ears. Surely, it wasn't the postman – here on the train. But before he had the chance to hear any more, the door flew open and he tumbled out, colliding face first with the rather rotund belly of an old man.

"My goodness," the gentleman said. "Did you not lock the door?"

George didn't answer. "Who was here?" he asked, grabbing the man by the arm. "Which way did they go?"

He peered through the doors towards the buffet car. He could just make out the back of someone's head disappearing into the crowd. Jet black hair poked out from beneath a dark green beanie. He pushed past the startled old man and tried to follow the hat. The buffet car was full, and he had to weave his way past several passengers, staggering from side to side as the train rocked and swayed.

He was just making ground when everything around him seemed to shift. The light suddenly changed, and the noise of the train seemed to bear down on him, loud and intimidating. He glanced out of the window – they'd entered the tunnel. When he looked back, the hat had gone.

"Damn!" he cursed to himself, hesitating midway down the carriage.

I'm supposed to stay away from trouble.

"What are you doing all the way down here?"

George turned to see Madame Dupont glowering down at him. Up close, she was disturbingly tall. George looked down to see if she wore heels and was horrified to see her gnarled, misshapen toes escaping from the tight constraints of a well-worn pair of flat, strappy sandals. They reminded George of play dough when you squeezed it out of your fist and it oozed through your fingers. He shuddered.

"Did you hear what I said, or are you deaf as well as disorientated?" she asked, placing her bony fingers on her protruding hips.

Even without heels, she towered over George so much that he could see right up her rather large nose. She smelt heavily of lavender, and her face was caked in powder, which is why she probably looked so pale.

"I was just in the loo – took a wrong turn, I guess," he said, trying to hold his nerve.

"The school party is that way," she said.

"Is there a problem here?" Mr Steckler had finally re-appeared.

Madame Dupont looked him up and down. "One of your students seems to have got lost. I'd keep better tabs on him if I were you." With that, she stuck her nose in the air and marched off.

"What you up to, George?" Mr Steckler said, as they made their way back towards their carriage. "I promised your dad that I'd keep an eye on you. We haven't even reached Paris yet and you're causing trouble."

"Sorry, Mr Steckler. It's just that I thought I saw—"

George glanced back down the corridor, and the man in the beanie was coming back his way.

"What? What did you see?" Mr Steckler asked, looking excited.

George's shoulders sank. It wasn't the postman, after all. The man looked Spanish alright, and he did vaguely remind George of the postman, but he was older and meaner looking.

"Nothing," George sighed. "It was nothing."

George watched the man as he got closer. He was tall and beefy with silver streaks running through his raven hair and bushy beard. The closer he got, the more his chin dropped and his eyes sank beneath the peak of his beanie. There was something about him that made George stare.

George turned to say something to Mr Steckler, but before he could open his mouth, all the lights went out, and the train was thrown into total darkness.

From: Anonymous
To: J21
Re: Bird of Prey {Encrypted}

I have uncovered the details of a possible attack, but we are also stumbling across conflicting reports and false information that I believe has been fed to my sources to put us off the scent.

I am worried that we are being watched.
I am not comfortable continuing to correspond on this Comms network – even if it is encrypted.

My sources tell me that you are off to Paris – I will find a way to get you the intel.

End.

From: J21
To: Anonymous
Re: Bird of Prey {Encrypted}

We must do whatever it takes.
This weapon has the potential to cause mass devastation and is almost impossible to trace.
It won't be easy stopping an attack without prior knowledge of the target and the delivery method.

Your sources are worryingly well-informed. I have arrived in Paris and will wait to receive details of the location of the intel drop.

End.

Chapter 9: Friend or Foe

The darkness didn't last for long, but in that short moment, chaos seemed to break out. George tried to grab hold of Mr Steckler as they were hurled down the carriage by the force of the rapidly braking train. His shoulder braced his fall as he smashed into the glass doors. He could hear old Steckler groaning and voices from within the carriage calling out in panic.

Before George could pull himself back onto his feet, someone had him by the arm. They said nothing, but the stranger picked him up and pulled his dishevelled blazer back over his shoulders, patting and dusting him down.

"Mr Steckler?" he called out into the void, but no one responded. As he steadied himself against the wall, he couldn't help noticing a whiff of lavender. Before he could say anything, the emergency lights flickered on, casting a ghostly green glow throughout the train. He searched in the gloom, but Dupont was nowhere to be seen.

"George, give me a hand here," Mr Steckler groaned. He was crumpled in the corner and struggling to get up.

George squatted down beside him. "Are you hurt?"

"I've had worse – just shaken up a bit."

George lifted him to his feet. "What happened?"

"No idea," Mr Steckler said, just as the speakers crackled to life.

"Ladies and Gentlemen, this is your driver speaking. We apologise for the sudden loss of lights and the rather dramatic stop. We seem to have experienced an isolated loss of power. Nothing to worry about. We have identified the problem and should be back up and running in a few moments. Again, please accept our apologies."

"Bloomin' trains – never liked them," Mr Steckler said, straightening himself out.

With that, Felix appeared from the other side of the doors.

"You OK?" he asked, looking concerned.

"Yeah, just about. Everyone OK in there?" George said, peering through the gap.

"Think so. A few people panicked but no injuries."

"Let's get you two back to your seats," Mr Steckler said. "I don't need to be calling your dad and telling him that you've got injured on the damn train."

As they wandered back through the carriage, George saw that Madame Dupont was sitting back in her seat: calm, composed and doing a crossword. George stared at her as he passed, but she didn't look up.

"She's a bit odd, that Dupont," he whispered to Felix, once they were back at their seats.

"You think everyone is odd," Felix said, rolling his eyes.

"Oh, George," Lauren said, as they sat down, "you've torn your blazer."

George strained to look over his shoulder. The sleeve was half detached from the body. "Great! I've only had it a week."

"It will fix easily enough," Lauren said, placing a hand on his arm. "I can do it for you. I'm sure I've got one of those travel sewing kits in my bag somewhere. I'm quite good with a needle. Here, slip it off and I can do it now."

George could feel his cheeks flare up. "Um, great, thanks." He could also sense Felix trying to contain his amusement.

The lights came back on to a feeble cheer, and George decided to take his dad's advice and stay put for the rest of the journey, which passed by without any further incidents.

It wasn't long before they were offloading at Gare du Nord. Madame Dupont addressed them again, but George missed most of what she was saying because he was too busy watching her body language and trying to suss her out.

"She's definitely a bit weird though, don't you think?" he said to Felix, as they wound their way across the airy station concourse.

"She's just some French tour guide, George. You need to stop assuming everyone's out to get you. Are you gonna' tackle her to the ground too?"

"Maybe," he mumbled to himself. "But I actually heard–"

"George." Felix stopped and grabbed him by the shoulders. "We're here to have a day out. Take a break from playing detective, and try to chill and enjoy yourself. Can you do that?"

George sighed. "Yeah – OK – you're right."

They caught up with the others, who were hanging out by some of the concession stands while the teachers went outside to organise the minibuses that were going to ferry them down to the Louvre

George stood to the side. He wasn't interested in shopping. Too many things were nagging at him. He lent up against the back of a jewellery stand and closed his eyes. He wanted to clear his mind but couldn't control the random thoughts from floating in and out of his consciousness – a mole inside MI5, a dodgy postman, an oddly behaved tour guide colluding with a bearded stranger, Victor planning some kind of attack and his dad mysteriously sent over to Paris, leaving Freddie to head up the case. He sighed, blew all the air out of his cheeks and stared up at the ceiling.

Does any of it mean anything, or am I just losing the plot?

Before he could answer his own question, he was suddenly aware of the rapid sound of clicking. He turned to his left and found himself peering into the lens of a camera. A short oriental woman with a bleached-blond bob, held back by a ridiculous red bow, was snapping photos of him.

"You so cute," she said, grinning at George.

"Er, that's not cool," George replied, holding his hand up in front of her lens.

"It OK," she said in broken English. "You buy photo on web."

"What?"

With that, she shoved a business card into George's hand and scuttled off. George stood dazed. The card was blood-red with a small emblem delicately painted on the front, as if in liquid gold. It looked like a moth. He flipped it over. There was no name, number or web address. Puzzled, he looked back up, searching the concourse for any sign of her, but she had somehow dissolved into the crowd.

"There you are!" Felix was sauntering towards him proudly carrying a rather large metal replica of the Eiffel Tower. George opened his mouth to tell him about the Chinese woman but stopped himself. It was obvious that Felix was getting tired of George's paranoia.

"What is that?" George asked instead.

"It's cool, huh? It was only twenty-five Euros!"

"Bargain," George said, raising an eyebrow. "What exactly are you going to do with it?"

"You lot are next," Mrs Stone called, waving in their direction.

Josh and Jess dragged Francesca and Lauren away from their shopping, and they hurried over to the exit.

"Where's Will?" Jess said, as they pushed open the doors.

"I thought he was with you," Josh replied.

"Have we lost something?" Mrs Stone asked.

"Will," Jess said.

"I'm sure he's coming," Felix said. "He was by the gift shop."

"My bag!" George cried. "I left it by the stalls."

"Oh, my goodness! Is there anything else we've left behind? Go back in and get it, please – and drag Will out with you."

George quickly turned and dashed back towards the doors. He ducked inside and raced over to where he'd been standing. His bag sat undisturbed. He grabbed it and turned to look for Will but instead spotted the Chinese lady with the camera, and she was talking to Madame Dupont. George rubbed his eyes and looked again. He could just make out the back of Dupont's head but could see the photographer's face. He tried to read her lips, but her English was so poor, and he wasn't even sure if it was English they were speaking.

I need to get closer.

Slipping his bag on his back, he snuck around the back of the stalls and dived behind a stand full of umbrellas. He could now see both of them clearly and almost hear them. The Chinese woman was handing something to Dupont. George couldn't make out what it was.

Maybe it's one of her business cards.

He leaned out a little further and felt the stand start to topple. Grabbing it with both hands, he just managed to steady it before it crashed to the floor. As he looked back up, the two women were parting ways.

Dupont was striding towards the doors, but the other woman was coming his way. She looked up and stared straight into George's eyes. He jerked back behind the umbrellas, spun around and made a dash for the exit. As he threw open the door, he barged straight into Will who was loitering on the pavement with an armful of shiny, metal sports bottles. They clattered to the ground and rolled across the pavement in all directions.

"What on earth are you two doing?" Mrs Stone was standing on the steps of the minibus looking less than happy.

"Sorry, it was my fault," George said, looking over his shoulder to see if he'd been followed.

"William, I hope you paid for those, whatever they are," Mrs Stone said, as Will and George hurried to gather up the escaping bottles.

"No," Will said, grinning, "some guys were giving them away for free!"

George was on his knees, trying to reach a bottle that had rolled under the front wheel of the bus, when he found himself faced with Dupont's gruesome looking toes.

"Can I help you with that?" she said, sliding her foot under the wheel and kicking the bottle towards him.

George slowly stood up, opened his bag and stuffed the bottle inside. As he struggled to zip it up again, the red business card fluttered to the floor. He looked up and momentarily locked eyes with Dupont before she bent down and picked it up.

"I see that you met the rather overly-friendly photographer," she said, flicking the card over in her fingers.

"Er – yeah." George tried to avoid further eye contact.

"This city is filled with strangers, young man, and you should never trust a stranger," she said, handing the card back to him.

"Right, of course."

George watched her as she steadily mounted the steps to the bus.

What's the deal with her?

"Come on, George," Mrs Stone said, as he finally got on the bus. "We're already trailing behind the others. Find a seat. Will, you can finish handing the bottles out later."

George collapsed into a seat at the front and tried to focus on Mrs Stone's voice as she rattled through a brief history of Paris over the bus' microphone. He could tell it was going to be a long day, so he resolved himself to paying attention and trying to learn something. If nothing else, it might just help him to stop fixating on the investigation and his ever-growing list of suspicious characters.

Chapter 10: The Art of Deception

The sun had broken through the thin layer of clouds by the time they reached the Louvre. George had seen photos of it in magazines and on the internet, but it was far more impressive up close and in person. Its iconic glass pyramid rose up from the surrounding pools like a perfectly chiselled iceberg. It shimmered in the morning sun, and George could see the reflection of the clouds racing across its gleaming face.

He took a deep breath and turned full circle, taking in the vista and trying to remind himself that he was in Paris – a world away from Chiddingham.

"Gather around!" Madame Dupont called, interrupting George's moment of peace. "We will be going around the museum in small groups, and each group will be allocated a guide. As I call your name, please follow your guide into La Pyramide du Louvre and through security."

George was hoping that they wouldn't have to stay in the company of Dupont. He eyed up the handful of guides that had appeared from within the pyramid. They were a mixed bunch.

"Hope we don't get the moody looking one on the end," Will said, sidling up beside George.

"I was hoping we could choose who we could go around with," Francesca said. "It would be more fun if we could stay with our friends."

"Knowing our luck, they'll split us up," Josh said.

"Yeah, especially after what happened in London," Will added.

"What exactly did happen in London?" Lauren asked, making the others fall silent.

"We got a bit … lost, shall we say," Jess replied.

"I heard you skipped the science fair and ended up getting arrested," Lauren said, fiddling with her blazer button, again.

"Um … I wouldn't say we were arrested, exactly," Will said.

Jess kicked him in the shins. "We were nothing of the sort!"

"Group D!" Madame Dupont was screeching at them. "Are you even listening?"

Somehow, they'd been put together. Will, Jess, Francesca, Josh, Felix and George.

"What are the chances of that?" Felix said, glancing at George. Lauren looked peeved.

"Must be the good luck charm I bought," Jess said, holding up a leather strap with a rabbit's foot attached.

"That's horrendous!" Francesca squealed. "What on earth–"

"Will you lot hurry up," Mrs Stone said, striding over towards them. "Your guide is waiting."

"Sorry, Mum," Jess said.

Mrs Stone shook her head, and her heavily rimmed glasses slid down her nose. She peered over the top of them, looking at each of them in turn. "You're not filling me with confidence – you need to behave yourselves today. We don't need a repeat of last time. I won't hesitate to split you up."

"Miss, can I go with them, please?" Lauren asked, just as Dupont was calling her name. George looked over at Group E, which currently consisted of Liam, Hayley and Jake.

"Please, Mrs Stone," he pleaded.

"OK, fine. Just stay with your guide – no … exploring."

Lauren beamed at George and pecked him on the cheek. "Thank you!"

George felt his forehead go sweaty and a lump lodge in his throat. "No worries," he croaked, and before he could embarrass himself further, he broke into a jog to catch up with the others.

They managed to find their guide: a young, athletic looking guy in skinny jeans and a tailored jacket. His dark afro hair was tightly braided and pulled back. He looked barely older than sixteen. He was French, but spoke perfect English.

"He's cool," Francesca whispered to Lauren.

Josh frowned. "Bet he's no good at rugby. He looks like he'd break in half."

"My name is Jean-Pierre, but you can call me JP if that's easier," he said, smiling.

George glanced over at Josh again, who was now puffing out his chest. He obviously wasn't used to the competition.

Welcome to my world, George thought.

They made their way towards security and had to slide their bags through a scanner.

"What's in these bottles?" the guard asked, holding up one of Will's freebies.

"Just water," Will said, shrugging.

The guard insisted on opening them all up and sniffing the contents. He even made Will drink from his.

"What's he so jumpy about?" Will said, as he shoved his bottle back into his bag.

"We've had the odd … incident," JP explained. "In fact, someone once threw acid at the Mona Lisa."

"That's awful," Francesca said, as they dived into the depths of the vast museum.

The teachers spread themselves between the groups. Mr Steckler was quick to attach himself to the back of their group, but he seemed to have a hanger-on. Madame Dupont was hovering on his shoulder. George couldn't help laughing. Poor Mr Steckler looked tiny compared to her, and it looked like she wasn't letting him get a word in edgeways.

The tour took them past the famous Mona Lisa and several other high profile pieces that looked vaguely familiar to George. Slowly the groups were spreading out as they snaked their way along the wide art-covered corridors and high-ceilinged halls. George tried to focus on what JP was saying, but couldn't help getting distracted by Dupont. Every time he looked back, she was dragging Mr Steckler off in one direction or another to admire some masterpiece.

As the morning progressed, the museum got busier, and before long, it wasn't easy to keep together, even in their small group.

"Try not to drift off," JP kept calling from up ahead.

The boys were dragging behind as they slowly lost interest in '19th Century French Impressionism'.

"Man, I'm starving," Josh said, lumbering along beside George. "When do we get a break?"

"God knows. It's too hot in here too," Will complained, loosening his tie.

"I'm exhausted and we've still got the cathedral and the Eiffel Tower to go," Felix said, yawning.

"Am I boring you?" JP had stopped and was standing in front of them with the girls at his side. "You guys want to see something a little more exciting?"

"Sure," said Will.

"Like a café?" Josh asked.

JP completely ignored him. "Well, it's not on the tour, but if we sneak off, we can maybe go and see something that you might find more … stimulating."

"Ooh, like what?" Lauren asked, looking intrigued.

"Follow me," JP said, changing his saunter to a stride.

"Er, hang on, guys," George said, searching behind him for any sign of Mr Steckler or the rest of year nine.

He could just make out Steckler and Dupont in the previous hall, admiring a large canvas of a harvest landscape. Dupont had actually linked arms with old Steckler and seemed to have his full attention. "Er … I think we'll have Dupont on our case if we take a detour." Although, he wasn't sure that she'd even notice.

"I thought you wanted to get away from her?" Felix said. "Come on."

"We'll be gone ten minutes, no more," JP said. "No one will even realise we've gone."

They ducked out of the hall they were in and were soon descending a set of wide stone stairs. Something about being in the basement of a museum – the artificial light, the dust hanging in the stale air – something about being underground made George uneasy.

"What exactly are we doing down here?" he asked, pushing forwards to question JP.

"We have a special exhibit for one month only," JP said, taking his ID off his lanyard and swiping it through a reader. "It's a collection of Rothko's. You would normally have to pay extra to get in, but luckily for you, I can sneak us in through this staff entrance."

George looked around at his friends. None of them looked worried. In fact, they looked positively excited to be doing something they weren't supposed to be.

Relax, George.

They passed through a thin corridor and at JP's instruction, slipped into the dimly lit room one by one. George could see that it certainly was different from all the historic oil paintings they'd seen upstairs. Eight large canvases hung from the walls, each lit from above by a single beam of light. In an otherwise featureless room, you couldn't help but be drawn to the striking vision of colours that each piece displayed.

Reds, greens, blues, oranges of all hues reached out and grabbed you.

"Wow, they're incredible," Francesca said, moving further into the room.

"Huh – I could do that," Josh said, shrugging.

"Maybe," JP said, "but would yours sell for over a hundred million dollars?"

"What?"

"This Rothko dude must be one happy guy," Will said.

"You'd think so," JP said. "But actually, he's dead – he killed himself, in fact."

"That's so sad," Lauren said.

"I don't get it," Josh said, still puzzled. "What's so special about them? They're just a bunch of different colours."

"Ah!" JP turned to admire the first canvas. "What's so special? Well, exactly that. They are simple and devoid of any central focus, yet they draw you in and fill you with emotion – emotion that is unique to you as the viewer."

Felix stood next to him and scrunched up his nose, tilted his head from one side to the other and then shrugged, making George laugh out loud.

"Shh!" A lady at the next canvas hushed at them and frowned.

"People come to immerse themselves in the colour and texture," JP whispered, moving to the next painting. "Have a wander around and see what you … feel."

It was a single, rectangular hall with an arched exit at each end, roped off and guarded. There were quite a few people in the room and a queue of people entering in drabs at one end as others exited from the other. George drifted around trying to find a piece that might move him but was suddenly distracted by a flash of red moving between the crowd. He could see a head – platinum-blond hair and a bright red bow.

It can't be!

George dodged between several visitors to get a better view. She was moving quite fast and then stopped, right next to JP. George froze.

What on earth?

JP was looking at his watch while she stood with her back turned, pointing her camera at one of the paintings. George moved again to get a better view. It was definitely the lady from the station, and she was talking to herself – or was it to JP?

With that, JP strode forwards and started gathering the group back together. George saw Felix and made a beeline for him just as JP and the rest of the group were also heading his way.

"I think we've outstayed our welcome," JP said, nervously eyeing up the guarded entrance. "We should probably re-join the rest of your group."

As they were making their way back towards the exit, the sound of someone shouting broke through the otherwise calm ambience. George twisted to see what the commotion was. Somebody was arguing with one of the guards, and that somebody looked a lot like Mr Steckler, but before George could say anything, a sharp and shrill alarm exploded in his ears.

"Quick, this way, guys," JP yelled over the noise, as he directed them back towards the staff door at the side of the room.

George glanced back. All the other visitors were rushing in the opposite direction and a metal gate was slowly descending from the ceiling, sealing the archways in and out.

"Wait! Shouldn't we go that way?" George shouted.

"It's too late," JP barked. "They're closing the security gates. There's a short cut to the gardens through the staff bay. Come on!"

George looked back one last time as JP hurried them through the door. He could see Mr Steckler's face squashed up against the metal mesh; a security guard wrestling with his flailing arms.

From: TDP
To: Anonymous
Re: Tracker {Encrypted}

The contact gave me the list of wanted assets. They have been grouped together and handed to their guide.

The transfer is underway. You should be able to track them as requested.

Everything went smoothly; however, we did have one slight issue. There was a chaperone who got very close to interrupting the handover.

I have neutralised him for now, but he may have the ability to alert J21.

End.

From: Anonymous
To: TDP
Re: Tracker {Encrypted}

This is great. I will track them from my end. I won't let them out of my sight. Send me a copy of the list. I need to know who they are and how many?

In reference to the chaperone – was it an elderly gentleman with a missing finger? If so, he is no longer in active service and should be easy enough to deal with.

Do not worry about him alerting J21. We have sent him to the intel drop and told him to turn off all GPS and cell traceable devices. He will be out of contact.

End.

Chapter 11: Déjà-vu

The sound of the alarms melted into the distance as George and his friends followed JP back out into the deserted corridor.

"What was that all about?" Jess said, stopping to wait for George, who was trailing behind.

"I have no idea," George said, under his breath, "but I don't trust this guy. Why did we have to come this way?"

Will had also hung back. "Don't stress, this leads us back up to where the others were."

"It better do," George grumbled. "Mr Steckler was stuck on the other side of that security barrier, and he looked pretty peed off. Mrs Stone will be freaking out."

"We can't hang around here," JP called from the stairwell. "We'll have to make our way to an evacuation point and try to meet up with the rest of your party. Follow me."

With that, he turned and started to head down another flight of stairs.

"Hang on!" yelled George. "We're supposed to go up." But as he reached the stairwell, he could see that the doorway to the galleries was also now blocked off.

Francesca had stopped. "I don't like this, at all. Why are the alarms going off in the first place?"

"I don't know," George said, "but I think it's time we found out." He pushed ahead and leapt down the steps after JP. "Hey, wait!"

"Keep up, guys," JP called back. "We need to get out before total shut down."

"Hang on!" George bellowed, pushing past Felix and Lauren who were racing to keep up with JP. "Just wait one minute. We're not going anywhere until you tell us what's going on."

JP stopped, and George could see him tense up. He took a deep breath before swivelling around to face them all. "It's probably nothing serious – there are several reasons for a full shut down. There's no need to panic, but it really is better if we just get outside, and then we can find everyone else." His eyes drifted across their concerned faces. "I promise this is the easiest and safest way back to the concourse."

"By going down?" Jess said, her hands on her hips.

JP swallowed. George watched his Adam's Apple rise and fall.

He's lying.

"I don't believe you," George said.

"George!" Lauren said, looking embarrassed. "JP is trying to help us."

George didn't expect her to understand. "We could have easily gone with all the other visitors, but he shoved us through that side door, and now we're trapped down here, and we have no idea where he's leading us."

"George, come on, mate" Felix said, giving him a look of exasperation.

George had had enough of Felix's scepticism. He looked to the others for support.

"I don't see why we can't just go back the other way?" Jess said, looking back up the stairs.

JP sighed. "Guys, why would I lie to you? It's me that's going to get in trouble if my boss finds me down in a restricted area with a bunch of visitors. I swear – look, this staircase leads us down through storage and then up and out into the loading bay. Just come to the bottom and you'll see the signs."

Lauren was already padding further down the steps. "I just want to get out."

The others stayed where they were. "I say we go back up," Will said, looking to George for agreement.

"You can't!" JP snapped. "You won't get back up there without staff access."

"You need to give us that ID card, then," Jess said.

"Yeah," Will added, "we'll let ourselves back up."

"I'd lose my job if I did that." JP was getting twitchy.

George could see beads of glistening sweat starting to gather on the bridge of his nose.

"Then we'll just have to go back up and shout until someone hears us," Francesca said.

George swung his bag off his back. "Better still, we'll call someone." He grabbed his mobile from the front pocket and started bounding back up the steps. The others quickly followed his lead, leaving Felix and Lauren at the bottom with an anxious looking JP.

"Who you gonna' call?" Will asked, climbing up behind him.

"My dad."

"What good is that? We need to call someone who's upstairs. Have you got anyone else's number?"

But before George had time to answer, the sound of Lauren's scream was reverberating off the walls and echoing up the stairwell. They all whipped around. JP had her; the cord of his lanyard wrapped around her neck.

"I didn't want to do this, but you've left me no choice." JP's cool, suave exterior had vanished, and all that remained was a look of anger and panic. "I'll throttle her, I swear it." He was obviously thinking on his feet. Whatever he was supposed to do, it wasn't going to plan. His eyes flitted from George, who was now at the top of the stairs, and back to Felix, who was only feet away. The others had stopped, strewn across the staircase. George tried to catch Felix's eye, but he was frozen still, staring in disbelief at JP's sudden turn of character.

"Please don't hurt her," Francesca said, starting to inch back down towards him.

"You don't have to do this," Jess said, coming down at him from the other side.

George wasted no time scanning through his contacts. *Damn! Why didn't I put Dad's number in the stupid speed dial?*

"Stay there!" JP was backing away. "And drop that phone!" He pulled the cord tighter. Lauren's eyes grew wide, her face was turning red and her legs were starting to give way.

"You'll kill her!" Francesca screamed. "Please stop!"

"Let her go!" Jess was now taking two steps at a time towards JP, Josh and Will close on her heels. They were closing in on him. Surely they could overpower him. He backed further away, dragging Lauren with him.

"Felix, do something!" George was screaming, but the words had barely left his lips before someone was on him from behind. He was grabbed by the hair, his head yanked back and something hard and sharp jabbed into the flesh just below his chin.

"You keep still now," a Chinese voice whispered in his ear. George's heart sank. He should have guessed. "You all stop!" she screeched.

George could see them twisting to see who the newcomer was.

Will was only a few steps away. "Who the hell are you?"

"I am Jin-é and you are doing precisely what I say."

JP had relaxed the noose around Lauren's neck. She was gasping for breath. "I was handling it," he spat. "I don't need your help." George looked down at him. He looked like a sullen teenager, annoyed that the grown up had taken charge.

"Looks like only thing you handling is little girl's windpipe," she said. "You only had one job."

"And I'm doing it," JP growled. "They are coming with me."

"We're going nowhere with either of you," Jess said.

"You will do it," Jin-é said, "or I kill."

She pulled George's head to the side, and he could just make out the tip of a long, thin, metal spike. It looked like a knitting needle and felt sharp enough to break his skin. She scraped it up his neck and towards his ear. He closed his eyes.

This is not happening again. I won't let it happen.

Without thinking twice, he took a deep breath, twisted in her grip and smashed his heel into the side of her kneecap. She crumpled to the floor and barrelled forwards, clattering down the steps.

George's phone had toppled from his grasp. He lunged for it, just as Will was charging back up the stairs towards Jin-é, but she bounced up like a spring. Before Will could take a swipe at her, she kicked him full blast in the chest, sending him flying into Josh and them both cascading down the stairwell.

George's fear and anger, boiled over. Determined not to let her win, he put his head down and charged at her from the steps above, trying to rugby tackle her around the waist, but she was up on her toes and saw him coming. She simply spun out of his way at the last moment, leaving him with nothing to break his fall. His already sore shoulder crashed into the iron bannister, his footing slid on the smooth stone and he ended up face down, belly sliding down the steps.

As he came to a stop, he could see Josh clambering up the steps towards him, but before he could get back on his feet, his head was slammed against the cold, hard stone and a burning pain shot down his neck and up to his temple.

"Stop!" she screamed. "I drive this through ear canal and into brain!" She had him pinned to the floor and the end of her needle shoved hard into his ear. George closed his eyes and took a deep breath. It all felt far too familiar. "This is painful death," she warned. "You all do what I say, or he die." Silence descended, and everyone stood frozen still. "We move down, now." She dragged George to his feet, slung one arm around his neck and held the needle steady in his ear.

The pain blurred George's vision. His eyes watered, and he struggled to find the edge of the steps with his toes. He glanced at Will, who was on the balls of his feet with his fists bunched. He caught George's eye, but Jin-é must have seen it too.

"I watching you," she said. "I not hesitate to kill him – I only need six of you."

Will backed down and traipsed down the stairs after the others.

George tried to keep his head level as they moved. With every step, his ear screamed out, sending a searing pain across his forehead. As they shuffled through several rooms stacked high with crated art, he wondered whether he could somehow outwit her. They were seven against two. How had they got themselves into this mess – again?

They finally arrived in the loading bay, just as JP had promised. He stopped at the door and checked that the bay was empty – everyone had evacuated. Dragging Lauren with him, he went ahead and punched a code into a wall-mounted panel. A large set of metal doors rumbled up and over their heads, revealing the back of a heavily armoured truck. It reminded George of those bullet-proof security vehicles that carry large amounts of cash.

"Open up!" Jin-é ordered, checking over her shoulder that they were still alone.

JP shoved Lauren towards the others. Francesca just caught her as her knees gave way. Without hesitation, JP slammed his fist against the back doors – one, two, three. The driver's door flew open, and someone leapt out, head to toe in baggy blue overalls and a full-face helmet.

"Get in!" a muffled voice said from beneath the darkened visor. Whoever he was, he was carrying a menacing looking handgun. He waved it towards the back doors.

"You get in with them," he said to JP, handing him a spare gun. "Keep them quiet."

JP looked down at the gun and back up at the guard. "That wasn't part of the deal. You said–"

"You'll do as you're told," the guard said. "We'll tell you when you're done. Now get in."

JP turned the gun over in his hands and then lifted it towards George and his friends. "Go on, you heard what he said."

George was the last to be shoved into the truck. As Jin-é released him from her grasp, he grabbed at his ear. The pain had left him with a throbbing headache, and his watering eyes were streaming down his cheeks. He stumbled on the rough metal flooring and staggered to one side, colliding with a thin wooden crate.

"I've got you," Will said, grabbing him and helping him to sit down with his back to the wall of the truck.

JP clambered on last before Jin-é, who was now also wearing a full-face helmet, slammed the doors shut, making the whole cabin shake.

There were no windows, and only metal hooks and loose bungee straps hung from the walls. George wiped his eyes to clear his vision. The few wooden crates that were keeping them company had the same emblem on as Jin-é's business card – the golden moth.

Who the hell is she?

The front doors slammed, the engine started and they slowly pulled out of the Louvre.

"Where are they taking us?" Jess said, staring at JP.

"Be quiet," he mumbled. He was sat with his back to the doors – his gun in one hand, his other hand cradling his head. "I wish you'd all just done as I asked. This isn't what was supposed to happen."

George looked at him. Sat down with his knees pulled up, he looked no older than them. A teenager, barely old enough to hold down a job – how was he caught up in all this?

"What *was* supposed to happen, then?" George asked.

JP looked up and scowled at him. "I was just meant to deliver you to the loading bay, that was all. I wasn't supposed to be in here with … this," he said, looking down at the gun in his hand like it was some vile creature.

Jess glanced at George and back to JP. "Why don't you put it down, then?"

"Yeah, do you even know how to use it?" Will asked. "I mean, you wouldn't actually want to shoot one of us, would you?"

JP looked down at the gun again. It looked heavy and awkward in his hands. "I'll do what I have to – I have no choice," he said, glaring at Will.

"Maybe we can help you get out of this mess," Jess said, her voice soft.

"Yeah, and maybe you can help us get out of here," Will said. "What have you got to lose?"

"Everything!" JP shouted, pointing the gun at Will, his hands shaking. "You have no idea who these people are – what they're capable of."

"OK, you're right," Will said, holding up his hands. "We have no idea."

"I think we do, actually," George said, still massaging his ear. "I think we know exactly who they are."

Jess turned to look at him. "You don't think…"

"Well, does anyone else have a strong sense of déjà-vu?" George said, raising his head and looking around at the others.

"You're right," said Will, "this stinks of Victor."

"Who's Victor?" Lauren said. She had recovered her voice but was curled up in a ball with Francesca's arm around her shoulders.

"It's not important," George said. "What's important is that Steckler and Dupont will know we're missing. We need to—"

"Dupont won't help you," JP laughed. "Who do you think put you together in your group and gave you to me? She'll be doing everything she can to distract your teachers."

"I knew it," George said, looking at Felix. "I told you she was dodgy."

Felix shrank further into his corner. "I'm sorry, I just thought—"

"It's irrelevant," JP said, as the truck bounced over a speed-bump. "The people behind all this – you can't mess with them – they have a way of getting exactly what they want." His chin had sunk down onto his knees.

"What exactly does Victor want with us?" George asked.

"Yeah, start talking JP," Josh added.

"I have no idea who you're talking about," JP replied, not bothering to lift his gaze. "I've not met any Victor. Jiné and the guy up front – they're the ones that wanted you guys – they said you owed them."

"Owed them!" Jess was indignant. "How do we owe them anything?"

JP shrugged. "Why do you think I'm here? I'm repaying a debt."

"Maybe he's after us because we rumbled him," Josh said.

"Yeah, and because George and Felix got Philippe and Jefferson caught," Will said.

"But I thought Victor got what he wanted," Josh said. "I mean, he broke out his team, set fire to the school and got into those tunnels."

"Yeah, why would he want to come back for us?" Jess asked. George and Felix exchanged looks, and it wasn't lost on Jess. "What? What do you guys know?"

"Nothing," George replied, a little too snappily.

"What aren't you telling us?"

"I swear, it's nothing." George hated lying but didn't think that telling them about the weapon and the potential attack would help the situation much, and anyway, it would be impossible to explain it all without exposing his dad. "We don't know any more than you."

"You need to be quiet, now," JP said. "You'll soon find out who's behind this – we're here. I suggest you do exactly as they say."

The truck reversed and came to a stop. JP stood up, and the back doors flew open. The helmeted guard stood sentry as Jin-é ushered them out and towards a small archway. George tried to snatch a glimpse of their surroundings. All he could make out was the smooth, curved stonework above their heads; a squat, wooden doorway, buried in a low arch ahead of them and the slap and rush of water.

We must be under a bridge.

"Keep moving," Jin-é whispered, shoving George in the back. She had removed her helmet and had slung a tool belt around her tiny waist. George could see her needle and a collection of knives and paintbrushes.

As they ducked under the archway and through the door, something caught the light – a golden moth etched onto a plaque on the wall. It was small and discreet but unmistakable.

"Inside – inside," Jin-é said, pushing the last of them into the small room, pulling the doors closed behind her.

George looked around the room – brickwork walls, covered in art; a cobbled floor and dim rays of light that filtered down from small glazed holes in the ceiling above. They were bundled in together in the gloom. He could feel Lauren snivelling beside him. He reached down and squeezed her hand. "It's gonna' be OK, I promise," he said, but the sound of a familiar voice punched a hole in George's confidence.

"So good to see you, again."

Chapter 12: A Reticent Reunion

It had only been a few weeks, but seeing Alex Allaman standing there in front of them, made everything that had happened to George since, concertina into a heartbeat. There he stood, his pencil moustache and slick hair as formal and motionless as ever.

"You!" Will spat.

"Thought you'd seen the back of us?" Alex said, gliding towards them.

"More like, hoped!"

"Silence!" Alex barked. "Or I'll gag you."

Lauren was trying to stifle her sobs. She was trembling all over. George squeezed her hand tighter and tried to catch her eye, but she was staring at her feet, her head shaking from side to side. Francesca lent over to comfort her.

"Step away!" Alex said, striding towards her.

"Leave her alone!" Francesca squealed. "You're frightening her!"

He stopped and glared at Francesca. "The only thing you need to be frightened of is what I'll do to you if you speak again. As long as she keeps her mouth shut, she will be just fine." He looked down his elongated nose at them and eyed each one in turn. "We only need six," he said, raising an eyebrow towards Jin-é.

"Bonus for you," she said, smiling back at him.

He frowned. "And you're late."

"JP's fault," she said, nodding towards the corner where JP was loitering in the shadows.

"What went wrong?" Alex asked.

"They … resisted," JP said, "but I had it under control."

Jin-é starting laughing. "Oh no, darling. Little kids have you surrounded."

JP lunged at her, taking her by surprise and knocking several brushes and knives from her belt.

"Get out of my way!" a muffled voice shouted from behind, pushing Jin-é and JP aside. It was the guard. He had rolled down his overalls to reveal a torn, black skull t-shirt and tattooed arms. "We've got work to do, and we're behind schedule," he said, pulling off his helmet.

George had already guessed.

Austin Van der Berg.

He had shaved off his dreadlocks but had several new piercings, including a large bolt through his eyebrow.

"Get them up to the workshop," Alex said to Jin-é. "Bind their hands, and do it well. They have a nasty habit of escaping." With that, he turned and followed Austin through a side door.

"You go," Jin-é said, shoving George in the back. "JP too."

They slowly filed across the room. George tried to see where the two men had gone. The door stood ajar, and Austin was sat at a desk, two large computer screens illuminating his face. One screen had a CCTV feed; the other had a collection of images – images of him and his friends at the station – the photos that Jin-é must have taken. Austin glanced up, caught George spying and kicked out at the door, slamming it shut.

"Up! Up!' Jin-é said, pushing them up a metal staircase into a cluttered room filled with crates and canvasses. Paint buckets, brushes and piles of old cloths littered every corner.

"Welcome – my workshop." Jin-é beamed with pride. "You never see such fine work – I am prodigy!" She spun around and bowed. "Thank you, my darlings."

"They're all copies," JP said, shrugging. "What's so special about that? Anyone can do a copy."

She growled at him. "You is imbecile – you know nothing of fine art. I am genius."

JP was smirking. She whipped her needle out of her belt and flicked her wrist. It flew through the air like a dart and lodged itself in the wall just behind JP's left ear. "You shut up now," she said, smiling.

JP went to grab at the needle, but Alex's voice was drifting up the stairwell.

"You kneel in line on floor," Jin-é quickly said, shoving George down to his knees.

One by one, their hands were tied. Lauren was sobbing again but stopped as Alex appeared on the stairs.

"We're ready," he said to Jin-é. "You two need to help Austin to load the truck. We will only have a small window of time to make the delivery. JP, you will then stay here to help escort the kids."

"I'm supposed to be back at the museum. They'll notice I've gone."

"I don't care. We need you to help take the kids to the drop off."

"That wasn't the deal. I'll lose my job."

Alex laughed. "I think that's inevitable."

JP fumed. "You said that all I had to do was drop them at the loading bay. I didn't sign up to any of the rest of this. You said that would repay the debt!"

"Your father owes us, and we will keep taking back from him until we are even."

"But–"

"But nothing! You can tell your father, next time he crawls out from whichever rock he's hiding under, that we will decide when he has paid his dues. Now get downstairs!"

JP kicked out at a bucket, sending it flying across the room and rebounding off one of the canvases.

"That my hard work!" Jin-é steamed. "You have more respect for my art!"

JP stormed down the stairs, spitting at a picture that hung from the wall as he went. Jin-é screamed at him. "You nasty boy! I get you with my needle!"

Alex was shaking his head.

They sat in silence as Alex busied himself on his phone. George could hear movement downstairs, doors opening and closing, Jin-é barking orders. He looked at his friends. He and Will were still balancing on their knees, but the others had slumped to the floor.

They need to stay alert.

He wasn't sure where they would be taken next, but they needed to be ready to take any opportunity to escape.

With that, something crashed below. Alex sighed and shook his head again. "I'm going downstairs. No one try anything funny. Don't forget, I only need six of you, so I'm more than happy to make a sacrifice if anyone steps out of line."

They listened to the sound of his boots clanging off the metal steps as he disappeared from sight. Lauren immediately started crying again, but Will was up on his feet. "We need to get the hell out of here."

"You don't say?" Josh said. "And how do you suggest we do that?"

"I don't know, but I'm not being part of whatever it is they're planning on doing to us."

"Well, I don't exactly *plan* to hang around for the after party, but I don't see any way out."

"Instead of whining – start thinking."

"That's exactly what I was doing before you started waffling!"

"Oh good, coz' your contributions are always *so* valuable!*"

"Guys, guys," George said, interrupting the storm of insults. "We need to stay calm and focused."

"Calm?" Will said. "How can we stay calm? Have you forgotten what happened in London?"

George lowered his voice further. "Look, JP is going to escort us. I think we can work on him."

"I agree," said Jess. "He wants to be out of here as much as we do."

"George," Felix said, "what happened to your phone?"

"It's gone," George replied. "I dropped it when Jin-é wiped me out."

"I think she picked it up," Lauren squeaked. "She must have it."

"Either way, it's gone."

The sound of the truck's engine starting signalled that their time was up. Alex and JP were coming back up the stairs.

"Remember," George whispered, "calm and focused."

But as Alex reappeared with JP dragging behind, George realised that it wasn't going to be easy.

"Hood them," Alex said, passing JP a handful of black, fabric sacks. "They mustn't see where we're going."

George could feel the panic stifle the air in the room. Terror flashed across Lauren's eyes as Alex thrust the first hood down over her head – every inch of her was shaking.

JP started halfway along the line and soon reached George. "We're one short."

"Find something else," Alex barked. "Get them downstairs. I will prepare the boat."

George watched JP as he ripped up an old, paint-splattered sheet. He came at George and paused in front of him.

"You can help us," George whispered. "Please?"

JP looked into George's eyes. "I'm sorry," he muttered, before enveloping George's face in the dust-filled cloth.

They jostled and stumbled, trying to find their footing, as JP herded them down the stairs. George felt his way to the edge of each step, stretching his toes out ahead of him. He could hear raspy breathing all around. With his hands tied, he had no way of maintaining his balance on the handrail. He felt like he was at sea.

The smell of paint filled his nose, and the dust scratched at his eyes, but the fabric was thin, and he could just make out shadows – light and dark. Someone ahead of him tripped, sending bodies tumbling down the stairwell.

"Get up!" Alex yelled. "We will be getting into a boat. Do exactly as you're told, and no one will get hurt. When I say, we will walk out of the doors and onto the jetty. You will step down into the boat and lie flat on your stomachs."

George could feel the rush of fresh air as the doors opened. The light flooded in, and he could see even more – contrasting shapes and colours.

"Just follow my voice," JP said, leading the way.

They shuffled forwards – one by one lunging off the jetty. George could see their faint silhouettes plunge from view. He was next. His heart rate spiked and his breath sucked the makeshift hood in and out as he crept to the edge. He hesitated. He couldn't see what was below his feet – a dark mass. He strained his eyes.

"Jump," Alex growled.

It felt like he was about to leap into the abyss. Would he hit water? He hadn't heard the others splash.

"Just step down," JP said in his ear. "You'll hit the boat."

George took a deep breath and stepped out into nothing.

"Argh!"

He landed on something soft – a body. "Sorry."

"Get down, now!" Alex barked.

George sank his head down. He could feel legs and knees; elbows digging into his back. He tried to look up towards the light, but before he could get his bearings, a large, black, rubber sheet buried them all in total darkness. The outboard motor rattled to life, and they were soon bouncing down the Seine like smuggled contraband.

They can't have gone very far before the boat swerved, tipping and sending them all rolling to one side. The sound of the engine dulled, and they slowed. All of a sudden, the noises seemed to echo around them, as if they were inside – but inside what?

They were gliding – gliding through calmer waters. An eerie silence cocooned George's ears. He shifted his weight.

"Careful," Will's voice warned from behind him.

"Sorry," George whispered back. "Where are we?"

"Inside something," Jess breathed from somewhere towards his feet.

"Égouts de Paris," Felix said.

George could barely hear him. "What?"

Felix wriggled and turned until he was almost face to face with George. "The ancient sewers of Paris – under the streets – miles of them."

Something was digging into George's back. His bag had slid off his shoulders and was buried beneath him, and his arms were awkwardly wedged under the bag. He tried to shift again.

"Ow! You're kicking me!"

"Quiet!" Alex's voice only just penetrated the thick rubber sheeting. "We're nearly there."

The motor died, and the boat bumped up against something. George was now face up, and as the sheet was yanked back, he could see shadows moving above him – bodies moving in front of a bright light.

"Get up!" Alex said.

They squirmed and fumbled, unable to lift themselves from the seesawing boat. George managed to get to his feet but was surrounded by bodies. He stumbled and lurched forwards. Bracing himself, he tried to protect his head, which came down first, but it simply bounced off the side of the boat.

A rubber dinghy, he thought, *just like the one we found Gran in.*

"This is ridiculous," Alex said. "Help them out."

JP grabbed George by the shoulders. "This way."

One by one they were dragged out of the boat and onto a concrete dock. George could smell stagnant water and something worse. He twisted his head to try to make out his surroundings. They were inside; enclosed somehow. It was dark except for a single light that dangled above them. Water dripped somewhere nearby, but wherever they were, the water wasn't moving fast.

He didn't have to wait long to satisfy his curiosity. Someone snatched at his hood and whipped it off.

"They can't go any further with these on," Alex said, ripping each hood off in turn.

They squinted as their eyes readjusted to the light. A floodlight had been hung from a pipe above their heads. George looked around. The dinghy was tied to a rusted railing alongside another smaller boat. The water beneath them was thick and dark, like rippling oil, and the narrow concrete sewer spread out into the darkness in both directions.

Pipes and cables drooped overhead, and a thin, raised walkway followed the sewer's path. A flimsy chain balustrade was all that was saving them from plunging back into the water.

"What do you want with us?" Francesca said, her voice catching in her throat.

"I'm done with you," Alex said. "I'm just here to drop you off."

He grabbed a bag from the dinghy, took out a set of overalls and pulled them on over his clothes. He yanked off his boots and slipped on a pair of waterproof shoes. "Put this on!" he said, hurling a head-torch in JP's direction.

JP fumbled as he caught it. "What? Where are we—"

"Just put it on," Alex said.

"I'm not going any further. I'm going back."

"You're not going anywhere until I tell you."

"No! If I haven't repaid the debt … you can take it up with my father … I'm done."

"You'll do as I say, or you'll never see your father again!" Alex drew his gun from inside his overalls and glared at JP. "Do you understand?"

JP backed up. He dropped the torch and pulled his gun out of his back pocket. "I'm leaving!" he shouted at Alex, gripping the gun in both hands to steady his aim. "You can't stop me!"

Alex smirked. "You going to shoot me?"

"I want out!"

"Put the gun down. It's no use to you – you think we would actually give you a loaded weapon?"

JP looked down at the gun. He pointed it towards the water and fired. *Click.* Nothing. *Click. Click.*

"Argh!" he screamed, hurling it into the water.

Alex chuckled to himself. "Now, I suggest you do as you're told. We will drop them off, and then you'll be done."

JP hung his head, but George couldn't help noticing him running his fingers over a bulge in his pocket.

"Get up! Let's go – single file," Alex ordered. "Stragglers won't be tolerated, so keep up."

Without looking back, Alex strode ahead, his small head-torch lighting the way along the path. George glanced back and could see JP staring down at the boats. He looked up and caught George's eye. George knew exactly what he was thinking, he just hoped that his plans of escape included helping them out – if not, George would have to somehow beat him to it.

Chapter 13: Dead and Buried

They walked until George thought his legs might buckle, venturing deeper and deeper into the crumbling sewer. Soon the water began to dry up, and all that remained were shallow pools and stranded puddles, strewn with rubbish and the remnants of the water's cargo.

The footpath soon ended, and they were forced to slosh their way through the tepid stew at the sewer's base. George looked down at his feet; another pair of ruined school shoes glared back up at him.

Great!

"Stop!" Alex bellowed from up front. "We're here."

George craned his neck to look around the line of heads, but he couldn't see anything but more tunnel.

"What are we doing here?" Will shouted back.

"Shh," Felix said from behind him, "he said to keep quiet."

"I don't care. If we're gonna' die down here, I'm not going quietly."

"Shut up!" Alex yelled. "You're going in there." George's eyes followed his outstretched finger. He was pointing towards a hole in the tunnel wall, no bigger than a manhole cover. It was roughly round and at about knee height.

"That's tiny," Jess said. "We can't get in there."

"I won't go – I can't – it's too small – I don't want to go…" Lauren was backing into George, crushing his toes. "You can't make me…"

Alex raised his gun. "Someone control that young lady before I dispose of her."

"Shh," George said, "please, Lauren."

She spun around and buried her face in his chest. "I can't do it, George … I can't."

"You can – I'll be right behind you," he said, trying to comfort her.

Her breathing slowed, but she didn't move. George prayed that she would keep calm.

"I'm going to untie your hands," Alex said. "You'll pass through one at a time. Push your bags through with you."

"Why don't they just dump their bags here?" JP called from the back of the line.

"No, everything goes through," Alex replied.

He drew a long, curved knife from inside his overalls and came at Francesca. She screamed, barging backwards into Jess.

"Stand still or I'll cut you." He slashed at her wrists, slicing through the cable that bound them. "Now, JP will go first. It's not far, but there's a small drop the other side."

JP pushed forwards, grabbed the edge of the hole and went feet first. Just as he was about to disappear from view, Alex grabbed him by his braids. "Don't get any ideas of running off. There's someone waiting for you on the other side."

George watched him wriggle out of sight, and the others steadily followed his lead until it was Lauren's turn. She had taken hold of George's hand and was gripping it tightly. She leaned forwards and peered into the dark hole as Will disappeared from view.

"Please, George," she whispered. "I can't."

"It's not far. I'm right here, and the others are just the other side."

"Do I have to force you?" Alex said, grabbing her by the arm.

"No," George said, stepping between them. "She can do it. She just needs a moment."

"We don't have a moment," Alex growled.

George turned back and helped her into the narrow hole. "Just wriggle through. You don't have to let go of my hand until the very last minute."

With that she took a deep breath, closed her eyes and was gone. He could hear her sobs drift back up towards him. He took one last look at Alex before he climbed in himself. "How do you sleep at night?" But George didn't wait for an answer. He pushed off the edge of the opening and began shuffling through the concrete tube.

His head hadn't been inside for more than a few seconds before someone was tugging at his ankles. He tumbled out, dragging his bag with him. It walloped him on the head as it followed his descent. He barely had time to push his bag aside, when two giant hands were heaving him from the ground. His eyes glided up until they came to rest at the huge bosom of Sabrina Fraulove. She towered over him like a giant ogre.

"Zat is ze last?" she bellowed back through the hole, her booming voice making the whole passageway shudder.

"Yes," Alex said, as he slid from the hole like an eel.

"I've been waiting," she huffed.

"I know ... we had some hold ups."

Sabrina growled and her chest vibrated. "Move out!"

They had entered a passageway, narrower and more roughly mined than the sewer. It was cut from the surrounding rock, pale and ragged. As Sabrina surged ahead, she ducked and turned to squeeze her bulk past the jutting rocks and below the broken stalactites. Even hunched and stooped, she filled the void ahead.

The others followed with JP and Alex at the rear. Soon the passageway opened out, and the tunnels divided off – so many paths, all of varying sizes and shapes. There was no order. It was like a rabbit warren. In places, the paths ended and more holes could be seen, either round like the one through which they'd entered or slivers of gaps, sandwiched between plates of rock, barely wide enough to squeeze a body through.

The walls were plastered with graffiti and tags. Names, images, warnings: '*Do not pass – you who fear death.*' Arrows of different colours pointed in all directions. They stumbled over abandoned shoes, discarded cans, rotting food and more. People came down here, moved in the depths, unseen to the world above.

As they journeyed deeper into the maze, the graffiti began to thin, the air grew stiller and there were fewer signs of life. George couldn't help noticing that one tag remained – the wings of a bird, stencilled onto the walls at every turn. Sabrina was following them like a beacon.

Victor!

The ground beneath their feet was uneven and damp in places. George's ankles turned and twisted as he tried to match Sabrina's fearsome stride. Lauren was struggling ahead of him. They were falling behind.

"Keep up!" Alex shouted again.

George tried to quicken his pace, but they were soon wading through water again, cloudy and full of grit. His calves were cramping up, and he could feel tiny bits of sand scratching at his heels and between his toes.

"How much further?" Will grumbled.

"Quiet," Sabrina said. "You'll wake 'ze dead."

Soon the water vanished again, and they were left crunching something underfoot. George looked down, but the light from Alex and JPs' head-torches was bouncing around as they moved, making it impossible to see clearly.

"What is this?" Francesca was murmuring.

"Oh God!" Josh exclaimed from up ahead. "It's bones!"

Everyone stopped. JP must have glanced down too, his torch lighting the ground at George's feet. The path was inches deep in bones, fragmented, shattered and whole.

"Are those … human?" Lauren said, grabbing hold of George again.

"I don't–"

"Keep moving!" Sabrina barked. "Or you'll be added to 'ze pile!"

They passed through a final slip of a hole and entered a large lit cavern.

"No!" Francesca gasped.

They stood in silence, taking in the sheer horror of what surrounded them. Every wall was, floor to ceiling, lined in skulls – human skulls. Jammed in, stacked one on top of the other, their hollow eyes and vacant stares peering out at those who dared enter. At one end stood an altar, carved from the rock, and in the centre of the room, a giant column of skulls loomed over them, ten feet wide – like a barrel of death.

"What is this place?" Lauren asked, edging backwards.

"Welcome to the Catacombs of Paris – the resting place of the dead!"

They swivelled around to see Jose Gonzalez sauntering towards them, cigar smoke engulfing his bulbous form. It had taken no time for him to regain a measure of his impressive waistline since escaping prison. His curls bounced off his shoulders as he waddled closer. George could feel hatred festering inside him. The more of them he saw, the closer he felt to Victor and the greater his sense of rage. George's whole body tensed. He wanted to fly at him, but Lauren held him back.

"Calm and focused," she whispered in his ear.

"Over six million to be precise," Jose continued, as he curved around the barrel of skulls, running his fingers over their ivory facades. "Six million dead, lining hundreds of miles of tunnels and caves. You are surrounded!" He belly laughed. "Literally and figuratively."

"Zat's enough," Sabrina said, throwing a stray bone at Jose's head. "We have work to do. Get z'em ready."

Jose smiled. "Yes, now our delivery has arrived."

"Wait! Z'ere are seven of z'em," Sabrina said.

"Yes, you have a spare," Alex said. "Deal with it."

"And what about him?" Jose asked, pointing his glowing cigar towards JP. "The rat's son – what happens to him?"

JP was loitering by the entrance, one foot still on the threshold. George could just make out something behind his back. A bone – a foot long, with a splintered end.

Alex must have seen it too. He laughed. "You going to batter us all to death with that?"

"It's a … s … souvenir," JP stammered.

"Leave," Alex said, "before I decide to bury you down here for your insolence."

"He cannot go," Sabrina said, storming towards JP. "He know'z where we are." She grabbed him below the shoulders with both of her man-sized hands and dragged him towards Jose. His ribs seemed to collapse inwards under the pressure of her crushing grip. "We will deal wi'z him."

"No! Please! I … I've done everything you've asked," he squealed. "Far more than was agreed. I won't tell a soul – I swear it."

"We can't take z'at chance." She stood behind him and yanked his arms back. George swore he heard a crack as JP screamed out in pain. Jose was lifting a knife from his belt.

"Drop him," Alex said. "He can take a message back to his father, Marcel."

"But–"

"No."

Jose slid the knife back into its sheath. "You are no fun."

Alex turned to JP. "If you get out of this maze alive, you can tell your father that we will be waiting for him as soon as his head pops out from under that stone of his. Now go!"

"Go? Go where? How am I supposed to get back to the boat?" JP said, edging away from Sabrina.

George tried to catch his eye. Maybe he would come back for them.

"Go now!" Alex said, whipping his knife back out. "Before I change my mind."

With that, JP scuttled across the bone-strewn floor. Skittling past the others, he tripped and slammed straight into George, sending him crunching to the ground. He looked George dead in the eyes.

"I'm sorry," he whispered, and then pressed something familiar into George's hand.

My phone!

Chapter 14: Over a Barrel

Jose and Sabrina wasted no time taking over from Alex. They stripped them all of their bags, dumping them in a side passage, and made them stand with their backs to the barrel of skulls. Alex stood guard while Sabrina and Jose bound their wrists in front of them and then tied them to the barrel with one long length of rope at their chests and another at their feet. Pinned to the barrel, spread around its circumference, they looked like human sacrifices.

George could feel the sharp edges of broken chins at his back; fractured eye sockets glaring over his shoulder. Missing teeth, dangling jaws – he tried not to think about who they had been or how long they'd been dead.

"I'm done. I need to get back to Austin," Alex said. "Don't forget the cargo needs to be well secured. Be at the pier when we agreed – you'll get a call when we're ready for them."

"We'll be ready," Jose said, lighting up another cigar.

"Just make sure you are. The timings have to be exact."

George watched Alex leave and wondered whether JP had managed to steal a lead and make it back to the boat. Had he seen the falcon's wings that Sabrina had followed? He prayed that JP would find help. But would he be able to get back to them before it was too late?

Sabrina and Jose busied themselves, in and out of side passages, carrying boxes and equipment. George took the opportunity to pull at his restraints, with no success. Around the curve of skulls, he could just make out Will to his left and Jess to his right.

"How tight is your rope?" he whispered to Will.

Will raised his bound hands and looked down at the rope that circled his chest. "I can barely breathe it's so tight."

"Psst, hey, Jess."

"What?"

"How tight are your ropes?"

"We can't get out of this one, George," she whispered back. "We're not only tied to the barrel but tied to each other."

George was about to respond when he became aware of a faint beeping sound.

"Someone's tripped the alarm," Jose yelled from somewhere behind the barrel. "Check it out!"

"You check it!" Sabrina called from elsewhere. "I'm busy!"

"No! I went last time."

George tried to twist to see where the sound was coming from and could just make out Sabrina's shadow stomping towards one of the passageways with what looked like a rifle slung over her shoulder.

"Goddamn Cataphiles!" she cursed.

With one of them gone, George reckoned now was as good a time as any to try again to free himself. He started moving his chest from side to side to see if he could loosen the rope's grip.

"Who's doing that?" Josh's voice floated around from the other side of the barrel.

"Stop it," Jess said. "Every time you move, you're tightening our ropes."

"What?" George said.

"That's what I was trying to say. We're all tied together. If you try to loosen your ropes, you tighten ours."

"There must be a way," George thought out loud, but his thoughts were interrupted by Jose's chuckling.

"You really think you can wriggle your way out?" He strolled towards George, flicking the blade of his knife over and over between his chunky knuckles. "We won't let you get away so easily this time … we have a job for you."

"What sort of job?"

"You'll soon see." Jose smiled, blowing smoke rings up into the still air. He was rolling his head back and taking another drag when a distant crack echoed behind the walls and raced out into the cave. *Crack!* And another.

"What the…" Jose grabbed another rifle and lumbered over towards the passage. "Sabrina!" he roared into the void, but there was no response.

He glanced back at his hostages. *Crack!* Another shot and the beeping returned. Someone was triggering the alarms, and it sounded like Sabrina had run into trouble.

"Grr, don't move," Jose growled at them, "or these bullets will have your name on them." Then he turned and squeezed out into the warren.

The beeping continued, but George didn't stop to worry about who was coming. All he cared about was getting himself and his friends out alive. He started again at his ropes.

"George!" Jess yelled. "It doesn't work."

"Your crushing my ribs," Will called from the other side.

"But this is our chance!" George insisted. "We have to get out, now!"

"Wait!" Lauren's voice bounced off the stone walls. "The skulls."

"What about them?" George said, stopping to listen.

"They're sharp – maybe a broken edge would cut through the rope."

George could see a skull to his left that was practically broken in half, split right down the middle. The nose cavity was jutting out; a sharp edge just in reach. He leaned over and slid the rope that tied his hands into the curve of the cavity. It caught and he began to saw.

"Oh my God," Francesca squealed, "the teeth are falling out!"

"It's gonna' be too fragile," Josh said.

"No, human bone is really tough," Felix said. "Just find a decent edge."

George continued to hack away at the rope – small movements, jerky at first, until he got the rhythm and a notch began to form. "It's working!"

"As fast as you can!" Will screamed. "We don't know when they'll be back."

"Or who else is out there," Jess added.

For several minutes, all George could hear was the sound of frenetic puffing and cursing. The rope around his chest felt tight as he was pulled from one side to the other. His forearms were tiring and cramping as he pumped them back and forth. He was about to stop to take a break when the rope around his chest fell loose.

"I did it!" Lauren screeched. "It broke through!"

George wriggled and freed his chest.

"Has anyone got their hands out?" Josh asked, between frantic breaths.

"Nearly," George panted, "nearly … nearly … yes!" The knot sprang apart and he ripped open his sweating palms, sending the rope flying.

"Get your feet out, George," Jess said. She was bent down trying to release her own feet with her hands still bound.

George squatted down. The rope at his feet was wound in a figure of eight about each ankle. It was tight to his socks and was rubbing as he moved. He tried to get his fingers between the rope, but it was impossible.

"Take your shoes off," Jess said.

He pulled the first shoe off and tried again, but the rope got entangled with his sock. He yanked off the sock. His foot was damp, and the rope tore at his skin. "Stop moving," he yelled. "Just for a minute – hold completely still."

They all froze and the rope seemed to slacken. He forced it millimetre by millimetre until it popped over the back of his heel and the rest of his foot was free.

"I'm out!" he screamed.

After slipping his other foot out and shoving his shoe back on, he ran around the barrel helping the others. Soon, the ropes lay abandoned on the floor like slain serpents.

"Ha! We did it!" shouted Josh.

"Lauren did it," said George, smiling in her direction.

"We can hand out medals later," said Jess. "We need to get moving and like, now." The words had only just left her lips when the alarms were bleating again.

"We're gonna' need torches," said Will.

"I've got one in my bag," said Felix.

"Where did they–"

"Guys, we need to hurry!" Jess was peering into the dark after Jose, a long thighbone in her hands. "Spread out and search the side passages. I'll keep watch."

George dived towards the passage that Jose and Sabrina had come in from and couldn't believe what he saw. The room was made up like a den: thin mattresses piled up with blankets and sleeping bags, a large sagging sofa, towers of water canisters and crates of dried food. In one corner stood a small generator that powered a fridge and what looked like a couple of laptop stations and a printer. Wires drooped overhead, and a double-ringed camping stove stood balanced on a rickety old table.

"They've been living down here," he said, standing in the doorway, taking it all in.

"Yeah – I think I found the toilets," Felix grimaced, coming up behind him.

George scanned the small room. Piles of boxes, marked with the falcon's wings, occupied every corner.

What have they been doing down here?

Jess pushed past George. "Guys, I can hear noises in the tunnels – we don't have time. Just find the bags and let's go."

The others piled into the room.

"There, under the table," Francesca said.

"Come on," said Jess, grabbing hers.

George's bag was at the bottom of the heap. He picked it up last and turned to leave, just as the printer buzzed to life. George stood staring at it as a single sheet of paper rolled out and fluttered towards the floor. He caught it in mid-air. It was a map of one section of Paris, and several addresses had been highlighted.

"Come on, George!" someone yelled.

He stuffed the map into his bag and dashed from the room, joining the others as they scampered back out into the cave.

"Which way?" asked Josh, looking around.

"The way we came in," said George. "Follow the falcon's wings – the tags on the walls."

With that, they raced from the cave, crunched through the corridor of bones and were soon fleeing through the maze, with Felix lighting up the rear and Will and Josh steaming ahead with a couple of stolen head-torches.

"Are you sure we should go this way?" Lauren asked, as she fell into line behind George. "What if we come across the other guy?"

"It's our best hope of getting out," George panted over his shoulder.

"Yeah, and anyway, Alex was on his way back to the art studio," Felix said from behind her.

"He'll have taken the boat though," Lauren said, skipping around the puddles at her feet. "The other boat was too small for us all. How will we get out of the sewers?"

"We'll have to figure that out when we get there," George said, picking up the pace to keep up with the others. "We just need to get as far away from Sabrina and Jose as we can."

"Guys," Jess called back, "try to keep your voices down. We have no idea who else is down here."

But it was too late. As they fell silent, someone else's voice was echoing down the tunnel towards them.

"Stop," Josh whispered from up front. "Lights off."

They plunged themselves into darkness and pressed their backs up against the curve of the tunnel wall. A light was coming from a T-junction ahead.

"What do we do?" Lauren squeaked.

"Shh!" Jess hushed.

"They're coming this way – we'll have to go back," Josh whispered.

"No, not back. Jose and Sabrina are–" George said.

"Get down!" Josh ducked, just as a beam of light bounced around the corner and glanced off the wall above his head.

They all collapsed to the floor and sank into the gritty puddles as the light swept back and forth.

"Par ici," someone said.

"Non – nous allons tout droit," another voice answered.

George could feel the water creeping up his legs as it soaked into his trousers. His knees were curled up beneath him and he dared not move, but he could feel the cramp coming again so lifted his head and tried to shift his position. In the gloom, their huddled forms looked like a pile of boulders, caved in from above. The torchlight seemed to vanish as quickly as it had appeared, and they were thrown back into darkness.

Will was the first to speak. "Who was that?"

"It wasn't Jose," said Josh.

"Or Alex," said Jess.

"Maybe they could have helped us?" said Lauren.

"Cataphiles," Felix said, sliding back up the wall and wringing out the ends of his trousers.

"What the hell are Cataphiles?" asked Josh, turning his torch back on.

"Yeah – they sound like some kind of sewer mutants," Will said.

"No," Felix replied, "urban adventurers – they hang out down in the catacombs … exploring."

"People actually come down here for fun?" Josh said, helping Francesca to her feet.

"Yes – although they don't always make it out alive – one guy recently–"

"OK, I think we've heard enough," said George.

"So, if they're Cataphiles, they can help us," Lauren said, standing up. "They can show us the way out."

She filled her lungs and was about to call out, but George lunged out and clamped his palm over her open mouth. "No!" He recoiled. "I ... I'm sorry. It's just ... I think it's best if we avoid contact with anyone else."

"I'm sorry," she said, staring at her feet. "I just thought ... I just..."

"It's OK." He felt awful. "I think we can do it ourselves – we just need to follow the falcons and get back to the sewer."

"Agreed," said Jess, taking charge. She picked up the bone that she'd been carrying and looked up over George's head. He saw her squint into the distance behind him, but before he had a chance to follow her gaze, there was a sudden splash. Felix whipped around, and his torch lit up the passageway, revealing the huge hulk of a figure that was storming towards them.

"Go, go, go!" George screamed, but the words had barely left his lips before a bullet blew a chunk out of the rock right above Felix's head. "Ruuuuun!"

George put his head down and sprinted. He could feel the adrenalin exploding through his muscles. Felix's torch beam bounced around like a strobe, making it impossible to see what was ahead. George tried to focus on Jess' backpack. Her rabbit's foot swung about madly as she bounced off the walls and tried to stay on her feet.

George dared not look back as they rounded the curve of the bend and surged towards the T-junction. *Crack!* Another bullet ricocheted off the wall to his left, Jess stumbled ahead of him and he crashed into her, throwing them both to the ground. *Crack!* They scrabbled to get back up. He lifted her to her feet and shoved her forwards. "Keep going!"

The T-junction was feet away. George kept running, following the others, not stopping to check for the falcon's wings, not stopping to look back. They raced on, turning and taking any path that got them away from the flying bullets. George's lungs burnt, his shins cried out as his ankles turned, and his hands were raw from bracing himself against the rocks, as they clattered through the tangled maze.

They turned another corner and another. Splashing through water, squeezing through crevices, ducking down tunnels until finally their legs gave up.

"Stop!" Francesca cried. "We need to stop."

George creased over. With every ounce of his energy spent, he tumbled against the cold wall and bolstered himself as he caught his breath.

"Did we lose them?" Josh wheezed.

"I think so," said Will, slumping to the floor.

Everything around them seemed to still. George closed his eyes and tried to steady his breathing.

"Wait!" Francesca squealed, puncturing the silence. "Where are the others?"

George looked up. "No!"

He staggered back to the last turning, but there was no sign of them – Felix and Lauren were gone.

From: Anonymous
To: TDP
Cc: Alpha
Re: Tracker {Encrypted}

We need to perform an immediate extraction. The tracker you installed has led me directly to the nest where the bird's flock have been hiding.

The children are on the move down there – they are no longer contained. I will extract them at the first possible opportunity and drop them back with you for re-insertion.

I have sent Alpha team into the catacombs.

Await my signal.

End.

From: TDP
To: Anonymous
Cc: Alpha
Re: Tracker {Encrypted}

You may need support.
Shall I pull Beta from his post?

End.

From: Anonymous
To: TDP
Cc: Alpha

Re: Tracker {Encrypted}

No, Beta has gone to rendezvous with J21 at the intel drop.
Beta needs to exchange intel with J21 and get back to us. I'm waiting for his call.

End.

Chapter 15: The Fallen

"Where the hell did they go?" yelled Will, as he came back to where George stood gaping down the tunnel.

"I don't know," George said. "They were right behind me."

"How did you lose them?"

"I didn't exactly have time to stop and check that they were keeping up."

"Jeez!" Will cursed, kicking at the rubble at his feet.

"We'll have to go back – re-trace our steps," Francesca said.

"What? No!" Will said. "We've just escaped death – you want us to go back in?"

"We can't leave them – they're our friends!"

"They could be anywhere! Did you see the number of goddamn twists and turns this hell-hole has? We'll never find them!"

"You can't abandon them!" Francesca squeaked in disbelief. "They'll never get out … we can't leave them!" She was shaking, trying to hold back the tears. "George, please – we have to go back."

Josh took Francesca by the shoulders and she turned to look at him. "Josh, you agree with me – please tell me you agree."

He held her tight. "I … we shouldn't leave them – it's not right, but they could be anywhere."

"George," Will said, turning to him. "What d'you say?"

George peered back into the inky void behind them, desperately hoping to see Felix miraculously appear with Lauren at his side, but there was nothing – not a whisper. He tried to imagine where they could be, where he had lost them but could only envisage Lauren's bright green eyes, filled with fear. He could almost feel her trembling hand in his. Then he thought of his best friend Felix with his goofy smile. He thought of all the times Felix had bailed him out. He knew he wanted to go back and find them. It was his fault that they were caught up in this mess in the first place. Lauren wouldn't have even been in their group if George hadn't have pleaded with Mrs Stone.

"George?"

He bit down hard on his lip. "It may not feel right, but the best thing we can do for them is to find a way back out and get help. We're no use to them dead and buried down here."

He knew that what he said made sense, but it didn't stop a large lump from lodging itself in his throat. The thought of them down here, alone, made him want to vomit.

"No, George – you can't!" Francesca cried.

"That's two for and two against," said Will. "Jess, you have the deciding vote."

But Jess hadn't said a word. She was still bent over; slumped on the floor.

"Jess," George called, "you OK?"

She nodded but barely lifted her head. Her hand was clutching at her stomach.

Will dashed to her side. "You got a stitch?"

She pulled her hand away and it was stained red. "Oh my God … what happened? Were you shot?"

"No, no," she croaked, "it's nothing – just a scratch."

"Let me see."

The others had crowded around. Will pulled at her blazer.

"Get off," she snapped. "I said I'm fine!"

"You're not fine, you're bleeding. Stop being so bloomin' stubborn."

She glared up at him. Her fierce, steely-grey eyes warned him to back off.

Francesca gently encouraged Will aside. "Give us ladies a minute, will you, boys?" she said, crouching down beside her. "Can I just survey the damage; maybe just see if you need a bandage?"

Jess glanced towards the boys.

Francesca coughed. "Uh-hum, a little privacy please." She gently lifted Jess' blouse. "That's a … nasty scratch. How did you get that?"

"I fell … on that stupid thing," she said, pointing at the long shard of bone that now lay tossed in a puddle.

Francesca inspected the gash. "It seems clean enough. I suggest we just patch it up – stop the bleeding." She slipped her bag off her back and pulled out a delicate blue scarf. "This should do the job." She covered the wound site with tissue and then stretched out the scarf and wrapped it around Jess' waist, pulling it as tight as she could without causing any further pain.

"You just bought that," Jess said, wincing. "It'll be ruined."

Francesca smiled and tied a double knot. "I don't think I want any souvenirs to remind me of this trip."

Jess smiled back. "Fair point. In fact … this can go too." She ripped the rabbit's foot from her bag and threw it into the puddle alongside the bone. "It didn't exactly bring me any luck."

"I guess luck is a question of perspective," Francesca said, standing up. "I mean, we're lucky we're still alive."

Jess chuckled. "Fair point again. Thank you."

"You're most welcome."

"So," Jess said, pushing herself to her feet, "have you boys made a decision?"

"Look, Felix is smart, right?" George said. "He's got as good a chance of finding a way out as we have. In fact, probably a better chance." The others looked at their feet. "They've got water and a torch and hopefully … each other." He didn't want to think of the possibility of them having been separated. He looked at each of his friends in turn. They all nodded.

"I hope you're right," Francesca sighed.

George swallowed hard and took a deep breath. "Well, I reckon there's a decent amount of graffiti around here," he said, looking at the myriad of tags that surrounded them, "and that might mean we're not far from an exit."

"OK, any sign of the wings?" Will asked, scanning the walls.

"No, but if we're logical about the direction we move in, we should be able to work our way out."

"Mate, it could take us all day," Josh said. "The passages all look the same."

"How about this?" Francesca was pulling something else from her bag – a lipstick.

Josh raised an eyebrow. "Really?"

"Yes, really." She raised an eyebrow back. "We'll make our own tag. We'll mark the walls at every turn – on the left – and then we'll know if we've been down a passage before and in which direction."

"Genius," said Jess.

With that, they marched on, Francesca scrawling 'OM' in bright pink at regular intervals. They tried to follow the paths with the most graffiti, tried to search for the falcon's wings and tried not to lose hope.

The tunnel was damp, crumbling and uncomfortably narrow in places. Several times, they had to remove their backpacks and squeeze through side-on, but their spirits lifted as the graffiti grew thicker and brighter – fresher paint and regular tags. Francesca's technique seemed to be working. They only passed their own tag once and knew to turn back and try another fork. Before long, they began seeing more signs of life.

"People must have been down this way recently," Will said from up front. "There's a half eaten sandwich down here and ... wait!" Will's hand sprang up and stopped them all in their paths. He lowered his torch. "There's someone down there," he breathed.

George could barely hear him. He was pointing ahead of them. Someone was slumped against the wall of the tunnel – legs splayed out, head lolling to one side.

"Is he drunk?" Francesca whispered back.

"Er, guys…" George had a nasty suspicion that he knew who it was. "I think it's Alex."

Will shone his torch towards the body, and they shuffled forwards.

"Is he dead?" Francesca squeaked.

"He's not moving," Will said, pushing ahead.

"Be careful," George whispered. "It could be a trap."

Will reached down and grabbed a stray lump of limestone. He held it up high and inched towards Alex's body. He jabbed one of Alex's outstretched legs with his toe. No movement. The others came closer. Will stretched out again and shoved his foot into Alex's shoulder. With that, Alex's head flopped to the side and his limp body slid down the wall, leaving a crimson streak in its wake. He finally flopped forwards and slumped to the floor, revealing a bloody wound at the base of his neck.

Will bent down and felt for a pulse. He turned to the others and shook his head. "Definitely dead."

"Who did this?" Francesca said, peering back over her shoulder. "What sort of hell is this place?"

"I don't know," said Will, "but I reckon he didn't see them coming."

George squatted down beside Will. "I don't know. Look, his knuckles are bleeding too. Looks like he tried to fight back."

"There's blood over here, as well, guys." Josh had wandered further up the tunnel. He pushed something with his toe. "Er … I think I may know who attacked him."

"Who?" George asked, moving up to join him.

Josh pointed towards the floor. A long, thin bone lay at his feet, blood staining half its length.

"JP," George gasped. "JP must have ambushed him."

"That must mean we're on the right path," Jess said, joining them.

Josh shone his torch against the surrounding walls. "Look!" The falcon's wings were as clear as day.

"Let's go," said Jess, "before JP gets away with that boat."

George glanced back at Alex's body as they left. A part of him felt sad that more blood had been shed for Victor's cause, but he struggled to feel sorry for Alex and that sensation troubled him. Was he actually happy that Alex was dead? Was that right?

"George, come on!"

He tried to block it from his mind and rushed to keep up with the others, but no sooner had he caught up when they all stopped again.

"What's going on?" he called from the back.

"Quiet," Jess whispered. "Listen."

Someone was groaning up ahead. A dark figure sat crouched on the ground.

"Who do you think it is?" George whispered.

"I'd put money on it being JP," said Will.

"My God, it is!" Francesca was now running towards him, splashing through the stream of water that ran down the centre of the path.

"Be careful!" Josh shouted, pushing past Will and chasing after her.

By the time the others caught up, Francesca was on her knees, lifting his head in her hands. "JP, what happened?"

He looked up. "Guys, how did you…" he croaked.

"Er … Francesca," George was looking down at the tiny stream at his feet; it ran blood red. "He must have got injured when he attacked Alex."

JP leaned his head back against the rock wall. His hands were smeared with blood. "Alex's knife," he hissed through his teeth.

Francesca recoiled and fell backwards, slipping in the bloody water. JP's shirt was ripped aside. Blood was pulsing from a puncture in his chest. He coughed and added his bloody spit to the stream. His lip was cut and swollen.

"We need to help him," Francesca said.

"What can we do?" asked Josh, pulling her to her feet.

"I don't know, but we can't leave him here."

"What, like he left us," Will spat.

"He had little option!"

"In case you've already forgotten, it was him that got us into this mess, him that had Lauren around the neck, him that was pointing a gun at us in that truck!"

"That doesn't mean he deserves to die!"

George looked down at JP's crumpled form. However much he had hated Alex and felt no sadness for his death, he felt for JP. "We'll take him with us."

"What? George, man, seriously?" Will said.

"We can't be far from the boat. We can help him out of here."

"Most of the tunnels are single file. How do you propose we do that?"

"I don't know, but we have to try."

With that, George bent down and dug his shoulder beneath JP's armpit. Francesca stepped forwards, but Josh stopped her and took his other arm. They lifted him to his feet and something clattered to the ground – Alex's knife.

Jess bent down and scooped it up. "Wait, we need to stop the bleeding." She unwrapped Francesca's scarf, wiped the blood from the knife, cut the scarf in half and bandaged JP's chest before re-dressing her own wound and handing the knife to Will.

"I don't know if it will help much," she said, grimacing, "but it should help stem the flow of blood."

It wasn't easy going, propping JP up as they staggered through the tunnel, following Victor's tags. In places, they had to shuffle through shoulder first. It was like trying to run a three-legged race sideways, but with an extra person sandwiched in the middle, who was barely moving his own legs.

Before long, the path almost vanished as it snaked its way between two giant slabs of rock.

"We'll have to take our bags off to squeeze through," Jess said. "We're nearly there, I'm sure."

George held JP up as Josh took off his own backpack. JP groaned and his knees buckled, pulling George to one side and slamming him into the wall.

"How are we going to get him through there?" George said, eyeing up the slither between the rocks.

"He'll have to push his own way through," Will said. "There's not enough room to carry him."

"Can you do it?" George asked JP, while trying to prop him up against the wall.

"Leave me," he gargled in response.

His breathing was wet and raspy.

"That doesn't sound good," Francesca said. "It sounds like the blood has gone onto his lungs."

"He's not going to make it," Jess said. "We've still got to get through the hole and walk the sewer. He can barely breathe."

JP's knees gave way again, and he slid to the floor. "Go … leave me."

"We could drag him through," Josh suggested. "I mean, pull him, somehow."

JP was shaking his head and his chest heaved with the effort of every breath.

The others exchanged glances. George knelt down in front of him. "It's not much further. We can get you to a doctor."

JP grabbed him by the arm and shook his head again. "No," he spluttered and tried to drag air into his lungs. It gurgled and bubbled on its way down. "Leave."

"He can't make it," Jess said.

"But we can't…" George tried to protest, but JP coughed, splattering George's shirt with a spray of blood. George fell back and stared up at the others.

Jess was shaking her head. "I'm sorry, George. I think we've done all we can. Maybe if he rests here…"

"We can get help," Josh said. "If he just waits here."

George could feel despair trickling through him. He'd not only lost Felix and Lauren, but now he was going to abandon JP too. He sat forwards.

"We'll find help," he said, "we'll send back help, I promise. You need to hold on – wait here – we'll come back."

JP opened his eyes and strained to reach into the pocket of his jeans. His fingers fumbled several times before pulling out a bunch of keys and handing them to George. His arm fell back to the ground and his head dropped back against the wall.

"What are these?" George asked.

Will peered down at them. "The boat keys. He must have taken them from Alex. That's why he waited to jump him."

George looked back down at JP. Something else was poking out of his pocket – a photo. George gently plucked it out and couldn't believe it when a familiar face peered up at him.

"Who's that?" Will asked.

"It's her," George said, holding it up to show the others. "The woman from the science fair. The woman who was shooting at Victor in the vault in London – remember?"

It wasn't the clearest photo. It looked like it had been taken from a distance with a long lens. Her hair was longer, lighter, and she was sat across a table from a bearded man. George flipped the photo over. There was a number scrawled across the back.

"What's she got to do with JP?" Josh asked.

"Who is this?" George asked, holding the picture up for JP to see. "Where did you get this?"

"My dad," was all JP could get out before he coughed up another mouthful of bloody mucus. He fumbled again, this time into the inside pocket of his jacket. He pulled out a gun. George lurched backwards.

"Take it," JP coughed. "It's Alex's."

"No," said George, "I don't want it."

A vision of Philippe lying on the floor of the cave sprang into his mind.

"We might need it," Josh said.

"No, we don't," George snapped. "It's not worth it."

Francesca looked down at George. "George is right. JP should keep it. He can protect himself if Jose or Sabrina come looking for him."

"Yes, exactly," George said, relieved to have a reason to reject JP's offer.

JP lowered his arm and rested the gun in his lap.

"We'll send back help, I promise," George repeated.

"We should leave him some water," Francesca said, grabbing the metal bottle from her bag. She swallowed a few mouthfuls and then raised it to his lips. He took a few trembling sips but could barely swallow without choking up more blood.

"Go," he croaked, his voice barely audible.

She rested the bottle by his side, and they turned to leave. George could see tears in Francesca's eyes as she shuffled past him. He took one last look back at JP as they left him stranded in the darkness. He had meant what he said about sending back help, but as he squeezed his way through the gap in the rocks, he added JP to the list of the fallen.

Chapter 16: Rabbit in the Hole

They emerged the other side of the passage in solemn silence. George felt like he would never be able to feel happiness again. Every ounce of joy was being slowly sucked out of him. He was lost in his own thoughts when Jess called out, "The hole, we've made it to the hole!"

He felt a small spark of relief but couldn't overcome the feeling of having already lost.

As the others filed through the hole, he prayed that Lauren and Felix would at least be on the other side.

"George," Will's head was already half buried in the rock, "come on, you're the last."

"I'm coming … I'll be right behind you."

He stood for a moment trying to re-ignite his sense of hope.

We can find help. We'll get back for JP. We'll find Lauren and Felix.

He took a deep breath, shoved his bag through the hole and pulled himself, feet first, after it. But just as he was about to shuffle through, someone grabbed him by the hair.

"No!" he gasped, thrashing about, trying to fight against the sudden attack. He dug his heels into the rock, but the hands were now clamped to his blazer. He was hauled out backwards and tumbled to floor, his legs flipping over his head in a poor attempt at a backward roll. Before he had time to right himself, the hands were grabbing at him again, but he pushed against the rock wall and launched himself into his assailant's legs, which buckled under the force.

George snatched at the chance to flip himself over just in time to see Jose rebounding off the opposite wall.

"You're not getting away this time!" Jose snarled, flying back at him like a bull to a matador.

George scrabbled to get onto his feet and braced himself for the impact. They clashed, and George's face smashed against the wall. He felt the sting as his skin skimmed the rough rock.

Regaining his balance, he tried to grab at Jose's arms as they went for his neck, but Jose was too strong. George twisted in his grip, but only managed to make things worse – Jose's flabby arms were now smothering his face as he gripped him from behind. George tried to call out in the hope that Will and the others would come to his rescue, but all he could see was the hole disappearing from view as he was dragged backwards down the tunnel.

George squirmed and kicked out. He even tried to dig his nails into Jose's flesh, but nothing seemed to stop him. He was about to give up when Jose's arms suddenly went limp and his grasp slackened. George took his chance and pulled away. He spun around to defend himself only to see Jose's great hulk nose-dive forwards and slam into the dirt like an opening drawbridge. George couldn't believe his eyes – there, stood in the tunnel behind Jose, was Felix, his hefty Eiffel Tower wielded above his head.

"George!" Lauren screamed, pushing past Felix. She threw her arms around him and planted a kiss right on his lips. He stood stunned, his head spinning. "Your face," she said, pulling back. George could feel the sting from his run-in with the wall but didn't care.

"Guys, I … how…" he spluttered.

Felix grinned. "God, it's good to see you."

"The feeling's mutual," George said.

"George?" Will's head poked out of the hole, and his eyes lit up. "Guys," he called back through the hole, "George has found Felix and Lauren."

George could hear faint cheering.

"What happened?" Will asked, spying Jose's body.

"Felix saved my neck," George said.

"Is he dead?" Will asked.

"Don't think so – just out cold," Felix said.

"I'm not sure we should hang around to find out," Lauren said.

"Totally agree. Let's get out of here before he wakes up," George said, ushering Lauren and Felix after Will.

They shuffled through the hole and out into the sewer, where there were hugs all around. They were back out of the catacombs and back together. All they had to do now was make it to the boats and hope that Sabrina hadn't made it there before them.

"How did you find us?" Jess asked, jogging along beside Felix.

"I found this," he said, pulling her rabbit's foot out of his pocket. "We knew you couldn't be far away."

"Ha! Good luck after all," Jess beamed.

"Then Lauren spotted your tag."

"Seriously?"

"Yeah, OM – Oakfield Manor. Couldn't be anyone else."

"Did you see Alex … and JP?" Francesca asked, with a quiver of sadness in her voice.

"Yeah, that wasn't you guys … was it?" Felix asked hesitantly.

"Of course not," Will said. "They did it to each other."

"Was JP … alive?" Francesca asked.

They all seemed to slow – keen to hear the answer.

"We didn't stop to find out," Felix panted, coming to a halt. "We assumed … you know."

Jess nodded and George hung his head.

"We did everything we could," Josh said. "He needed a doctor, we couldn't have done more than we did."

They stood in silence for a moment, and George tried to gather his thoughts.

"You OK?" Lauren said, placing her hand gently in his. He nodded. "We're nearly there, George."

"I know … I just wish…" he croaked.

"Come on, it can't be far to the boats," she said, squeezing his hand.

He smiled. It felt so good to know that she was safe. He took a deep breath, cleared his throat and looked around. "I'm not sure we've come out at the same hole."

"Does it matter?" Will shrugged. "We're back in the sewers. The boats must be down here somewhere. We just need to keep moving."

They pushed on, keen to put distance between themselves and Jose. The puddles grew wider and deeper until they finally found the raised walkway. George was happy to get up out of the water, but as they rounded the corner, the tunnel split in two.

"I don't remember a fork in the tunnel," Francesca said, slowing down. "Which way do we go?"

"We should stick to the right," Jess said. "Even if we did come out of the hole too soon, we should still stay on this side."

The others agreed, and they picked up the pace again. Freedom began to feel tantalisingly close, but George felt a measure of dread in the pit of his stomach. With Alex dead and Jose temporarily unconscious, they only had Sabrina to worry about. But if he'd learned anything from his experience in London, it was that Victor's crew would stop at nothing.

"I can see deeper water – we're nearly there," Jess said, excitedly.

"Wait," George whispered. "We shouldn't just bowl up there."

The others slowed.

"We need to get to that boat before anyone else beats us to it," Jess said, as they huddled together.

"And that's exactly what they'll expect us to do." George took the keys from his pocket. "If I were Sabrina, I'd have come straight here the minute I'd realised we'd escaped."

"George is right," Josh said. "I bet her giant backside is plonked right in that boat, right now."

"So, what's the plan?" Jess asked.

They all looked at each other.

"I know," Josh said. "Will should go ahead. If Sabrina's there, he can peg it back down here, and we'll jump out and take her by surprise."

"Right," said Will, "great idea. So good of you to volunteer me."

"You're the fastest runner, and you've got Alex's knife," Josh said, shrugging.

"Cheers, that will help against her rifle."

"Well, what's your bright idea then, General Carter?"

"I suggest we charge at her, using you as a human shield," Will said, grinning sarcastically.

"Oh, shut up, both of you," Jess said. "Anyone got a more sensible idea?"

"I know," said George, pulling his phone from his pocket.

"Where d'you get that?" Will asked. "I thought Jin-é had it."

"JP shoved it into my hand. He must have swiped it from her when he knocked her over in the studio."

"I don't suppose you've got any signal down here?" Jess asked, hopefully.

"No, but if we put it on the path down that other fork and set off the alarm. Sabrina might come to investigate. Then we can slip back past her and make a dash for the boat."

"Brilliant idea," Lauren said, beaming at George.

"That's genius, George," Francesca added.

"Not bad," said Josh, nodding. "It might just work. And if all else fails we can still send Will to Karate chop his way out of trouble."

Nobody laughed, least of all Will. "It's taekwondo, you idiot."

"Come on," Jess said, rolling her eyes.

They crept back to the fork, and George slowly waded through the water to the other side, trying to make as little noise as possible. He placed the phone on the opposite walkway and set the alarm. By the time he re-joined the others, they were hiding in the curve of the sewer.

"You know, this means we're sacrificing the phone," Felix whispered.

"Yeah – but it's no good to us down here, anyway," George whispered back.

"If anything goes wrong, we will need to be ready to fight," Jess said.

"I'm ready," said Felix, clutching his Eiffel Tower.

Will had Alex's knife, and Jess had taken his lump of limestone. It wasn't much, but they needed anything they could get their hands on.

"OK, lights out," Jess instructed.

They squatted in silence, listening to the distant trickle of water and waiting for George's alarm. It seemed to take an age, but finally a cheesy, electronic melody echoed through the darkness.

George could hear Josh stifling a chuckle to his left.

"Shh," Jess hushed from his right.

The tune went around and around, getting louder and louder. George strained his ears to listen for any noise other than the embarrassing alarm tone. No one seemed to be coming.

Maybe she's not there?

But just as he was about to break the silence, he heard a faint grunting noise. Each grunt came faster and faster, closer and closer. Soon the sound of footsteps joined the rhythm, and a bouncing beam of light rounded the corner.

George flattened his back against the cold concrete.

It's working.

Sabrina must have held her torch at her side because her huge shadow stretched its way up the curved sewer wall, making it look like King Kong was storming towards them. George held his breath. He could feel Josh tense up beside him, getting ready to run.

Sabrina jumped down into the thigh-deep water and waded across the fork, holding her rifle out ahead of her. They waited until she had forged her way deep into the tunnel, and then George was up.

"Go!"

Will and Josh flicked the torches back on, and they sprinted for their lives. No one wanted to be left behind. They almost tripped each other up as they stormed down the narrow walkway. George turned several times to make sure she wasn't on their tail and to check the line of runners, adamant that he wouldn't leave anyone behind, this time.

He clutched the boat keys in his fist, knowing that they'd only have moments to get the engine started and get out of Sabrina's firing range.

As they rocketed around the curve in the path, he could see the floodlight hanging from the pipework above the chain balustrade.

We've made it!

The water to his side looked deep and dark, just like it had done hours before. He turned back one more time and could just make out a faint light illuminating the tunnel behind them.

We don't have long.

"It's gone!" Jess screamed.

They all slammed to a halt at the makeshift dock. George stared down at the tiny two-man boat that bobbed about beneath them. He stared at the keys in his hand and back at the murky water.

"But we've got the keys," he said. "How?"

"Sabrina must have cut it loose," Will said. "She knew we'd come."

"What do we do now?" screeched Lauren.

"Er…" George tried to think.

"We run," yelled Felix from the back of the line. "She's coming!"

As the others turned and ran, George looked back. Sabrina was heaving herself out of the water like a ravenous monster – dripping wet and raging.

With no time to think and no other options, he hurtled down the path after the others, desperately hoping that it would get them all the way to the Seine.

It can't be that far.

They quickly put a distance between themselves and Sabrina. Her weight was her enemy and she quickly fell behind, but George's temporary relief was crushed when he heard the faint crackle of an engine spluttering to life.

"She's in the boat!' Felix cried. "Faster!"

They somehow found another level of pace, but George's thighs were beginning to scream out and a stitch was ballooning beneath his ribs.

Crack! He knew it wouldn't be long until she started firing. *Crack!* Her bullets were way off target, but then she needed them alive – at least, six of them.

As a corner loomed ahead, he dared to look over his shoulder.

"She's getting closer!" he yelled, as they surged around the bend, giving them temporary cover. But their moment of safety was soon cut short as the path abruptly ended, leaving them sandwiched between an advancing Sabrina and a sheer drop into a wide, fast-flowing canal.

"No!" Jess screamed.

George pushed to the front. "We have to jump in!"

"What?" Josh exclaimed.

"She can't drag us all from the water in that tiny boat. The current will help us swim."

"If we don't drown first!" Will yelled.

"Guuuuys," Felix said, "she's coming!"

The buzz of the Sabrina's motor was escalating, and George knew that they had no choice. He took a deep breath and prepared himself to jump, but as he looked down at the water, it began to ripple and then slosh.

What?

He looked up and realised that the noise of Sabrina's engine was rapidly being drowned out by the roar of another.

"Who's that?" Will shouted from behind.

A large, black rib was charging along the canal towards them, sending fountains of water splaying out on either side. It swerved violently and splashed up against the wall beneath them.

"Get in!" the driver screamed from under the peak of her cap.

George looked down and didn't hesitate. He leapt out, leaving the others to follow his lead.

Chapter 17: Unexpected Allies

Felix's backside had only just touched down when the captain rammed the throttle and threw them all backwards. George was up front. He grabbed the side of the rib, steadied himself and strained to look behind them. Sabrina was only metres away. Their motor was more powerful, but her boat was lighter, and even with her weighty mass more than filling it, it hurtled across the water like a skimming stone.

She looked like a grown adult riding a toddler's tricycle. Her elbows and knees hung over the edges of the tiny vessel. She had slung her rifle over her shoulder and retrieved a small handgun from within the boat. *Crack!* This time she was aiming to kill.

"Duck … and hang on tight!" their skipper shouted over the noise of the engine.

She yanked the wheel and turned their boat a full 180 degrees, taking Sabrina by complete surprise. Firing back, she made Sabrina duck and lose grip of her wheel, which sent her boat veering off course. Before Sabrina had time to get it back under control, they were coming back around. Their wake violently rocked her boat as they steamed back past her and cut in behind. She tried to fire at them again, but the barrage of harassing waves made it impossible for her to aim straight.

Once more they came at her. She stood and twisted to face them, firing madly. George had slipped down into the hull of the rib with only his forehead exposed. Huddled up next to his friends, he could feel the cold, damp spray whipping at his hair. He peeked over the rim just as one final wave slapped Sabrina's boat side-on and flipped it over, knocking her clean overboard into the soupy, green water.

As they sped off, all George could see were her giant arms thrashing about as her heavy, steel-capped boots and bulky rifle dragged her down into the water.

"Woohoo!" Josh hollered, punching the air. He half stood up and yelled back at her as she desperately tried to tread water, "See ya', sucker!"

Francesca grabbed at him and pulled him back down. "Behave yourself!"

George clambered back onto his seat and looked over at their skipper. She showed no emotion. Her eyes peered out from beneath the peak of her dark cap, scanning the water ahead as she hit the throttle once more and they powered up the canal. Her sharp black bob had been replaced with a long copper ponytail that protruded from the hole in the back of her cap and flapped about wildly in the breeze. Her dark eyes were now emerald green, and she'd sprouted freckles, but the disguise didn't fool him. He'd recognised her immediately – her restless eyes, her strong, slender frame and head to toe in black. She was the mysterious vigilante from London, but how had she managed to run into them, again?

"How did you find us?" he shouted over the crash of the water.

"Good fortune!" she shouted back, not shifting her gaze.

"Who are you?" Will asked from the row behind.

She ignored the question. "I'm taking you back to your teachers."

"How did you know we were in the canal?" Even after their timely rescue and the ingenious disposal of Sabrina, Will still didn't seem to trust her.

"I have sources," she replied. "You can ask all the questions you want when we hit land."

"Wait!" George screamed. "We have to go back – we have to get JP!"

She immediately slowed the boat. "What did you say?"

"We have to get JP – he needs a doctor – he's back in the tunnels, it's not far."

"But, George," Lauren said from behind. "I don't think—"

"Jean-Pierre Perron?" the skipper interrupted, cutting the engine completely.

"Er … I don't…"

"How do you know him?" Will asked, looking at her suspiciously.

She peered over her shoulder at him. "I know his father."

"That makes sense," George said, rifling in his pocket and pulling out the blurry photo he'd taken from JP. "He had this on him."

She took it from George and scanned both sides. George watched her rigid expression soften just a fraction. He swore he saw genuine concern flash across her face. "Where is he now?"

George described where they'd left him and what state he was in. She reached for her phone and barked something in French at the person on the other end of the line before restarting the engine.

"We'll find him," she said, nodding towards George. He didn't know whose side she was really on, but he believed her none-the-less.

It wasn't long before they broke out of the canal and into the glistening sun. George could feel all his muscles relax. The air was filled with the smell of the silty water and the oily fumes from the other boats that went about their daily chug up and down the Seine. It seemed impossible to imagine that life had been bustling along above them, unaffected, as they had fought for their lives beneath the streets of Paris. He was sure of one thing though: Mr Steckler and the rest of their teachers were going to be spitting mad. How was he going to explain where they'd been?

What will Dad say?

"Dad!" he gasped, looking over at the skipper's phone. "I need to call my dad." She said nothing. "I need to tell him where I am. Can I use–?"

"I don't think that's a great idea," she said.

"What … why not?"

"We're here – you can contact him once you're back with your group."

With that, they glided beneath one of Paris' many bridges and pulled up to a small jetty. George was about to protest when he caught sight of a tall, pale figure waiting for them on the bank.

"Dupont!" Will yelled. "What the hell is she doing here?"

"She's here to escort you back," the skipper said, as they bumped up against the wooden dock.

Will was on his feet, rocking the boat. "I'm not going anywhere with her! It's her fault we ended up with JP!"

"Yeah, she's with Victor!" Josh spat.

"She's with *me*," the skipper said, calmly climbing from the rib and tying it to the dock. "You'll be safe with her."

"You're joking!" Will shouted. "JP told us she's one of them."

But the skipper wasn't listening. She jogged up the jetty and onto the bank to speak with Dupont.

The mood in the boat had swung from jubilation at being saved and watching Sabrina splash into the Seine, to a frosty disquiet.

"What the hell! Is this woman on our side or not?" Josh said, looking around at his friends.

"She just saved us," Lauren shrugged.

"Yeah, but she could have helped us out in London and she didn't," Will said. "She pretty much scarpered once things got messy. What's her deal?"

"I don't know," George said, "but she's never done us any harm. Maybe JP was wrong. Maybe Dupont is on our side."

George watched the two women as they seemed to exchange terse words. He certainly didn't trust Dupont, but his gut told him to trust their skipper.

"Why would she save us and then hand us back to Victor?" he thought out loud.

"I don't know, but I don't wanna' hang around to find out," Will said, clambering into the driver's seat. "I don't trust either of them."

"Me neither," said George, "but I think we should find out more before we do anything crazy. Give me two minutes." With that, he leapt out of the boat.

"George, wait!" Lauren called after him. "Be careful!"

But he was already half-way up the jetty.

"Hey!" he shouted. "We're not going anywhere until you explain what's going on."

Dupont rolled her eyes at the interruption, but the skipper turned to face him.

"Madam Dupont works with me," she said. "She's been acting as a double agent."

"And?" George said, as the others climbed from the boat and joined him.

"She has been keeping close to Victor's associates in order to keep us informed of their movements. She's the reason I knew where you were."

"And *how* exactly did she know where we were?" Jess asked.

"Yeah, good point," George said, pointing accusingly at Dupont. "And if she knew where we were, why didn't she try to help us out earlier?"

The skipper leaned forwards and grabbed at George's shoulder. She pulled hard and almost ripped the sleeve clean off his blazer. Before he could register what had happened, she had stuffed her hand inside the dangling sleeve and pulled out a small disc, the size of a button.

"She put a tracker on you," she said, holding it in front of his nose.

George looked at the tracker, down at his sleeve and over at Dupont. She was smirking.

"On the train!" he gasped. "It was you that lifted me up when the lights went out. You did it then, didn't you?" She said nothing. "But how … why?"

"We had intel to suggest that Victor would try to get to you," the skipper said. "We needed to know where he was planning on taking you."

"You *let* him take us!" Jess said in disbelief.

"We didn't know for sure," Dupont said. "We had to wait for the right moment."

"We could have died!" Francesca screeched.

"Victor isn't interested in killing you," Dupont said. "We knew you'd be safe."

"Safe!" Jess spat. "Is this safe?" She lifted up her blouse to reveal the bloodstained scarf.

"Or JP?" Francesca shouted. "What about him? Did you think he'd be safe too?"

Dupont locked eyes with the skipper. "He was supposed to be back at the Louvre. Where is he?"

"We've got eyes on him," the skipper said. "Alpha team are down in the catacombs now. We'll get him out."

"Wait," Will said, advancing on Dupont. "You knew everything. You used us. I should lay you out, right here, right now!"

Dupont didn't flinch. "I'd like to see you try."

"That's enough," the skipper said, stepping between them. "I suggest you stand down, young man."

Jess had him by the arm. "Calm down, Will."

George stared at the two women. He didn't like the fact that they'd been used as bait, but he couldn't help admiring the extent they'd gone to in order to hunt Victor down.

"You are in safe hands," the skipper explained. "This is a highly planned operation. I can assure you that we never put you at any unnecessary risk."

Will snorted. "Being shot at – is that 'necessary risk'?"

"You're alive, aren't you?" the skipper said, glaring at Will from beneath her cap.

Dupont scowled. "There was supposed to be zero risk. This is rapidly slipping through our fingers."

"It's OK," the skipper said. "We're still on track."

"On track?" Dupont said, frowning. "We've pulled them out, and we don't even know if we've snared Victor. Whoever had them down there, will be telling Victor right now that the kids have escaped and that the plan has gone wrong. They may even have spotted you!"

"Relax," the skipper said. "Alpha team have already sent their initial report."

"And?"

"The heat signatures only showed thirteen bodies. These seven and JP, means only five potential hostiles. They found two civilian cataphiles at one of the eastern exits. Sabrina is in the water back there. So, that leaves only two–"

"Alex and Jose," George interrupted.

"Alex is dead," Jess added. "JP killed him."

"And Jose is unconscious, not far from the sewers," Felix said, grinning.

"See," the skipper said, breaking into a hint of a smile.

Dupont's frown lifted. "I guess that's good news, but what about Victor? We're no wiser as to what he's planning or where he is."

"The map," George said, slinging his bag off his back. "I pulled it off their printer."

He unfolded the crumpled paper and flattened it out on the ground at their feet.

The skipper squatted down beside him. "What is this?"

George shrugged. She ran her finger over each note, following an invisible path between the highlighted streets.

"Hmm," she murmured.

"This doesn't look like much of a plan," Dupont said, looking unsure.

"It's a start," the skipper said. "Whatever he's planning, this could tell us where and when."

"But wait," Felix interrupted. "Alex said they needed us – six of us."

"Yeah," Jess added, "but we got away. If they needed us, then surely they can't go ahead with whatever they were planning without us."

"What were you supposed to do?" Dupont asked.

"We never found out," Felix answered.

The skipper looked worried. "That means we've got even less time. We need to search these addresses before Victor realises that the plan has collapsed. He may have intended to use them as mules."

"How do we know he'll be at any of these addresses?" Dupont asked.

"He'll avoid exposing himself, but I know Victor, and he won't want to be far away from witnessing his masterpiece. We need to get moving."

"Agreed," Dupont said.

"You take the kids back to meet up with the rest of their group. We mustn't raise any alarms yet – no police or authorities. Tell their teachers that they had left the Louvre via a fire exit and got lost trying to get back to the concourse."

"They won't fall for that," Jess said. "We've been gone for well over two hours."

"So convince them," she said, glaring at Jess. "The success of this whole operation relies on you *all* playing your part."

Jess folded her arms and glared back at the skipper. "Why should we help you?"

"Because, young lady, it's in everyone's interest to see Victor and his team behind bars."

"I know that," Jess huffed, "but I just don't think they're going to believe our story."

"That's my job," Dupont said. "We'll tell them you made your way to the boat jetty after you couldn't find us. I'll say that that's where I found you."

The skipper nodded. "OK, get moving. I need to contact Alpha team and get these addresses searched."

"Come on," Dupont said, ushering them up onto the bank.

They exchanged glances.

"We have to help anyway we can," George said. "We know what he's done and what he's capable of. If there's any chance of catching him and the rest of the crew…"

"I guess, but for the record, I still don't trust *her*." Will said, glaring at Dupont as they began to file past.

George hung back.

"Yes?" the skipper asked, looking up from her phone.

"Can I call my dad now?"

She hesitated. "He won't answer."

"What? How do you know?"

She watched the others trudge up onto the bank and along the footpath then lowered her voice. "His phone is off."

"Why?"

"I sent him to meet with one of my agents to exchange intel, and I was worried he'd be tracked, so I insisted he switched off his cell devices."

"But, maybe he's put them back on," George said.

"No, my agent was supposed to contact me as soon as the meet-up was complete."

With that, her phone rang. She looked down at the screen and up at George. "I have to take this. You need to go with Dupont."

She turned her back on George and answered the call.

"Yes … what do you mean he wasn't there? When? … For God's sake! No … ambushed … how?"

George froze. He could see Dupont and the others waiting for him on the path. Felix was waving for him to hurry up, but he knew that something had gone badly wrong and that it was something to do with his dad. He stepped around in front of the skipper just as she was hanging up.

"What's happened? Where's my dad?"

"Not where we sent him," she replied, looking frustrated.

"You said 'ambushed'. He's in trouble, isn't he?"

"No – we don't know that, we–"

"Give me the phone!"

"Calm down."

"I said give me the phone, now … or I'll … I'll…"

"OK, relax. Here, take it. Call your dad, but I don't suspect he'll pick up."

George grabbed the phone, rummaged inside his bag for the scrap of paper his dad had given him that morning and dialled the number. There was a long pause and several clicks.

"It's a secure line – it will take a while to re-direct," the skipper said, seeing the impatience bubbling inside him.

"It's ringing!" he shrieked.

She seemed surprised, but her shocked expression quickly turned to a face of worry.

George waited: five, six, seven rings.

Come on Dad, pick up.

Eight, nine, ten.

"We need to move on Victor," the skipper said. "I can't waste anymore–"

"Dad!" Someone had picked up. They breathed down the phone – short, sharp breaths, as if they'd been running. "Dad, it's me, George. Where are you?" Silence. "Dad?"

But before anyone could respond, the skipper snatched the phone back out of his hand, plucked out the SIM and threw the whole thing into the river.

"No!" George screamed. "He was there. I could hear him breathing."

"It wasn't him," she said. "And whoever it was on the other end, was just waiting for you to give up your location. We need to move out."

"But Dad…" George could feel his head spin again. "What have they done with my dad?"

Dupont had come back down the jetty. "What's the hold-up?"

"J21 has been compromised. I need to go and see what's happened. You take the kids back as planned. I'll get Alpha team to cover the addresses on the map. We'll be thinly stretched, but we'll have to make it work. I'll be on comms. Keep in constant contact."

"Will do," Dupont said. She looked down at George. "Let's go."

"No, I'm coming with *you*," he said, glaring at the skipper. "I'm coming to find my dad."

"That's not happening," the skipper said.

George could feel the panic writhe inside him. He couldn't possibly go back and re-join his fellow students, pretending to enjoy a trip down the Seine, while his dad's life sat in someone else's hands.

"I swear to you," he hissed through his teeth. "I've already lost one parent, and almost lost my Gran, because of Victor. I'm not losing anyone else. I'm coming with you, whether you like it or not."

As he said it, he realised how unlikely it was that she would agree. He stood facing her, trying to anticipate her response so he could bite back. But, to his complete surprise, she just smiled. There was a glimmer of respect in her eyes as they stilled and rested on his. For a moment they just stared at each other.

"I admire your determination," she finally said. "You can come … as long as you do exactly as I say."

George nodded.

"Are you serious?" Dupont said, looking stunned. "He's just a kid. This was not part of the plan."

"The plan is evolving."

Dupont looked uneasily at the skipper. "I heavily advise against this. We talked about the risk of … of this kind of exposure. You promised me that you'd—"

"I intend to keep my promises – all of them," the skipper said, grabbing George's bag from the floor. "He could be … of use."

"Use? You're playing with fire, Jay. You could jeopardise everything."

The skipper shot an icy look at Dupont. "Don't call me that," she warned. "I know what I'm doing. I suggest you do *your* part." With that she turned to George. "You sure you understand what you're getting yourself into?"

"Absolutely," George said. "I've done nothing but dream of taking Victor down since he first set foot into my world. I'm not letting him hurt my dad, and I'll do anything I can to help. I'm in."

Dupont shook her head. "And how am I supposed to explain his absence?"

"I'm sure you'll think of something," the skipper said. "You may have to recruit the ageing chaperone to your cause. Get him onside. He'll be more than excited to help you run a cover." With that, she stuffed the map into her jacket pocket and headed back towards the boat.

George glanced back up at his friends. He could see the look of concern on all their faces. He felt like he was abandoning them and wanted to explain why he was disappearing with a complete stranger, but however much they'd been through together, they couldn't possibly understand why he felt the way he did about stopping Victor – for him, it went beyond personal.

Chapter 18: Digging up the Past

There was something very strange about the silence between him and the skipper as their boat bounced along the Seine. George couldn't quite put his finger on it. They were strangers with very little to say to one another but bonded by a joint desire to snare Victor. It felt like an unsaid secret between them. He guessed that she knew why he hated Victor, but he could only imagine what her grievances were.

He watched her as she calmly steered the rib up the river. She filled him with a sense of safety and reassurance. Strong and wilful, in control and defiant; she was all the things he wished he could be. And yet, there was something vulnerable and awkward about her. Maybe it was the disguise or her constantly shifting gaze. Maybe she wasn't as assured as she made out.

"Who are you?" he asked, but she said nothing. "How do you know my dad?"

She continued to ignore him and focused instead on navigating past the ever-growing number of tour boats that littered their path.

"You could at least tell me your name," he pressed, but she just frowned. "Fine, don't tell me. Dupont called you Jay. I'll call you that."

"I'd rather you didn't," she said.

"Whatever," George huffed.

He wondered what it must be like to live a life under cover, constantly evading prying eyes and avoiding pressing questions.

Does she ever drop the disguise?

She must have sensed his frustration.

"Call me what you like," she said, passing him a cap and a lightweight jacket. "Just put these on – lose the blazer. We don't need to draw any unwanted attention."

He slung the torn blazer down at his feet, threw on the dark jacket and had to tighten the cap at the back to stop it from flying off.

They skimmed past several large boats. Jay buried her face further beneath her own cap as she spotted a group of onlookers snapping photos in their direction.

"Where are we going?" George asked.

"We need to meet with my agent. He's waiting for us near the intel drop."

"Has he ... seen my dad?"

"We'll find out what happened. Don't worry."

But he was worried. He tried to stop his mind from picturing his dad tied up and held somewhere, like Gran or Mrs Hodge or ... *stop it, George.*

He felt jumpy with impatience. Not knowing was the worst part. He needed to find his dad, and he was pinning all his hopes on this strange and evasive woman.

"Are you MI5?" he asked under his breath, even though no one else was within earshot.

"It's better if you don't ask any more questions," she said. "Better for both of us."

He took the hint and looked away, attempting to distract himself by watching the scenery flit past.

As the river narrowed, he could see Notre-Dame's imposing figure glide into view. It stood on its own island, splitting the Seine in two, like the speared helmet of an armoured knight, guarding the banks of Paris.

"Are we getting off here?" he asked, as they darted between more cruise boats and headed towards the bank.

"Yes, we'll have to pull up over there and come across the bridge. Keep your head down and stay close behind me. I don't know who is out there. It's dangerous to be this exposed."

"Exposed to what?"

"The enemy," she said, as she sprang from the boat. "Pass me the duffle bag … under the bench."

George squatted down and slid his arm under the seat. His fingers found fabric and he tugged. It was heavy. He yanked at it with two hands.

"What's in here?"

"My life," she said, leaning down, taking it from him and slinging the strap across her chest.

George grabbed his own bag, pulled the jacket tight around him and heaved himself out of the rib. She wasn't wasting any time. Head down and light on her feet, she danced between the tourists. George struggled to keep up. As she slipped between a couple that were sauntering along, arm in arm, he tried to follow her, but the crowd closed in and he was cut off. Quickly ducking left, he undercut a small group of elderly tourists but found his path blocked by a little man in a beret who was flapping a plastic folder at him.

"Portrait! Un portrait?" he was yelling at George over the surrounding chatter. "Dix minutes! Ten minutes – a beautiful portrait! Regardez!"

George tried to peer past the folder of artwork that was now almost smothering his face, but the momentary distraction had left him engulfed in a sea of bodies, and he'd lost sight of Jay completely.

"Viens, it's a great souvenir," the man insisted.

"Get off him!" Jay had reappeared as if from nowhere. She grabbed the man by the arm, making him drop his folder.

"Ow! Lâchez-moi!" the little man shouted, trying to wriggle from her grip, but before George had a chance to intervene, her other hand was disappearing inside her jacket.

Her gun!

"No, no," George yelped, trying to stop her. "It's OK. He's just an artist!"

Her fierce gaze didn't stray from the poor, withering man, but her hand slid back out, empty. George breathed a sigh of relief as she let go of the man's arm, and he rubbed at it while mumbling something in French.

"I'm sorry," George said, picking the folder up from the ground.

"Forget it!" he barked, snatching it back and storming off.

Jay glared at George. "I said, 'keep up'!"

"I was trying," he muttered.

By the time they had made it out into the gardens of the cathedral, George had worked up a sweat. The autumn sun was soft on his skin, but he could still feel a chill biting at his damp legs as they ducked into the shade of a large tree.

Jay stopped and pulled a small leather pouch from inside her duffle bag. George tried to see what it was, but she turned away and fiddled with it in the curtains of her jacket. Seconds later, she was murmuring something into the palm of her hand. She scratched at her ear, as if dislodging a lump of wax, and George caught a glimpse of a flesh-coloured earpiece wedged deep inside her ear canal.

She ignored George completely while she continued mumbling to herself and scanning her eyes across the crowd. He tried to follow her gaze and soon spotted the bearded man with the green beanie who was marching towards them.

"He was on our train!" George gasped. "Is he with you too?"

"Shh," she snapped. "I said no more questions."

"What took you so long?" the man asked, as he came to a stop on the other side of the tree trunk.

"Issues," she replied. "We're very exposed here."

"Why is *he* with you?" he asked, glancing at George.

"It doesn't matter. What's the latest?"

The bearded man looked at George again. George wasn't sure if he should say hi but thought better of opening his mouth again and just smiled at him. He reminded George of a cartoon sailor he'd seen in an old comic that Gran had given him. His tattooed forearms bulged; his dark, speckled beard swamped his lower face and his eyebrows were just as overgrown. His Spanish accent wasn't as pronounced as the postman's, but his skin was just as tanned. George could imagine him heaving fish-laden nets over the side of a creaking boat.

"I waited as long as I could, but J21 didn't show," he said. "I was exactly where you said I'd be in the note you left him at the airport."

"What makes you think he was ambushed?" Jay asked.

"This," he said, passing her a thin, blue envelope.

"Damn it! Where did you find it?"

"Inside."

Jay stuffed the envelope into her pocket. "Any signs of a struggle?"

"Not really, but it's not exactly empty down there. I got out as soon as I realised he was a no-show. I didn't want to risk being cornered."

"We'll have to go back down; see if there's anything to give us a clue as to who disturbed him. There's a small chance he just freaked out and left when he saw you."

George was watching the conversation bounce back and forth. He could see the sceptical look on the bearded man's face. "I don't know about that…"

"Is he … dead?" George spluttered.

"There's no sign to suggest that," Jay said, before the bearded man could respond.

"I want to come with you … to look for him," George said.

"I wasn't exactly going to leave you out here alone."

"So, what are we waiting for?" he said, a prickle of impatience running through him.

Jay frowned before turning back to the bearded man. "We'll follow close behind you."

With that, he nodded and strode off.

"Try to blend in," Jay said, as they began to forge their way through the thick of the crowd.

George peered up at the cathedral, trying to look like all the other visitors, but he was sure that they stood out like a pair of coffin bearers at a circus. He must have looked ridiculous in his oversized jacket, damp trousers and low slung cap, and he was sure no other tourists were prowling through the crowd like Jay was. She looked like a panther on the trail of her next kill.

George was expecting to go inside the cathedral, but their bearded associate passed it by, ducked down the side of the building and weaved across the plaza. The crowds thinned as they left the cathedral behind them, and soon they reached a set of steps that plunged down into the ancient crypts.

George wasn't sure what lay beneath the famous Notre-Dame. He imagined a dark, gloomy room full of dusty recesses and lonely stone coffins, but as they descended the steps, he was surprised to see that the crypt looked more like an archaeological dig. The rough stone, half-crumbled archways and layers of brickwork created an eerie maze. It was cool and quiet, with far fewer visitors. People sauntered between display cases and excavated stonework, reading up on the archaeological history of urban Paris.

"Keep up," Jay hissed at him from around the back of a small glass display.

He sped up, and they weaved their way between groups of enthusiastic visitors to the back of the dingy dungeon.

"Here," the bearded guy whispered. "This is where I found the letter." He pointed at the base of an alcove. "We were supposed to meet here."

Jay swung full circle, surveying the ground at her feet, but there was nothing obvious to suggest that there'd been a struggle.

George tried to picture his dad down here, skulking in the shadows, waiting to meet his contact. He tried to imagine what he'd have done next. He began drifting away from the other two, searching within crevices and behind bends. As he approached the very back of the room, a woman appeared out of the shadows.

"Bonjour, can I help you?" she asked, peering over George's shoulder at the other two, who were still searching the ground. "Have you lost something?"

George noticed her badge. She was the crypt's shift manager.

"Um – is there a gift shop?" he blurted out.

She looked at him quizzically. "Not back here, there isn't. Maybe your parents can take you up to the main cathedral."

George stared back at Jay and her Spanish colleague and almost laughed. "Er … they're not – um, thanks," he said, smiling.

The lady loitered a little longer, eyeing all three of them in turn, before ducking through one of the narrow arches. George peered after her. She swept left and seemed to slip between a fold in the rock wall. Curious, he shuffled after her. His eyes were just readjusting to the gloom when he felt something soft brush against his foot.

Dad?

Stooping down, he snatched up the faded blue cap that sat crumpled at his feet. It was unmistakably Sam's.

"What was he doing back here?"

"George?" Jay appeared behind him.

"He was here," he said, whipping around and shoving the cap under her nose. "This is his."

She gently took the cap from his grip. George pulled back his hands and his stomach flipped over backwards. Even in the gloom, he could see the glimmer of the cool, wet blood that stained his fingertips.

"No," he breathed. "What have they done?"

Trembling, he held them out for Jay to see. He looked at her, searching her eyes for any sign of reassurance. Any sign that she knew that his dad was OK. "Where is he?" he asked, the panic rising up inside him.

"I don't know, but we'll find him – I promise."

"How … how can you promise that?" George snapped. "I've seen what Victor does. He tried to kill my dad once already – why would it be any different now?"

"Try to keep your voice down," Jay said, glancing over her shoulder.

"What? This is all your fault – your plan, your intel drop, your–"

"Look at me. Control your breathing. If you want to help me find your dad, I need you to stay calm. The greatest test for any agent is to stay in control, whatever the circumstances."

"I'm not an agent. I'm not like you!" he shouted. "I'm just a kid!"

"No!" she barked back. "You're not a kid – not now. You're here because you said you could cope. You're here because you wanted to help. Now get a grip!"

George stared at her, lost for words.

"Do you want to help your dad?" she asked, lowering her voice.

"Of course."

"Then think smart and start behaving like an agent."

George bristled but knew that she was right. He tried to tame the tornado of rage and fear that was tearing at his insides. He sucked in a lungful of air and focused on blowing it out – slow and steady.

"Elías, get over here," Jay barked at the bearded man, but he was on his phone. "Elías!"

He ended his call and strode towards them.

"Alpha team have got eyes on Angelika Volkov," he said.

Jay's eyes lit up. "Where?"

"Place de la Bastille, but we don't have enough bodies to watch her and the addresses you sent them to, and if Victor is with Angelika, they'll definitely need more manpower."

Jay rubbed her forehead. "Damn it! We're stretched too thin. I need to find Sam. Looks like someone did get to him before us," she said, holding up the bloody cap.

"But our priority is Victor, surely…" Elías said, glancing at George.

But George wasn't listening to them. His mind was cartwheeling. He closed his eyes and tried to force the painful images and thoughts from his mind. He had to believe that his dad was OK. He hung his head and braced himself against the wall.

Breathe…

When he opened his eyes, the room was spinning, so he rested his forehead between his hands, only to find himself staring directly at a patch of blood-stained rock. He immediately glanced at his own fingers.

Was that me?

Standing upright and edging sideways, he tracked his eyes along the wall. Another red mark – barely visible – just a smudge.

"George?" He could hear Jay's voice calling him, like a distant echo, but his eyes were fixed on the trail. Moving further into the passageway, he searched for another mark.

There!

Millimetres from the gap in the wall that the shift manager had slipped through – and then another – a spot on the floor.

"George, wait!" Jay shouted, but George couldn't stop.

With every step and every new drop of blood, his heart rate ratcheted. He dashed through the passage that lay behind the gap and into a small corridor.

Which way?

He frantically searched for any more signs of blood, but there was nothing. He figured that whoever had taken his dad, wouldn't have hung around, so he shoved his way out of the door marked 'fire exit' and stepped out onto a narrow, concrete path that hovered only feet above the rush of the Seine. His breath caught in his throat as the cool air whistled past him.

As the door swung closed, it sent a shudder through him as metal clanged against metal. He was locked out but didn't care. Jay's muffled voice leaked from behind the solid door, and it sounded like she had disturbed the shift manager. She would have to deal with it herself. George had no intention of waiting for her.

He scanned the footpath in both directions. To his left, small rounded steps descended into the water. He swallowed hard.

Where did they take him?

To his right, the path was just wide enough for one body to pass, and there was no railing or rope to stop him from falling into the water, but he didn't let that slow him down. Feet pounding against the concrete, he rounded the bend at a sprint only to find himself heading towards a solid stone wall.

What the ...

All he could see ahead of him was the curving support of a low-slung bridge. It cast a heavy shadow across the water. He stared up at it as a small boat glided past filled with curious passengers. He turned away from them and faced the wall.

Where is he?

Edging closer to the bridge, trying not to look panicked, he scanned his eyes across the water and searched the concrete at his feet, looking for any more signs.

Bang! The door had been thrown back open. *Clang!* And slammed closed. Footsteps clattered behind him in the distance. "George, stop!" Jay bellowed.

But just then, he saw it, a gap in the wall to his right, and blood – more blood. He took one last glance down the river and then slid into the gap.

The passageway led beneath the bridge, right through the centre of the cold, ancient stone. Hazy rays of light filtered in through a scattering of grills, and the cool air flowed like water at his ankles. It took a moment for his eyes to adjust to the light, but then he saw him, creased over on the floor, his head in his hands.

"Dad!"

Sam gingerly raised his head. Blood had trickled down the back of his neck and soaked into his shirt.

"George, what are you…"

"Dad, what happened? Who did this to you?" George said, dropping to the floor beside him.

"I don't know. Someone set me up."

George ran his hands over his dad's torso, pulled aside his coat and checked for more blood.

"It's OK," Sam said, grabbing George's hand. "It's just my head."

"Just?"

"It looks worse than it is. I'll be fine, I promise."

With that, Jay and Elías appeared, blocking the light from the entrance.

"Help me," George pleaded.

"Who's there?" Sam said, straining to see past George and trying to push himself to his feet.

"Dad, relax, they're with me."

Jay turned to whisper something to Elías.

Sam was up, bracing himself against the wall. "Who are you?" he demanded. "Show yourselves!"

"Take it easy," George said, catching him as he stumbled forwards. "Just take a moment. You're concussed."

George stood in front of him, steadying him with both arms, but he continued to try to push past.

"I said show–" Sam said, stopping short. "Elías?"

Elías lowered his gaze beneath his beanie.

"What are you doing here – in Paris?" Sam went on, lurching closer.

"He's here helping catch Victor, Dad. Victor is here, in the city."

But Sam wasn't listening. He slid along the wall, forcing George backwards.

"They can explain, Dad," George said. "They've been hunting Victor down."

He turned to them for support, but before George could ask again, Elías had spun on his heels and sprinted away.

"Wait!" George called over his shoulder. "Where's he going?"

But Jay didn't answer. She stood watching him leave: her back turned, her neck rigid and her shoulders tense.

"I said, 'show – your – face'," Sam growled, fumbling around inside his jacket.

George looked back at Jay but she refused to face them. When he looked back, Sam had a taser gun in his hands.

"Dad, wait! She's with me – she helped me find you!"

George glanced over his shoulder again. He could see Jay filling her lungs. She lifted her head and slowly turned to face Sam. The shadows cloaked her dark frame, and all that George could see were her piercing green eyes peering out from beneath the peak of her cap.

"Take off your hat," Sam ordered, his taser tight in his grip.

She closed her eyes and slowly peeled off her cap, releasing her shock of copper hair.

Sam stood frozen, his eyes unblinking. "W…what?" he stammered.

She lifted her arms and pointed her gun straight at him. George saw something in her expression, something he couldn't read.

"Put down the taser," she said.

Sam staggered backwards. "You!"

Chapter 19: The Deception of the Dead

There was silence. George stood confused, a human barrier, soaking up the unseen force of tension and emotion that pulsed between them. On one side, he could feel a shockwave of horror and anger seep from every pore of his dad's body. On the other, Jay stood poised, on edge – as if waiting to duck a bullet.

"So it's true," Sam growled, "a traitor *and* a liar."

"Put the weapon down and we can talk like adults."

"You first!" Sam said through gritted teeth.

"Fine," she said, lowering her gun. "See."

George looked at his dad. "Please, Dad, she's on our side."

Sam slowly lowered his taser. "She set me up!"

"That's not what happened," she said.

"Really? So it wasn't you that sent me down here?"

"Yes, but I didn't know you'd be–"

"I should have guessed: an informant with inside knowledge of Victor's plans – who else could it have been?"

"Sam, please, we don't have much time. Victor is here in Paris. He has the weapon and he plans to use it. There's no time for explanations."

"Explanations! When did you last care about explaining your actions – or care about anything else for that matter? Why should I believe you?"

"Ask George," she replied. "Victor's already tried to get to him."

"He what?" Sam spluttered, turning to George. "Is that true?"

"Yes, but we got away and Jay saved us ... well ... actually, tracked us."

"What did you say?"

"She has a team following Victor, they put a tracker–"

"George, please," Jay interrupted. "Let me speak."

"You put a tracker on my son?"

"I can explain," Jay said, moving a step closer.

"Get back!" Sam shouted, pushing George behind him.

"Dad, please listen to her!"

"We had reason to believe that Victor wanted to get to him. I only used the tracker, so that we could follow–"

"You used my son as bait?"

"It was a calculated risk," Jay said, her face rigid.

"You haven't changed, have you?" Sam snapped back. "Haven't learned a goddamn thing – always happy to gamble, whatever the cost."

"I just take the necessary steps to get a job done. That was our training, unless you've forgotten."

"Always a step *too* far," Sam said. "That's exactly how you got us into this mess in the first place. I should arrest you now."

"Don't threaten me, Sam. Now is not the time. I know I've made mistakes, we both have, but our priority is Victor and that weapon."

"Mistakes? I don't think you can point any fingers at me."

"Dad, please," George begged. "She's right, we have to focus on stopping Victor."

"You've made plenty of mistakes," Jay sneered. "Your whole unit is a joke."

"Funny," Sam said, "those are the exact same words Victor used when I last saw him. Seems you two have a lot in common, which I guess makes sense, seeing as you've obviously been working with him this whole time."

"Don't you dare!" she roared. "You have no idea – no idea of what I've been through – what I've had to sacrifice!"

George struggled to keep up; to track the bullets as they flew between them. Had he made a mistake? Was she really the enemy? Her, Dupont, Elías, JP? Had he fallen for it all and led her straight to his dad?

"I don't understand," he said, trying to prise his way back in front of Sam. But neither of them were listening; both too intent on attacking each other.

"I lost everything," Jay said.

"Ha!" Sam laughed. "You should have thought of that before you decided to put your job before everything else that mattered."

George's brain was struggling to process his dad's words. They floated around in his consciousness like a feather that was just drifting out of reach. He tried to grab at it; to pin it down.

"Did you ever once stop to think about who else you were affecting – the trail of devastation you left behind?" Sam continued.

"Wait," George uttered under his breath.

"I've done nothing since but try to right my wrongs. Who do you think tipped off your source in Turkey?" Jay said.

"Wait," George said again, his mind reeling.

"Who gave you the location of the nest?" Jay went on. "It was *me* – I put my life on the line, just so you and your double-crossing chief could throw it all away in some cock-up of a sting! I risked everything: my cover, my freedom, my life – for what?"

"Yes, exactly," Sam said.

"Dad, listen to me," George pleaded, but Sam didn't stop.

"For what, Jay? We didn't ask you to risk your life for us. Not for me … and definitely not for your *son*!"

Time stood still. Sam's words hung in the air like a kestrel hovering above its prey. George's mind spiralled up to meet it. He looked it dead in the eye, searching for a glimmer of sense – reality. Everything else fell away: all thoughts, all feelings, all time. His breath was whisper still. Then something heavy dropped inside him and he plummeted to earth, crashing back down to the ground as everything flooded over him at once: the whine of the wind, the slap of the water, the thud of his heartbeat, the truth of what he'd heard.

When his head finally cleared, he found himself down on his knees, his dad by his side and Jay staring down at him – fear, pain and worry swirling in the pools of their eyes.

"George?" they both uttered in unison.

He struggled to find his voice. "I don't…"

Jay glared at her feet and swallowed hard. "George … I … I didn't want it to be this way, I…"

"No," Sam said, springing back up. "You don't get to do that. You don't get to creep back in here and speak to him like you have a right. You have no right!"

"Dad!"

"No, George, you can't trust her!"

"But, Dad," George said, pulling himself up.

"He's my son too," she said.

"You don't get to decide to be his mother now. You haven't earned that right. Seven years, Jay – you can't be absent for seven years and just–"

"I had little choice," she growled.

"You had one choice and you screwed it up."

"Victor gave me no choice. It was life as his hostage or death, and I chose life."

"You could have chosen life with us; you could have walked away," Sam said. "Instead, you chose to sell your soul for Victor."

"Stop," George said.

"You think it was easy!" she yelled. "You think there wasn't a day that went past when I didn't regret the decisions I'd made. For years, I was his hostage, dragged from one hideout to another, questioned, tortured, left for days with no idea of my fate. I had no choice but to win his trust. I went through hell!"

"Stop, please," George pleaded.

"And what did you have to do to win his trust, exactly? What part of your soul did you have left to sell him?" Sam pressed.

"That's ENOUGH!" George screamed. "Shut up – both of you! Neither of you win, no one wins! Everyone lost! And you *both* screwed up!"

"George!" Jay said, shocked.

"No – Dad's right. You aren't a mother to me. You've been dead to me for seven years. Seven years with no mother!"

"And you," he said turning to his dad. "You knew and never told me?"

"I had no proof, George. It was barely rumours, conspiracy, I…"

"Stop!" he said, standing between them. "None of that matters now. What matters is that Victor is out there, and so are my friends. You've both failed. But I have no intention of failing *them*."

His parents stood speechless; unable to look at each other, unable to look at him.

"You're right," Jay said, breaking the silence. She looked up at Sam, a shred of softness in her expression. "Whatever the past, we have a chance to fix it, here and now. The rest has to wait."

Sam struggled to respond. He couldn't even look at her. George turned to face him. He looked like a broken man; a man that had tried so hard to do his best, even though he was soaked through with anguish and regret. George could see the exhaustion lying heavy on his shoulders. He realised now that the conflict within his dad must have eaten away at him, every second of every day – never really knowing the truth, yet always knowing that he was keeping something from his only son. No wonder he was so withdrawn, so distant. But who had he been protecting – his son, himself, or both?

"Dad, we can do this, we can finish it."

"How?" Sam croaked.

"We think we might know Victor's targets."

"What?"

"He's here, in Paris," George said. "His team are planning something – something big."

Sam shook his head. "How can you be so sure?"

"George found this," Jay said, pulling the map from her pocket and tentatively passing it to Sam.

"Where did you get this?" Sam asked, snatching it from her.

"I pulled it off the printer in their hideout," George replied. "They were definitely preparing something – they had boxes and maps of Paris down there."

Sam looked up at George. "Where did they take you? Did they hurt you?"

"No … I mean, I'm fine. They just took us down into the Catacombs. They were hiding out down there, but, Dad, listen, we've already taken out Sabrina, Alex and Jose."

"And we know where Angelika is," Jay added.

Sam tried to look at her. "Really?"

"We're so close," she said.

"And you're sure Victor's actually here, in Paris?" Sam asked.

"I've spent enough time around him to know exactly what he's thinking," she replied. "Trust me, he's here. I can almost smell him."

Sam looked down at the map and back up at Jay. "How do I know I can trust you?"

"I've done nothing but plan for this moment. Through every hour sat alone in the dark, every overheard conversation, every mental note taken, I never stopped planning. I've watched him, studied him, infiltrated his networks, coerced his sources, bribed his allies – all so that I can finally be free of him and close the door on the past. I have no intention of cocking this up."

Sam turned away. He braced himself against the damp wall and looked at the ground. George could hear him breathing deeply.

"Dad?" George crept closer. "Dad, we need to stop him … please."

He turned back towards Jay; the map clenched tightly in his fist.

"You have to promise me – no risks," he said, glaring at her. "The focus is on stopping the attack, isolating that weapon, saving lives, public safety. I won't risk all that just to take him down. If we snare the bird then that's a bonus, but it's not the prime objective."

"Agreed," Jay said, holding up her hands. "But he won't stay hidden – he knows we're both here."

"What makes you so sure?"

"He knows I'm on his tail. He enjoys it; thinks it's a game. Since escaping, I've never been more than a few paces behind him. He lost track of me for a while, but he's sent me messages; left me warnings. He knows. And he definitely knows you're here – and George. Why else did he choose Paris?"

"Hang on," George interrupted. "How would he know that we were going to be here? I only found out last night that we were coming."

"He knew about your trip to Paris from your teacher, Mr Jefferson. He knew precisely where you'd be and when. And as for your dad," she said, turning to Sam. "Who assigned you to the summit?"

"Chief," Sam said, bluntly.

"Exactly! Convenient, don't you think? In fact, I'm guessing it was your chief who sent his minion to knock you out at the intel drop."

"That's a huge assumption. I didn't tell Chief anything."

"Well someone put a tail on you, and it wasn't me, so I'm guessing it's your mole."

"Hmm, maybe, but why would Victor risk exposing himself when he's surrounded by enemies?"

"He won't be able to resist, Sam. Both of us, together in Paris – that's just too much for his ego. He'll show himself – I can promise you that."

From: TDP
To: Anonymous
Re: Exposure {Encrypted}

Your cover is blown. They know you are here. Be careful.

End.

Chapter 20: Deciphering the Defence

As they made their way out from beneath the bridge, the faint afternoon sun had crept below its arches, sending warm, mellow rays bouncing off the undulating water. George looked at his shadow as it stretched along the path. There it lay, nestled between two others – a trident with all its prongs. Just like that – two had become three. In one sliver of a moment, he had been reunited with his dead mother. He felt like he should be flooded with questions, anger, sadness, relief.

What – what should I feel?

Something surely, but he felt empty – just a numbness – a void.

"What do we know so far?" Sam said, stopping to get a proper look at the map.

"We know he's been preparing the weapon," Jay said. "He had a lab set up here in Paris – ready to go. He took what he stole from you, and we're assuming that he's split it into several small loads."

"Enough to cause serious damage?"

"It only takes small amounts. That's how it can travel undetected. We're pretty sure it needs a trigger though. It reacts in contact with oxygen, but it needs something else."

"We knew that already," Sam said impatiently. "What's new?"

Jay frowned at him. "We tracked several trucks leaving the lab last week. They were headed for Spain. They split up, but by the time we were able to get close enough, they'd been abandoned."

"What?"

"They were decoys – dummies – just empty boxes branded with the falcon's wings. He knew we were watching. He'd sent us on a wild goose chase."

"So, the real load got past you," Sam said smugly.

"Or maybe it didn't leave Paris at all," Jay said, forcing a smile. "When I heard that you were on your way here, I was convinced. Paris is the target. We set a plan in motion and soon had sources on the inside…"

"And?"

Jay touched her ear. "Wait … it's Elías. Give me two minutes." With that, she strode off down the path, whispering into the palm of her hand.

George watched her go. This woman, this stranger was his mother. He searched inside himself for some glimmer of recognition, some warmth, but found only a fog of confusion.

"George … I'm sorry," Sam said. "I know this must be a huge shock. I really–"

"No, Dad, *I'm* sorry. I didn't mean to say those things, I just–"

"But you're right. I don't win any prizes for … anything, but I promise you, all the evidence pointed towards your mother being dead."

He pulled a chain from beneath his shirt. A small worn medallion hung from it, swaying back and forth. Sam plucked it aside revealing a fine gold ring.

"This is all they sent me – after forensics had filtered through the ashes – just this."

George felt a lump in his throat. "You kept it?"

"Of course," he replied, turning the ring over in his fingers. "I held out hope that she was maybe alive, but it was killing me." He looked back up at George. "In that first year, we received several reports from contacts in the field that she'd been spotted, but they came to nothing. And the more I thought about it, the more the anger took over me. The thought of her alive and not fighting to come back to us, the deceit, the chance that maybe the rumours were true – that she'd double crossed us and joined Victor, traded secrets – it consumed me."

He slumped back against the wall.

"Did she?" George asked. "Did she really do all that?"

"I have no idea. I tried not to believe it. No one ever said it to my face of course, but they all thought it. Every time a new report of a sighting slid under the office door, they whispered it in the corridors: my wife – the traitor." He hung his head. "I'm sorry I never told you, but I couldn't put you through it. It was easier to accept that she'd gone."

George nodded. He understood, although deep down he realised that it was just another part of their life that had been kept from him. He looked at his dad and realised that he wasn't mad. He didn't blame him, if anything, he felt sorry for him.

"Do you trust her now?" he whispered.

"Honestly … I don't know. It seems strange that she's chosen to show up now, after all these years, and right when Victor is planning his comeback."

They both turned and watched her as she paced up and down, deep in conversation. "For now, I'll choose to trust her – for as long as she appears to be helping," Sam said. "But please – I know this must be very difficult to take in – but please don't forget – she's as much a stranger to you now as she was before. Don't take anything she says as the truth. I don't know where her allegiances truly lie. In fact, I don't know her at all anymore."

"So, what do we do now?" George asked.

"We piece together everything we know, and we find Victor before he hurts anyone else. I need you to tell me what happened. How did he get to you?"

George explained as best he could. He told Sam about JP and Jin-é, the art studio, the catacombs and Jay appearing in the canal.

"And you think they took you because…" Sam said.

"They said they needed six of us … to do something."

"Maybe he intended for you to carry the payload," Sam mumbled, looking down at George's map. "Six targets? There aren't six addresses on this map."

"I don't know, Dad. But they were definitely preparing for something."

Jay returned. She threw a small first aid kit at Sam.

"Sort your head out – we need to get moving."

"I'm fine," he said, tossing it back at her.

She shook her head. "Suit yourself."

"What did Elías say?"

"It looks like Angelika is loading up a truck full of equipment. She's moving out. We need to follow her."

"We need to take her in," Sam said.

"What? No, not yet. I don't want to throw Victor off track. I want him to follow through with his plan."

"The focus is on stopping the attack," Sam said. "Have you already forgotten?"

"No," she frowned, "but we actually have no idea of the full extent of the plan. Taking her out may not stop anything."

"His plan seems to be dissolving as we speak. If what George says is accurate, he's lost his mules, half his team and now Angelika is exposed."

"Yes, but there's a chance he isn't aware of all, if any, of that."

"You really believe that?" Sam laughed.

"We got to Alex and Jose first, Sabrina has been taken in by local police, so she'll have no way of contacting him, and Angelika doesn't exactly look like she's been spooked."

"You really think he'll press ahead with half his team down?" Sam asked.

"He'll have all his buyers watching – he intends to prove the versatility of the weapon. A failed test would leave him dead in the water. They won't tolerate another failure. And he won't back down. This plays into our hands. He'll be thinking on his feet and will have to raise his head and get his hands dirty."

Sam chewed at his lip and ran his hands through his beard. "I don't like this at all. If we know there's a threat of an attack, we should be informing the Parisian police, making arrests, doing everything we can to reduce the impact."

"What exactly should we tell them?" Jay snapped. "Which sites should we evacuate?"

Sam looked down at George's map again.

"I don't know. This doesn't feel right. These addresses – they're so random. I can't believe these are the targets."

"I thought the same, but I didn't take any chances – I've got a team down there."

"How on earth did you get a team together? And Elías of all people. I thought he was still in prison."

"Not everyone gave up on me," she said, smiling.

"I'm surprised you could find anyone who still trusted you."

George coughed. "The map – we were talking about the map."

Sam rubbed the back of his neck. Flecks of dried blood fluttered down onto the paper. He swept them aside.

"They don't look like targets to me. And these time stamps – there's no logic or sequence to them. Why would he hit such low grade sites, and at random times? We're missing something."

Sam ran his finger around the sites, just as Jay had done.

"I tried that," she said.

"And?"

"There's no hidden message. No meaningful central vector."

Sam raised one eyebrow and turned the paper upside down, up to the light, back to front.

George looked at him quizzically. "Dad?"

"Sometimes things aren't what they appear to be, George. Codes, hidden meanings. It's very unlikely that Victor just emailed a map of the targets to Jose. There'll be something … wait. Where's your phone?" Sam shoved his hand out in George's direction without lifting his eyes from the paper.

"Um … in a sewer," George said.

"What?"

"I used it – it doesn't matter. Where's yours?"

"He took it – whoever knocked me out. He took my gun, my tablet and my phone – just forgot to check for my taser. Jay, give me your phone?"

"It's in the Seine," she said.

"And … I'm sure you didn't just bring one device – what else have you got?"

"Nothing that I'd show you."

"Seriously?" Sam said, glaring at her.

"The feeling of mistrust is mutual," she said, smiling sweetly.

Sam shook his head. "And the first step to re-establishing trust is … lending someone your tablet," he grinned. "I just need to look up these addresses."

"Just addresses," she said, reluctantly handing over a small tablet from inside the side pocket of her duffle bag. "Nothing else."

Sam squatted down and spread the map out on the ground. "Hold it for me," he said to George, and then started tapping the addresses into the tablet's search engine.

George watched in silence as Sam drew his finger through the dust at their feet. 'L'

'A'

"You got something?" Jay asked.

"I was always better at code breaking than you," he said.

Jay frowned. "I was too busy catching the bad guys."

"And letting them get away again," he said without lifting his gaze.

'E'

'D'

'F'

"What is it?" George asked.

"These numbers – they're not times – they're pointing to a letter or number in an address. Look. This building – it's 2, Rue Sainte-Anne. The supposed time stamp is 18:08. The eighteenth digit is 'E' and the eighth digit is 'N'."

"Wow!" George exclaimed.

"This one is a number – sixteen." Sam said, continuing to draw in the dirt.

As Sam continued, George stared down at the collection of scrawlings. His eyes scanned across them, trying to piece them together into something that made some sense.

"Wait," he gasped, "La Défense! It spells 1600, La Défense!"

"The summit!" Sam said. "Of course – how could I be so blind? It's the perfect stage – every Head of Security in one place."

"That's no low-grade target," Jay said. "That's headline news. That's got Victor written all over it."

"But surely it's heaving with security," George said, standing up. "How would he get in?"

"Chief!" Sam and Jay said, at once.

"My God! This whole thing, Sam. You don't think it's just been one big charade, do you? He's had me running all over the city, tracking George, worrying about the whereabouts of his crew, following Angelika – all so that he can walk straight in there and deliver the weapon. God, he's probably creased over right now laughing at me."

"I have no idea, but I'm now here instead of there. I'm supposed to be heading up the security."

George was still marvelling at the deciphered code at his feet. "Hang on, what are the numbers for? 1600, is that a building number?"

"No," Jay said, looking down at her watch. "That's the drop time." She looked up at Sam. "We've got fifty minutes."

"There are hundreds of delegates in that building, let alone government officials in the offices. We need to evacuate, now." He lifted the tablet.

"Stop!" Jay barked. "You can't use my comms."

"What?" Sam said. "I need to call it in."

"No, I'm sorry, Sam. I can't let that device anywhere near official channels."

"Jay – no offence, but I don't really care about your privacy."

"Please, Sam. You don't understand. I'm a wanted woman. I've…" She glanced over at George. "You know that any call into official channels with the warning of an attack will trigger the download of a Trojan tracker. They'll access my files – all my contacts, all my sources. Everything is on there. I'll be risking too many covers, too many lives."

"We're talking about innocent people, Jay. That's the objective – remember – saving lives."

She pinched the bridge of her nose. "Is there anyone else? Anyone who is off-channel? Non-official?"

"Steckler!" George cried. "Contact Mr Steckler. He can call it in."

"Yes!" Jay said. "Perfect!"

"Yes, that would be great, but I don't tend to wander around with his contact details inked on the back of my hand," Sam said.

"Ahh!" Jay screamed in frustration.

"Dupont!" George said. "You told Dupont to get to Steckler. She can get a message to him."

"Great thinking," Jay said, snatching the tablet back from Sam. "*I'll* call it in."

"Dupont, Therese Dupont! My God, Jay, how many other low-lives have you been cosying up with? Ex-informants and con artists."

"Shut up! You need to get to La Défense and intercept your chief."

"And where exactly will you be?" Sam asked, frowning.

"I'll stay on Angelika. If Victor doesn't show at the target, then he'll be with her, for sure. I won't let her out of my sight."

Sam hesitated. "I have no way of contacting you."

"Take this," she said, handing Sam a small device from her bag. "You can message me directly on this. It's two way but a closed channel. You can only reach me – no one else."

"I want to know everything that happens," he said, turning it over in his hand.

"That goes both ways," she replied.

Sam looked up at her. "If Dupont doesn't respond, then you have to call it in – direct to French Intelligence. You have to promise me."

She nodded. "I promise. Just Go!"

With that, Sam and George raced off along the path, up a set of steps and out into the afternoon sun. The last thing George saw, as he glanced back down the river's edge, was his mother's back as she disappeared into the shadow of the bridge.

From: Anonymous
To: TDP
Cc: ALPHA, BETA
Re: Target {Encrypted}

The estimated drop time is 16:00.
J21 has gone to the target site at La Défense.

Get the chaperone to pass on the message to French
Security exactly as I dictated. We must stay in control. We
cannot afford for a full city lock down – we will have no
escape route.

I am joining BETA on surveillance.
ALPHA team are on standby; they will not risk breaking
their cover.
We must remain hidden – minimal exposure to any
authorities.

Isolate the children and the chaperone. Get them to Gare
du Nord and await my instructions.

If anything goes wrong, get out of the city. We will
rendezvous as discussed.

End.

From: TDP
To: Anonymous
Cc: ALPHA, BETA
Re: Target {Encrypted}

The chaperone seems more than happy to co-operate.

I am standing by for your instructions.
Be careful – you are very exposed. They will be coming for you.

Good luck.

End.

Chapter 21: The Burden of the Mule

The cab ride to La Défense would have taken an infuriating thirty minutes, but Sam had no intention of sitting stranded on Avenue des Champs-Élysées so collared the first police officer he could find and managed to convince them to blue-light him and George the full ten kilometres to the target. Leaving nothing to chance, he borrowed the officer's phone, called the security team at the summit and ordered the evacuation.

"I am deadly serious," he barked down the phone. "Yes, I know he's my superior, but he needs to be detained … Yes, I believe he's involved … I don't care, just get everyone out and get all dignitaries to a safe holding room … Yes, I know … Just follow protocol, Devant. I'll be there in two minutes."

As they pulled up to La Défense, the tiered plaza was teeming with people. The huge picture-framed structure of La Grande Arche stared down at them as they leapt from the car and sprinted up the steps.

George's heart was racing. The blue lights of the police car still flashed across his retinas; the blare of the siren still rang in his ears.

"Dad, how do we know where he'll hit? Look at all these people."

Tourists sat on the lowest steps, soaking up the autumn sun; street vendors loitered on the outskirts and teams of security guards patrolled behind barriers.

"He'll be after the delegates," Sam panted, "in the conference centre."

As they reached the entrance, people were being spat out of the revolving doors, flustered and disgruntled. Sam tried to push past, but they were coming thick and fast.

After several revolutions, he grabbed George, shoved him through a small gap in the flow and they squeezed their way through the doors and into the glass lobby.

"Just keep close to me," Sam said.

"Stop!" someone shouted. George looked past his dad. A security guard stood at a metal detector. "No one is allowed in," she said.

"I know," Sam said. "I ordered the evacuation. I need to speak with Abi Devant, your boss."

He pulled out his ID and flashed it in the woman's face.

"I'm sorry, I have strict instructions," she said.

"I'm the UK Head of Security. I need to get to where they are holding the delegates," Sam said, glancing down at his watch.

The woman hesitated, picked up her radio and spoke to someone at the other end. "OK, you have clearance."

Sam barely waited for the woman to finish her sentence before surging forwards.

"Wait! You have to go through the scanner."

"Argh!" Sam steamed, as he emptied what he had left in his pockets onto the belt next to George's bag and barged through the body scanner.

"Slow down," another guard said, as Sam tried to scoop up his belongings. "I need to go through this bag."

"I don't have time for that," Sam snapped, flashing his badge again. "I have official business to attend to and a suspect to arrest."

The guard glanced at the badge and turned to look for someone else to back him up, but it seemed that word was spreading of a possible security threat and most of the guards were making their way outside. Sam didn't wait for his response. He grabbed George's bag, and they dashed out into the rapidly emptying lobby.

George became very aware that he and his dad were the only ones going *into* the building.

"Er, Dad, where are we going?" he asked, as they made their way towards the elevators.

"I'm going to find Chief – you're going to the safe room."

"What? No, Dad, I want to stay with you."

Sam stopped and took George by the shoulders.

"George, I need you in that safe room. I can't risk anything happening to you."

"But, Dad—"

"But nothing, George."

"Officer Jenkins!" A dark, stocky woman was racing towards them.

"Devant!"

"Thank God you're here," she said. "It's chaos. Some of the delegates are refusing the safe room. They are insisting on leaving."

"Where are you holding them?" Sam asked.

"Downstairs, in the basement. It's part of the government offices."

"We can't risk them being out in the open until we know that the threat has passed."

"I know – but try telling them that. They all think they know better."

"And my chief?"

"I've got my officers going room by room, but there's no sign of him."

"He's either somewhere helping deliver the weapon or he's scarpered. My guess is he's vanished. Can you take my son to the safe room?"

"Of course."

"I'll do one last search. We need everything locked down before 16:00 hours. No later."

She glanced at her watch. "You've got ten minutes."

"I know. Please, just take George."

"Dad, no…"

"I'll be back at the safe room before four, I promise."

With that, he strode into the glass lift. George watched his face disappear up into the heady heights of the metal and glass that hung above them.

"Come on," Devant ordered, scuttling off towards the emergency stairwell, and George reluctantly followed.

The safe room was far bigger than George had imagined. It was the size of a large theatre and was lined with chairs that no one seemed to be using. It had no windows and was filled with the urgent chatter of voices in every conceivable language.

George insisted on waiting by the door, and Devant seemed more than happy to leave him as she dealt with angry delegates. He was the only one in the room under thirty and not in a suit and tie. He sank to the floor and watched all the shiny leather shoes pace back and forth.

Minutes ticked past, and George couldn't stop thinking about all the people outside – the guards, the tourists, the street vendors – his dad. He stared at the door handles.

With no watch or phone, he had no idea of the time. His knees bounced up and down as he rubbed his sweaty palms down the sides of his trousers.

Where is he?

"You OK?" a voice said from above a pair of maroon, patent heels.

"Huh?" he replied, looking up at the woman.

"We're safe here, you can relax."

"What time is it?"

She pushed up the sleeve of her suit jacket and looked at her watch. "Four, almost four."

George jumped up and was nearly knocked over as the door swung open and Sam burst in. Slamming the door behind him, he almost missed George entirely as he strode into the room.

"Dad, what happened?" George said, grabbing him by the arm.

"George! Nothing – and Chief has vanished – looks like he swiped out over an hour ago."

"So, did he let Victor in? Is Victor here?"

"I doubt it, George," Sam whispered. "Maybe you really did scupper his plans. Either you and your friends escaping or his team being taken out ... or maybe we've misread the whole thing."

"But the map, the codes – it can't be a coincidence that it led us here."

"No, I agree. That's why I've called the bomb squad in. They're going to go room by room looking for anything suspicious."

"What do we do?"

"We wait here – get comfy, I need to speak to Devant."

George sank back down to the floor. He could feel his anxiety ebbing away now that four o'clock was upon them and his dad was in the safe room. But it was replaced by something else, something that didn't sit right in his stomach.

George ran everything through his mind: the kidnapping, Victor's team hiding out in the catacombs, someone trying to stop Jay from sharing intel with his dad, the delivery that Jin-é and Austin were loading up and

Angelika sneaking around Paris. It all had to come to something.

He felt deflated, disappointed even. Had he wanted there to be an attack? Or was it that, actually, he really wanted to see Victor?

He sat up and looked around, ashamed, as if the people in the room could read his mind – what would they think?

I wanted him to be here. I wanted him to show himself. I wanted to have the chance to be there to take him down.

It was then that he thought of Jay, his mother, and realised that this is exactly how she must have felt – for all those years: a deep determination to make Victor pay, an addiction, driven by hatred and revenge, a desperate need to catch Victor, whatever the cost.

He felt embarrassed.

What really matters is that everyone is safe – no one was hurt.

He tried to shake off the feeling. Clear the thoughts from his mind.

"George." Sam had reappeared. "Do you need anything? We could be here a while."

"A drink?" George said.

"Of course, let me see what they've got down here."

"Actually," George said, as he spotted the woman with the maroon shoes again. She was drinking from a sports bottle – just like the one Will had given him. "I've got water."

He stuffed his hand inside his bag but couldn't feel it. He dug deeper, ripped open the zip fully and turfed the contents onto the floor. The bottle came out last, bumped to the floor and rolled away.

"George," Sam said, "what's that?"

George looked between his feet. A small white marble sat nestled amongst the rest of the junk from his bag.

Glossy, snow-white, perfectly smooth but for one tiny hole the size of a pinprick: it stared up at him – and then it flashed – blue. Bright, vivid and fresh, it woke and blinked at him like the eye of a hidden serpent, waiting for its prey to come within range.

"I … I have no idea," George stammered.

Pinned by its gaze, he could feel his pulse, the dryness in his throat, the panic circling in his gut. He looked up into his dad's eyes. "Dad … I think…"

"Is it yours?" Sam said, bluntly.

George shook his head.

"Arghh!" The woman with the maroon shoes was screaming. Her bottle clattered to the floor and she stumbled backwards. George stared in horror as a fine mist steamed up from the puddle that spread across the floor.

"Arghh!" – and another. Bottles were exploding all around them.

Hiss! His own bottle suddenly shuddered to life. George sprang to his feet, just as the smoke began to seep from below the lid. He stood paralysed as it coiled upwards and caught in the blue light from the marble. It looked acrid, deadly, venomous – ready to strike.

"Get out!" Sam shouted, grabbing George by the arm. He slammed his pass against the door's scanner and yanked it open. "GET OUT!" he screamed, shoving George through the exit.

George almost tumbled over his own feet as he staggered out backwards into the corridor. As he turned to run, he saw Sam, his mouth covered by his sleeve, grabbing the marble and diving for the door.

"Go!" he yelled at George, as they raced towards the stairs.

"Dad, drop it! Whatever it is, just drop it!"

"It's the detonator. I need to destroy it. Just get upstairs!"

"But…"

"Do as you're told!" Sam screamed, as the corridor behind them filled with the charge of pounding feet and the screams of panicked voices.

George sprinted up the stairs, not stopping to look back, not daring to take another breath until he burst out into the fresh air; the flood of bodies behind him sending the revolving doors spinning out of control.

Coughing, choking – people stumbled out, grasping at their throats, fighting for breath. George stood on the steps of the plaza gaping at the scene in front of him as it drifted in and out of his vision. His head swam, his throat tightened. He watched as people fell to their knees, doubled-over and vomiting, their eyes streaming, their faces bulging with fear.

What have I done?

He searched the crowd for his dad, for the woman with the maroon shoes, for any sign that what he'd done hadn't killed them all.

"George!" It was Devant. "Come with me – now! I need to get you out of here."

"But Dad, I need to wait for Dad!"

"He's coming."

With that, she dragged him down the side of the building and threw him into the back of a black people carrier.

From: J21
To: Anonymous
Re: URGENT {Encrypted}

Gas attack at La Défense at 16:00.

The weapon was hidden inside over a dozen metal sports
bottles – silver, bullet shaped, domed lid.
From what I can tell so far, the bottles were handed to
delegates as they entered the plaza.

A proximity detonator, disguised as a single white marble,
was buried in <u>the mule's</u> bag.
We walked it right through the goddamn front door!

Get Dupont to check the other mules and destroy any
other detonators, then get the whole group to safety and
await my instructions.

La Défense is on lock down.
Update me from your end, ASAP.

End.

Chapter 22: The Tourist Trap

George sat in the back of Devant's van with his face pressed up against the blacked-out window. He watched as emergency vehicles of every kind descended on the plaza. Delegates sat on the steps: some in tears, some coughing, some already hooked up to oxygen masks.

George stared in horror as bomb squad officials suited up and made their way into the building, as others cordoned off the area and herded victims into containment pens. He had done this. He had done exactly what Victor had wanted.

How can I have been so stupid? Why didn't I check my bag?

"Oh my God!" he suddenly shouted from the back seat. "My friends, my friends all had these things in their bags." Devant was on the phone, up front. "Devant!"

"What?" she snapped, looking over her shoulder.

"Where's my dad?" He tried to slide open the side door, but it was locked. "Let me out!"

"Your father wants you to stay here."

"Let me out – my friends are in danger!"

He started to bang on the window.

"Stop that!" Devant said.

"But my friends – they all have the bottles and the marble and – just call my dad, please."

George tried to clamber over the boxes and cases that were wedged into the back seats of the vehicle. Devant just gawped at him, as he squeezed himself over the front headrests and landed head first in the passenger seat.

"What on earth are you doing?" she asked, looking astonished.

"Getting out!" he snarled.

"Your father won't be very happy if I let you leave."

"I need to find him," he said, yanking on the handle, but it didn't budge. "Let me out!" he shouted, turning on Devant and grabbing her by the collar.

Her eyes nearly popped out of her head. "I suggest you refrain from assaulting me."

"Then let me out!"

"Fine!" she said, looking over his shoulder.

Next thing he knew, he was tumbling out of the door backwards. As he landed on the pavement, he could see his dad staring down at him.

"George, what do you think you're doing?"

"Dad," George gasped, struggling to right himself. "My friends – they all had one – in their bag."

"A detonator? Yes, I had assumed that," Sam said, lifting George to his feet.

"Yes, but we all had a bottle too."

"You didn't get that here?"

"No, Will got them – from Gare du Nord."

Sam's eyes widened. "Jesus! Devant, give me your phone."

She had exited the van and come to join them. "I'll leave you with it – I need to get back over there," she said, handing Sam the phone and heading for the plaza.

Sam called French Security. "Yes, I know … Five, five more detonators. Yes – and evacuate Gare du Nord … No! When? … What's the damage?"

George watched his dad as he ran his hands through his hair. The call seemed to last an age, and George felt like he'd held his breath the whole time.

Sam finally hung up and braced himself against the side of the van.

"What? Dad, what happened?"

"It was simultaneous. Gare du Nord was triggered at the exact same time."

"What? But my friends – my friends weren't there, were they?"

"I don't know, but I guess we have to assume…" Sam said, pulling the device that Jay had given him from his pocket.

"Assume! It must have been them, Dad – they had the detonators… Dad!"

But Sam wasn't listening. "Where the hell is she?"

"What? Where's who?"

"Your mother. She's gone silent."

"What about Dupont, Steckler – can you get through to them?"

"Sorry, George – I can't get hold of anyone," Sam said.

"But my friends – I need to know!" George said, falling against the van's side. "What have I done?"

Sam shoved the tablet back into his pocket and stood in front of him. "This wasn't your fault. You couldn't possibly have known."

"But my bag – I should have checked my bag."

"No, *I* should have – I didn't stop to think. I was so knocked off course by your mother appearing – I wasn't thinking clearly. Jose must have loaded you all with the detonators before you escaped. They must have intended on dropping you each at the target sites."

"But we got away, we …"

"Just had to be in close proximity to the bottles at the drop time. That's all he needed."

"But what are the chances of us having ended up here and the others at the station – how have we…"

"Done it for him?" Sam said.

"How, Dad? How has this happened?"

"I don't know. I mean, it's my fault. I brought you here, I should have stopped and thought through all the possibilities." He slammed his palms against the van's side. "I'm such an idiot! I wasn't focused. Your mother – she threw me off! If I hadn't have listened to her – if I hadn't have…" Sam's head snapped up. "My God … she played us! It was her – she told us to come here. She sent us straight to the target!"

"What? No," George said, lost for words. "I … I don't understand."

"She knew … she knew I'd take you right in there," Sam said, throwing his arm out towards the conference centre.

"But…"

"There may have been several targets, George, but you can bet that the summit was the only one Victor really cared about." Sam kicked out at the tyre of Devant's van. "God, I'm so stupid! That's why she intercepted you. When you escaped, she knew because she'd tracked you. Then she picked you up and brought you to me, knowing that I'd bring you here with me. God, she knew every move I'd make. In fact, they needed me to walk you in there – you wouldn't have got that close to the delegates without me."

George felt everything inside him shift. His own mother – a traitor, a liar – working for Victor.

I don't believe it.

"But why? Why would she do that?" he said, his voice barely a whisper. "Why would she kill all those people? And … and my friends…"

He stumbled backwards into the gutter. He felt so sick, so mad. He hated them all: Jose, Sabrina, Alex, Victor and now, his own mother. He wanted to scream. He'd been so sure that he could trust her; so sure that she was on their side. He balled up his fists.

"We have to get them, Dad. Victor, Angelika – we have to get them all – every one of them!"

"We will – I won't let her get away with this." Sam's attention was back on his phone.

George closed his eyes. He could see her face; her eyes. He could feel something – her presence. He now knew how it felt to be near her – the reassurance, the feeling of safety. He screwed up his face.

You're so stupid, George.

How could he have trusted her – a complete stranger?

The tears forced their way up and filled his head. He tried desperately to hold them back. He didn't want to feel sadness – only anger, rage. He so badly wanted to stop them all and he'd failed.

"George … George." Sam was holding him. "George, listen to me!" George looked into his dad's eyes. "I know you're scared and angry, but we need to use that anger – we need to use it to focus."

"How?" George spluttered. "What can we possibly do?"

"We take what we know, and we follow the leads."

"What leads?" George said, wiping the tears from his cheeks.

"There's only one way to find Victor now and that's to find out where those bottles came from. I need to know – where did Will get them from?"

"The station," George said, straightening up. "Some guys were giving them away at the station."

"Did Will say anything about who they were – any more details?"

"Not really – I mean – they were freebies, giveaways."

With that, Devant reappeared. "I need a word."

"What?" Sam asked.

"We've apprehended someone that may be of interest."

"Yes?"

She nodded over to a colleague who dragged behind her a gangly looking teenager. The young man wore beaten-up baseball boots, ripped jeans and a gleaming white, perfectly pressed, straight-out-of-the-packet t-shirt that had a tiny logo printed on the front. George squinted at it – it looked like a bird carrying a bullet.

"We caught this young man trying to run away from the plaza, forcing his way past the security line," Devant said. "He was in quite a rush."

George tapped his dad's shoulder. "The logo," he whispered.

Sam was frowning at the young man, who was shaking from head to toe. "Does he speak English?"

"Yes, perfectly well. Tell them what you told me," she said, turning to him.

He went to open his mouth and hesitated. He looked at George.

"The bottles," George said, "you were handing out the bottles, weren't you?"

He nodded. "I didn't know – I swear."

"Where did you get them?" Sam asked, bearing down on him.

"A lock-up – I swear we just picked them up this morning – I really had no idea … I didn't, I–"

"Get control," Sam snapped. "You're not in trouble – yet. Who employed you to hand them out?"

"Never met anyone," he said. "Just an e-mail with the lock-up address and a list of locations. All the merchandise and t-shirts – it was all in the lock-up."

"Which locations?"

"Six – six locations for setting up the pop-up stalls – we were just told where to go and when to—"

"Which locations?" Sam pressed.

The young man listed off six top tourist sites in Paris, "Er … here, Eiffel Tower, Gare du Nord, Le Louvre…"

"Shut them all down," Sam said, turning to Devant. "We can't take any risks. Get them all evacuated."

Devant nodded. "What do we do with him? Do I take him in?"

Sam looked at the nervous wreck in front of him.

"Take his details. We may need more information from him later. For now, all we need is that lock-up address."

Devant handed Sam a piece of paper. "It's a printout of the email they were sent. Address is all there. You want me to send a team over?"

"Leave it to me," Sam said.

"I know this is your case, but the jurisdiction really lies with French Security."

"Let's get Paris safe first and try to track down those responsible. We can talk jurisdiction later," Sam said.

Devant nodded. "Take my van," she said, throwing Sam the keys. "I'll get Paris locked down – they won't get away – not on my watch."

Chapter 23: True Colours

George sat motionless in the front seat of the van as he and Sam pushed their way through the streets of Paris. He watched in awe as bodies swarmed out of buildings, spilled off pavements and scurried down side-alleys. With all the major tourist sites on lock-down and word of an attack spreading fast, everyone had taken to the streets.

The blue light and siren hidden in Devant's van made little difference to their progress. They picked up speed once they hit the Champs-Élysées, but the exits to the Metro were spewing out crowds like erupting volcanoes, all spreading out onto the already over-laden sidewalks.

George gawped at the sheer number of people that one city held – usually hidden beneath the ground or stashed away behind gleaming windows.

"The city's in chaos," he said, his breath fogging up the window.

"That's exactly what Victor wanted," Sam said. "He thrives off it. He loves to watch the ripples he makes spread far and wide, like some great tsunami."

"You think we'll find any clues at this lock-up?"

"I doubt it, but we have to start somewhere."

George sat back and thought about his friends. Were they safe? He hated not knowing. If his mother was really with Victor, then surely Dupont was too. Would she have abandoned his friends – left them stranded amongst the chaos? Would Steckler have had the sense to react – to get them out, like his dad did for him? The unanswered questions pin-balled around inside his brain. *Buzz!* Devant's phone vibrated in his lap.

She has news!

He answered it without hesitation. "Hello!"

"Where's Sam?" He put it on speaker.

"I'm listening," Sam said, turning off the siren.

"There's something you need to know," Devant said.

"Yes?"

"The gas – it seems to be a form of tear gas."

"What?" George and Sam said together.

"Unpleasant, yes, but not deadly."

"Right," Sam said, looking confused. "No fatalities?"

"We've had one blue light to hospital – an asthmatic – nothing else."

Sam looked blankly into the distance. "Right, thank you," he said. "Stay in contact."

George hung up. "I don't get it."

"Hmm," Sam murmured, his mind obviously elsewhere. "I told you, George … things aren't always what they seem."

"But I don't understand – if he didn't use the real weapon – what was it all for?"

"There'll be a reason – you can be sure of that," Sam said. "The chaos won't only please his ego – it will be a cover, a means to some other end. He's somewhere in the city, right now, doing something that none of us are watching because we've been far too busy falling for his tricks."

"Like the fire at my school," George said.

"Precisely. Let's get to this lock-up," Sam said, flicking the siren back on and hitting the accelerator.

George sat relieved but confused. Did that mean that his friends would be OK?

Tear gas?

He wound his mind backwards through everything that had happened: the attack, his mother at Notre-Dame, being held in the catacombs, Jess injured and bleeding; he thought about being tied to the barrel, dragged through the sewers, hooded by Alex and ambushed by JP and Jin-é at the Louvre.

"The Louvre," he whispered to himself.

He closed his eyes and could see JP strangling Lauren with his lanyard, he could see Jin-é whispering to JP and the bright colours of the Rothkos.

"Dad," George said, sitting up. "You don't think … I mean, I think I may know … it might be…"

"Spit it out, George."

"The Louvre – I think that's what they're after."

Sam turned to look at him. "What makes you think that?"

"Jin-é, the woman that helped kidnap us, she had a studio – she's an artist. She bragged about it – she does copies of famous pieces. JP and her, they met in a gallery – the gallery that we were taken from."

"And?"

"It was full of these paintings – these Rothkos."

"The Russian painter?" Sam said, slowing the van.

"They're worth millions, Dad – like multi-millions."

Sam pulled up to a red light and flicked off the siren again. He sat and stared out of the window.

"Art," he said with a look on his face like he was chewing something over – deciding if he liked its taste. "Stealing art? Victor? And Rothkos – I mean, selling on stolen art isn't easy. I don't know, George."

"But that's it, Dad. I think Jin-é was going to replace them. She and Austin were loading these crates up. Big ones. What if they plan to switch them? Fakes for the real ones. How long would it take for anyone to realise?"

"Huh! But what would he do with them? Unless, he already has a buyer lined up. Someone who is specifically after Rothkos – stolen to order." Sam looked a little more convinced. "Where did you say this studio was?"

"Er, not far from the Louvre … but we were inside a truck … I … I don't know … I'm sorry," George said, slumping back into his seat.

"Don't give up," Sam said. "Think. What *can* you remember?"

George closed his eyes and tried to picture the journey. "I remember we went over a speed bump. Um … the road seemed uneven – not like smooth tarmac."

Sam was fiddling with the phone that Devant had given him. The traffic light ahead turned green. "Keep going, George – what else?"

Someone beeped their horn.

"Um … when we got out of the truck, we were under a bridge – the studio was in an archway. It was dark, but daylight came from above – you know, like there was a street above it. When we went upstairs–"

"Got it!" Sam cried. "Canal Saint-Martin. It's right by Bastille – where Angelika was. Look!"

He passed the phone to George. The map showed a small canal that ran down from Bastille and into the Seine.

"It's about three kilometers from the Louvre. Does that sound about right?"

"Maybe, yes, I guess," George said.

More horns blasted but Sam was oblivious.

"There's a line of privately-owned studios, right there on the bank," he said, pointing at a spot on the map. "You can only access them from this side road, see? It's private, and look." He switched to street view. "A barrier and a speed bump – at the entrance." He grinned a full-face grin, and George couldn't help smiling back. "Ha! They think they've outwitted us, George. But we're coming up right behind them."

With that, someone beeped their horn and yelled out of their window as they swerved past the van. Sam put his siren back on, made a sharp right, across the heavy traffic, and headed for the studios.

"I hope we're not too late," he said, swerving between the cars that were squirming around, trying to get out of his way. "I need to get hold of someone at the museum. Call Devant."

"Me?"

"Yes, George. Tell her what you told me. Tell her to get hold of museum security and to get a team over to the studio – we may need backup."

George did as he was told. It felt a little odd telling a French Security Officer what to do, but she seemed to take it well. By the time he'd hung up, they were bumping down the cobbled side streets, blue lights and siren off.

Sam pulled up a block away from the barrier with the line of studios just within sight.

"I'll have to go the rest of the way on foot. Stay here. If anything goes wrong, call Devant again."

"But, Dad, what if they're in there? In the studio? You can't take them on by yourself."

"I'm just staking it out. I'll make a quick surveillance and come back here if there's any sign of them. We can wait for Devant and her team before we go in."

"Please don't go in on your own," George said, seeing the excitement in his dad's eyes.

"Stay on the phone. Devant may call back with news from the Louvre."

With that, he leapt out of the truck and scurried across the street, ducking to one side to avoid the prying eyes of a

CCTV camera. George watched him as he slipped under the barrier and disappeared into the shadow of the archways.

George sat waiting; the phone sweaty in his palms. The narrow streets were mainly in shade as the sun was rapidly diving behind the cluttered horizon. He looked up and down the street. With very few doors and little space for parking, it was pretty much deserted. It was good to be away from the chaos of the plaza and the overcrowded city centre, but he felt uneasy sitting alone in the quiet.

He strained to see if his dad was coming back but was held down by his belt, so he unclipped it, just as the rattle of a vehicle's engine crept up behind him. He threw the belt off and sank down into his seat.

As the truck trundled past, he lifted his head just enough to see over the rim of the door. It was a security truck, just like the one Jin-é and Austin had used.

They're coming back! Dad!

He watched it pull up to the barrier and to his surprise, Angelika jumped out, punched a code into the key pad and leapt back into the truck.

Oh God!

George looked at the phone.

Where is Devant?

He punched re-dial and waited as it rang.

Voicemail! You're kidding me!

He dialled again … and again. By the fourth time, his hands were struggling to hold the phone still. Still no answer.

"Argh!" he screamed out loud.

He looked back past the barrier. He could make out the bridge and the jetty. The truck had pulled over at the far end of the run of archways, and Angelika was getting out.

She turned and looked back towards him. He dived back down so quickly that he nearly slid all the way into the footwell.

He stayed there, frozen still, not daring to breathe, not daring to look up. *Slam!* A door had been hurled shut. He counted to ten and slowly inched up sideways so that only his ear and the side of his eyeball were exposed. She had gone – but where? He twisted to look out of all of the van's windows – had she come to get him? Or had she gone inside?

Dad! I need to warn him.

Sam had been gone too long. George knew he had to do something.

I can't exactly storm in there.

He searched around the van, not knowing what he was really looking for.

Maybe I can cause a diversion.

He flicked open the glove box, but there was nothing but a box of tissues and some tablets.

Damn!

He thought of his dad's van and all of the useful things stashed inside it. Then he looked behind him. The boxes that filled half the van's back-end stared back at him. Clambering over the headrests again, he landed on top of them. They were sealed shut. He tore at one. Pamphlets! The next one opened more easily. Bags of pens!

What sort of Security vehicle is this?

He plunged into the next box just as the roar of another engine shook the sides of the van. His head sprang up. Riding past, straddled over the back of a motorcycle, hugging Elías, was his mother; her copper hair trailing from beneath her helmet.

George knew he should hide but couldn't take his eyes off her as she glided past his window. He wanted to call out. For what? Out of instinct? It was his mother, after all. But as he opened his mouth, she turned and stared straight at the van. With no time to duck, he stared right back at her, but her expression didn't change. Her eyes skimmed past his.

She can't see me.

The blacked-out windows hid him from her view, but she had registered the van, just like Angelika had.

They know we're here.

Elías brought the motorbike to a stop a few feet passed the entrance to the side road but didn't go down towards the barrier. Instead, they both hopped off and slid along the wall. They squatted in the shadows with their eyes firmly fixed on the back of Angelika's truck.

George sat with his mouth still open.

What are they doing?

For a moment, he forgot all about his dad, but then *Bang!* something slammed shut. Next thing George saw was Angelika heading back out to the truck with Jin-é hot on her heels. They stopped in the lane and seemed to be arguing. Jin-é threw her arms in the air, but Angelika ignored her, yanked open the back doors of the truck and motioned to someone else. A second later, Austin appeared pushing a large crate on wheels. They struggled between the three of them to load it into the back and then scarpered back into the studio.

Where the hell is Dad?

George looked back towards Elías and his mother. They had shrunk even deeper into the shadows. He ran his hands through his hair.

What do I do?

But before he had time to think, the truck's rear lights lit up, and Angelika began reversing back down the lane towards him.

Damn it!

He turned to look for his mother, but she and Elías were back on the bike and already disappearing up the hill.

They're all leaving!

Angelika's truck was backing out of the lane and heading his way. He threw himself into the opened boxes, just as she made a three-point turn and her headlights pierced through the blackened windows, lighting up everything inside. George waited, pens digging into his side, until her lights had passed and the rumble of her engine had faded. He was about to lift his head when a second truck charged up the lane with Austin at the wheel. George ducked back down, only raising his head as Austin's rear lights bounced up the lane after Angelika's.

He looked in the shadows for any sign of his dad.

Where the hell is he?

He looked back at the fading tail-lights.

We're losing them.

He looked into the driver's seat where the keys dangled from the ignition.

You can't let them get away.

Chapter 24: Tail to Tail

George dragged open the back door, leapt out of the van and clambered into the front seat. He fumbled for the keys; his fingers jittering.

What am I thinking?

He yanked the keys from the ignition and leapt back out onto the pavement. He stood staring up the hill. He had to go and find his dad but knew that losing sight of the trucks would mean giving up on any chance of finding Victor. He slammed the door shut and rounded the front bumper, just as someone started screaming his name.

"George, get back in!"

"Dad!"

"Come on, we can't lose them!"

George stood in the middle of the road as Sam sprinted towards him. "What happened?"

"Just get in!"

Before George had the chance to ask anything else, they were both back in the van and storming up the hill.

"Which way?" Sam asked.

"That way," George said, pointing. "Just a moment ago. They all turned left."

"Great!" Sam threw the van around the corner, and the back end slid out, making the whole thing shudder.

"Dad!"

"You were right – great big art crates, George. Who'd have thought?"

"Yes, I know, Dad. But listen, Mum was with them."

Sam didn't flinch. "In the truck?" he asked, pushing his foot to the ground.

"N … No, on a m … motorbike, with … Elías," George tried to say, his voice vibrating as they clattered over the cobbles at top speed.

Sam shook his head. "I should never have trusted her." He slammed on the brake, and George was thrown forwards. "Put your belt on!" he shouted. "Where did they go?"

George yanked his belt back around himself and peered out of the window. The trucks were nowhere to be seen.

"No!" Sam shouted, slamming the steering wheel in frustration.

With that, a motorbike steamed past, Jay's hair flapping about behind her.

"There!" George yelled. "That's them!"

Sam stamped on the accelerator again and flew out onto the main road. The traffic was heavy ahead, and Elías was weaving between the crawling cars.

"Dad, they're getting away!"

Sam turned on his siren and ploughed his way through the parting sea of cars. Jay twisted. Holding onto Elías with one arm, she lifted her hand to shield her eyes from the glare of the low sun. She must have seen them. They were only metres away.

"You're not getting away now," Sam growled.

But to George's complete surprise, Elías slowed, making Sam stamp on his brake.

"What's she playing at?" Sam said.

"Pull back!" she screamed at them.

"What? No!" Sam yelled, winding the window down. "It's over."

"Drop back!" she screamed again, waving her free hand at Sam.

"I'm not falling for that!" Sam said, pushing his foot down.

He came within inches of their back wheel.

"Dad, be careful!" George said, gripping onto the dashboard as he was thrown about in his seat.

Elías pumped the throttle and pulled away again. Jay took one last look over her shoulder, tucked her arms around Elías' waist and they zigzagged away through the traffic.

"She thinks I'm stupid. I'm not falling for any more of her games – hers or Victor's."

"Maybe we were wrong," George tried to say, as they swerved to miss a small truck that was trundling along in front of them.

Sam slammed his hand into the horn. "Get out of the way!"

George tried again. "She and Elías – they were just watching Angelika – like they were … staking her out or something. Maybe she *is* trying to stop them."

He could see the motorbike weaving its way towards a junction. The lights were amber. Elías almost took out the back of another bike as he surged forwards, making it through the lights just before they turned red. The traffic stopped dead, and Sam was screaming again, siren blaring. "Move over!"

As they squeezed their way between frustrated looking locals, George peered ahead. His mother was disappearing up a wide, open road. He looked beyond them.

"There!" he shouted. "The trucks, look!"

Sam had broken free of the junction. He picked up speed and soon had both trucks and the bike in clear view. He turned off the siren and kept a constant distance.

"She knows we're behind her but she's not trying to get away," Sam said.

"I told you, I think she's trying to follow them," George said.

"She's guilty, George. I promise you!"

"Dad, it was you that told me: 'Never make assumptions, a good detective never jumps to conclusions.' Remember? It can blind you from the truth."

Sam glanced over at George and frowned.

"Call Devant again – she needs to know where we're going. I don't know where we'll end up, so get her to track this cell."

But as George went to dial, the phone rang.

"It's Devant," he said, holding it out to his dad.

"So, answer it."

George picked up and put it on speakerphone again.

"Where are you?" Sam asked, his eyes on the targets ahead.

"Right behind you," Devant replied.

"What, how?" George asked.

"That's my phone, remember? When you weren't at the studio, I tracked the cell."

"Good," Sam said. "We're going to need all the manpower we can get."

"I've left half my team at the studio. I assume you're following the suspects."

"Yes," Sam replied. "Two trucks, up ahead. Can you see them?"

"The security vehicles?"

"Yes, we believe they may have the stolen art."

"Sam, there's no sign of a break-in at the Louvre. The whole place was evacuated and locked down. Are you sure it's art they're carrying?" Devant asked. "All the CCTV and alarms seemed clear."

"Austin was in the CCTV," George said. "I saw it, in the studio, he had access on his computer."

"Devant, these criminals are the best in their class. I wouldn't put anything past them. There's a chance they already had access and control of the security systems. Get the Louvre to check the Rothkos – every one of them. I'm convinced they'll find at least one fake."

"That'll take time," Devant replied.

"Look!" George cried. "They're splitting up!"

He was right. Angelika's truck was headed for an exit, but Austin was still steaming ahead.

"What's the plan?" Devant asked, still on speakerphone.

Sam hesitated – his eyes firmly fixed on Elías and Jay. "Dad?"

"Where's she going?" Sam muttered to himself.

"Sam, you still there?" Devant pushed. "Who am I following?"

Elías swerved across the traffic and ducked towards the exit.

"You stay on the one ahead," Sam said, shifting lanes. "Follow that truck and see where he ends up. If he tries to make a dash for it, pull him over and arrest him."

"OK," Devant replied. "And you?"

"I'm on the other truck. Be careful, it's very likely that he's armed and dangerous."

With that, Devant hung up and they watched her car speed past them as they rolled off the main road after Elías and Jay.

Sam kept his distance, but George could see the tension in his dad's arms as he clung to the steering wheel. He looked deep in thought.

"Dad, what's the plan?"

"I don't know. If I take out Jay and Elías, I'm risking losing the truck. If I go for Angelika, your mother will…"

George knew what he was thinking. Sam had been wounded – twice – by his own wife. Deceived, double-crossed. He was understandably desperate not to let her get away. But even George knew that that wasn't the objective.

"Dad, surely the truck is the priority?" he said, calmly.

Sam sighed and his grip loosened on the wheel. He sat back in his seat.

"Are you going to pull them over, then?" George asked.

Sam drummed his fingers against the wheel.

"No … it's too risky here. They won't go down easily. I can't risk a fire fight in public."

They continued to follow behind as the convoy made its way out of the city. The roads grew quieter and the terrain changed. It wasn't long before they were passing through residential streets and out into the shrubby suburbs. George was starting to think that they'd be driving all the way back to Russia, when Angelika's truck suddenly turned off the road and disappeared from view.

Elías slowed right down, and George and Sam watched from a distance as he slowly pulled up to the entrance to the narrow track. Sam gently pressed the brake and pulled up to the kerb.

"Where have they gone?" George asked.

"Your mother's holding back," Sam said, looking unsure.

But with that, Jay looked over her shoulder at them and Elías pulled off and turned down the track after Angelika, dust flying up as the bike's wheels spun in the dirt.

Sam didn't wait long to follow. As they pulled into the lane, it was obvious that they were near to their destination. The narrow, rutted track couldn't lead to much.

"George," Sam said, "Use the phone and find our location on a map. I need to know where this track goes?"

"Woods," George said, trying to zoom in on the map. "And some buildings … looks like … wait … an airfield – it's an old airfield!"

"They're flying out!" Sam cried.

With that, he hit the pedal and the van stormed down the lane following the trail of tyre tracks.

"How many ways in and out?" Sam asked, as he tried to dodge the potholes.

"Er … just this one," George replied.

"How close are we?"

"I don't know … few hundred feet maybe."

"We can't just pull up to the airfield, we're hopelessly outnumbered. Wait!"

Sam slammed on the brakes opposite a small clearing in the trees. Dust hung in the air and clung to the surrounding branches. He threw the van into reverse, spun it ninety degrees and bumped through the narrow passage, the branches screeching down the van's paintwork as they passed.

At the end of the tiny path was a shed. And leaned up against the shed door was Elías' bike.

Sam peered out of the window and George scanned the surrounding trees. There was no sign of them.

"They can't have gone far," Sam said, pulling the van up behind the shed to mask it from the road.

He popped the door handle and gently pushed it open.

"Dad," George whispered. "We're totally outnumbered, remember. What are you doing?"

"Look," he said, pointing past the shed. "You can see the hangar and the airstrip from here. I'm just going to take a look. Stay here."

George watched as his dad pulled his taser from his pocket, slid around the shed and disappeared into the cover of the trees.

Seriously!

George sank into his seat and tried to look between the tree trunks to see what was happening on the airfield, but the shed blocked his view. Frustrated, he hopped down from the van and slunk to the corner of the shed. He could just make out Angelika's truck jutting out from behind the small hangar. He could see a figure moving across the tarmac. But before he had a chance to investigate further, someone had him by the collar.

"What are you doing?" his mother whispered, looking back at the van. "Where's your father?"

George hesitated. "Um…"

"Right here!" Sam jumped out behind her and took her around the neck, his taser jabbed into her side. "Don't try anything funny."

"Dad!" But George was too late, Elías was on Sam in a flash. He grabbed Sam by the hair and held a gun to his temple.

"Let her go," he growled in Sam's ear.

Sam released Jay at once and she turned to face him.

"What do you think you're playing at? You're jeopardising the whole operation."

"You're with them," Sam spat. "You sent us to La Défense. You knew we'd walk the detonator right into the heart of the target. Don't deny it!"

"That's rubbish!" she said. "I knew as much as you did."

"How do you expect me to believe that?"

"You'll just have to trust me, which is something you're obviously struggling with."

"Do you blame me?"

Elías pulled at Sam's hair, yanking his head further back.

"Stop it – you're hurting him!" George said.

"We'll put him down as soon as he stops being an idiot," Jay said. "You really think I'm working against you?"

"Why wouldn't I? You went silent," Sam said, straining his neck to look at her. "You promised you'd stay in contact. You didn't even respond after the attack."

"I was busy."

"What could possibly be more important?"

"Dupont was at Gare du Nord when the attack triggered. I had to get my team to get her and the kids out."

"My friends," George gasped, "are they OK?"

"They'll be fine," Jay said. "She's holding them somewhere safe."

"You're full of it," Sam snapped. "Always got an answer for everything. Why should we believe anything you say? What are you really up to?"

"I'm doing exactly what I set out to do – stopping him, once and for all."

"Really? So how come you let Angelika leave the studio?"

"Because, Samuel, I'm pretty sure she'll be heading directly to Victor."

"You think Victor's really here? There's been no trace of him. You're risking everything, just in the vain hope that he'll show up."

Jay was jumpy. She kept glancing towards the hangar.

"He's here," she said. "And he's waiting for whatever Angelika's got in that truck."

"It's art," George blurted out.

"What?" Jay said, turning to him.

"They've stolen it – from the Louvre," George went on.

She looked at Sam. "Art?"

"We don't know that for sure, but we're guessing they went into the Louvre as soon as the place was evacuated," Sam said.

"Art?" Jay repeated, looking over at the hangar again. "What does Victor want with art?"

"We think it's Rothkos," George said.

His mother's eyes widened. "Rothkos?"

"That mean anything to you?" Sam asked, seeing the change in her expression.

"Maybe…"

Something rumbled in the distance. An engine. They all turned to see a car careering down the lane. Jay and Elías dived behind the cover of the shed, pulling Sam down with them. George was left at the shed's corner, his back pressed up against it.

"What can you see, George?" Jay whispered.

He poked his head out. "A car is arriving," he whispered back. "It's heading towards the hangar." A dull rattling noise filled the air. "Wait! It's opening – the hangar doors are opening."

"Who's in the car?" Jay asked, sliding past Elías and Sam to join George.

"I can't see – they're getting out on the other side."

Jay was now on her knees, crawling through the undergrowth. She pulled a small set of binoculars from her pocket.

"Damn it! I can't see who it is!"

"Does it matter?" Sam asked. "We need to stop them from getting away, Victor or no Victor."

Jay crawled back behind the shed.

"We have no idea how many hostiles are in there."

"I can call in back-up," said Sam. "I'll get Devant to send a team."

"We don't have time for that," Jay snapped. "There's only one way off the airfield. Elías and I can go in – you cover the exit."

"Er, guys," George interrupted. "I don't think they'll be leaving on the ground."

The hangar doors had fully opened, and a small jet was making its way out onto the tarmac.

"It's now or never," Jay said, looking over at the jet as it taxied towards the runway. "Can I trust you to behave?" she asked, looking at Sam.

He scowled at her. "Can I trust you to be honest?"

She didn't answer. "Elías and I will skirt around the woods on the left. We'll try and take out their access to the jet. You cover the lane. Use the van to block it if you have to then sit in the trees and wait to take out anyone who gets off the airfield. Agreed?"

"That's great," Sam said, "but firstly, George and I are only armed with a short-range taser, and secondly, how can I be sure that you're not planning on jumping on that jet with them?"

"Argh!" Jay fumed. "When will you get it through your head?"

She stormed off and returned with her bag. "Here! This solves both your issues," she said, throwing a gun at his feet. "Let him go, Elías. Now, see, you're armed and, if you really distrust me that much, feel free to shoot me right here."

George gaped at her. She stood with her hands above her head. Elías looked uneasy. He didn't lower his own gun. Sam glanced at the gun at his feet and back at Elías. He slowly bent down, picked it up, checked that the cartridge was full of bullets and snapped it shut.

He stood staring at his wife. "Tell Elías to drop his weapon."

She nodded at Elías. "Seriously?" he said.

"Do it," she replied.

Elías shrugged and placed his gun on the floor. He held his hands up too.

"So, arrest us both now or put it all behind you and help us stop them," Jay said.

George held his breath. He realised that he had no idea what was going through his dad's mind, no idea of what he'd do. Sam looked at Jay and then over at the hangar and, to George's surprise, he looked straight at him.

"George," he said. "What do you think?"

George looked at all three of them. These grown adults. They all looked back at him, waiting for his decision.

"Honestly," he said, looking at his dad. "I don't care what she has or hasn't done. I just want to stop Victor. If there's any chance that he's in there, then I want him flushed out and taken down."

Jay actually laughed. "Smart boy."

Sam sighed. "Don't make me regret this. You owe it to him, to George, to make this right."

She nodded. "You do your part; I'll do mine."

With that she backed away into the cover of the trees, her bag slung across her back. Elías grabbed his gun and came face to face with Sam.

"I never liked you," he snarled at Sam before he turned and left.

Chapter 25: Fight or Flight

Sam and George stayed crouched in amongst the rotting leaves as they watched for any sign that Elías and Jay had made it to the airfield. George had tried to keep them in view as they picked their way through the trees and along the fence-line that skirted the perimeter, but he had lost sight of them now. He gave up scanning the distant undergrowth and focused on the hangar instead. He could see figures moving inside. The car still sat with its far door open, which partially blocked his view, but he figured he could make out at least three individuals.

"Angelika, Jin-é – who's the other one?" he asked his dad. "Do you think it's Victor?"

"Don't know," Sam said. "But we can't assume that they're the only ones, either."

Sam looked worried.

"Dad, she's got to be on our side. This whole time, even in the vault in London, I–"

"That's not what worries me," Sam said.

"What then?"

"It feels too easy. I mean, they must have twigged by now that they're being tailed. And yet they've led us right here. They don't even look like they're in a rush."

George looked back at the hangar. There was still no sign of Jay and Elías.

"I'm calling Devant," Sam said, digging the phone out of his pocket. "We're going to need back-up, whatever side your mother's on."

George kept his eyes on the hangar. He so badly wanted to be right, so badly wanted to trust her, but as the minutes passed by, he became more and more anxious.

"You're still tailing him?" Sam was on to Devant. "Yes … He may head for the border. I doubt he's carrying anything of significance … a decoy, maybe … No, keep your distance for now. We don't want him alerting the others … No, they seem pretty relaxed. They're not showing any signs of knowing that we're here. Yes … an airfield. That sounds about right." He flicked back to the map. "Yes, that's the one … I understand … That'll have to do … OK, I'll let you know once we've made our move here, then take him in."

With that, he hung up.

"Is she coming?" George asked.

"She's still on Austin's tail. She'll call in another team, but they're currently spread all over the city."

"So, should we wait – I mean, until they get here?"

But before Sam could answer, the sound of gunfire raced across the airfield, startling George and making him topple backwards into the damp earth.

Crack!

"Mum!" George scrabbled back to his feet. "We have to help her!"

"Get down!" Sam yelled, pulling him back to the ground. "She's trying to flush them out. We wait and see if any of them make a dash for the jet."

Crack! Crack! The rapid blasts filled the air like fireworks.

"Dad, please!"

"We have to stick to the plan, George. If we charge in there, we'll be useless to her. From here we can stop anyone from driving away. That was the plan."

"But, Dad, she could be in trouble. Don't you want to help? Don't you care?"

Sam grabbed George by the arm. "I am not risking your life, or mine, for her, George. She's the one who wanted to go in there without back-up; she's the one who decided to hold back in the hope that she could get her hands on Victor!"

"But, Dad…"

Crack! Crack!

"Look," Sam said, "someone's coming around the side."

A figure was crouched at the corner of the hangar.

"It's Elías." George could see his large frame, his bulky arms and just make out the shadow of his beard. "Where's Mum?"

"Wait," Sam replied. "She must be trying to force them into the open so Elías can take them out."

George squinted and shaded his eyes from the glare of the sun that bounced off the pale sides of the hangar. Someone was coming out. It looked like Angelika. She moved with speed and precision as she dashed for the cover of the car and slid around its back end. Elías was edging out too. He saw her and fired a single shot before ducking back behind the cover of the building. Angelika fired back. Her aim was perfect. Chunks of brick dust flew from the wall, barely centimetres from where Elías' head had been. She fired again. He daren't move. They exchanged more shots. Glass flew from the windows of the car and Angelika dropped back.

George couldn't take his eyes off them. *Bang!* Something made Elías turn around and suddenly he was making a run from behind the building and throwing himself towards a mountain of tyres.

"What is he doing?" George screamed.

Sam was on his feet. "No!"

Someone had come from behind Elías while his attention had been on Angelika. *Crack!*

George watched in horror as he tumbled to the ground, shoulder first, but before his attacker could shoot again, someone was firing from above.

George looked up. Shots were coming from high up in the hangar. Bullets flew as the person who'd shot Elías scrambled towards the car. Angelika was firing over the bonnet, aiming up into the rafters of the hangar.

"This is a complete cock-up!" Sam shouted.

"It's Mum, look!" George yelled.

He could see someone high up on the gantry of the hangar, her dark silhouette sharp against the white sheeting that hung in drapes from the ceiling. She was moving fast, drawing their fire.

George looked back to where Elías had fallen, but he had vanished.

"What do we do now?" he said, looking to his dad, but before Sam could answer, the hangar doors were rumbling closed.

"No!" George shouted. "They're shutting her in. She'll be trapped."

Sam kicked out at the stump of the tree.

"Argh!" he bellowed. "Why does she have to take these risks?" He glanced towards the van. "Wait here!"

"What? What are you going to do?"

Sam marched over to the van, dragged open the side door and started up-ending the boxes onto the floor.

"Dad, I've looked in those – there's nothing…"

But Sam wasn't interested in the boxes. He emptied them all out of the van, and to George's surprise, he slammed the door shut, stood back and fired a single shot at the window.

George instinctively ducked, but the glass didn't break, it simply fractured like ice on a pond.

"Good," Sam said, heaving the door open again, "get in."

"What?"

"It's bullet-proof. I want you to lie flat on the floor, in the back. Don't raise your head for a second, no matter what happens."

George looked at his dad.

"What is going to happen?" he asked, as he approached the van door.

"We're going to help your mother – let's just hope she's grateful."

"We're gonna' just drive up there?"

"We're safer driving up in this thing then *walking* into a gunfight, and I have no intention of leaving you here on your own."

George climbed in.

Sam was about to close the door but stalled.

"Take this," he said, handing George the taser. "If anything happens to me, stay hidden in here until Devant's team arrive. If anyone comes near you, point this at them and pull this trigger. It will disable them for long enough for you to get away, but remember, you only get one shot."

"Dad…" George was speechless. "I…"

"Just keep your head down."

With that, he slung two of the empty boxes back over George and slammed the door shut.

George lay with his stomach pressed to the rough carpet. He could feel the vibrations of the engine and the shudder of the suspension as they charged down the track. He held his hands over his head and could just hear the muffled sounds of his dad's voice updating Devant on the phone.

He spun it all around and around in his head.

What are we doing? We must be mad.

He had all but forced his dad to charge full face into a gun fight to save his mother – a mother he barely knew, a mother he owed nothing to, a mother who had abandoned him and thrown herself into danger, for what? Glory? Revenge? Was he not now doing just what she had done? Did it really matter if Victor got away? With some stupid paintings! Was it worth risking his life for, his dad's life for?

"Stop!" George shouted, as he erupted from beneath the broken boxes. "Dad, we don't need to do this!"

The van slowly stopped, and George peered carefully over the headrests. Somehow they were still amongst the trees.

"Where are we?"

"I found another track. It's taken us around the back of the hangar."

George sat up onto the seat. "What can you see?"

"Not much, but I also can't hear any more gunfire."

He turned to look at George, with a look of apology.

"You don't think … is she?"

Crack! George's heart almost burst from inside his chest as the window in front of his face cracked and fissured like a spider's web – a tiny hole at its very centre.

"Get down!" Sam screamed. *Crack!* Another hit Sam's window. "It's Angelika!"

George was down in the foot well, curled up into a ball, his whole body shaking.

Sam fumbled with the gear stick and the van kangarooed forwards.

"Arghhh!"

He pushed the accelerator again and it surged ahead.

Crack! George heard the metal at his feet ping as another bullet hit. He could hear the van twang and screech as it scraped against branches and bounced over whatever lay in their path.

They were charging through the woods, but the gunshots kept coming.

This is my fault!

Crack!

How are we not getting away?

Smack!

He was thrown against the back of the seats in front and something fell, like a shower of dust, onto his ankles. He looked up. The window was still in place but completely crazed; glass dust covered the seats and his trousers.

Thud! A door slammed shut, and George lifted his head to see his dad running for the trees.

"No! Dad! NO!"

The shots stopped hitting the van, but the trees were now exploding in Sam's wake – one at a time, splinters of wood flying into the air. George sat helpless as his dad vanished into the thick of the trees, and then … silence.

George waited two, three minutes, no more. He had sunk back to the floor, flat on his back with the taser gripped in both hands. He could feel the fear in his gut and the tears trying to come, but his mind raced.

He told me to stay in the van.

His legs shook; his hands were slick with sweat.

The van creaked and something hissed. George tried to calm his breathing. The air was rich with fumes as he sucked it in through his nostrils.

Petrol.

He could smell petrol.

We must have hit something. The tank...

He tried to think straight.

What do I do? Think ... think like ... them.

He rolled onto his front and pulled his knees underneath him. Slowly, he edged up to the window. There was very little clear glass left, but he found a spot and peered through it, looking for any movement. The smell of petrol now filled the van.

I have to get out.

Grabbing the taser tightly, he carefully moved towards the door, blew the glass dust from the handle and squeezed it, steadily rolling open the door. He poked his head out and scanned the surrounding trees. The air had fallen silent; all he could hear was the drip of petrol and the sound of his own breathing.

Sliding out head first, he slipped to the floor and crawled to the front of the van. He could see now what had caused them to stop. A half-buried tree stump was wedged into the front bumper, caving it in and lifting the front tyres clean off the ground.

George peered around the van and could see the side of the hangar. There was a small door, and the boundary fence had fallen flat, leaving a clear path to the entrance, barely fifty feet away.

He sat with his back to the van and rested his head on the warm metal. He considered his options: stay hidden and hope that no one comes back to check, or make a run back to the road and try to get help. Maybe he would intercept Devant's team or maybe even find his dad.

But ... Mum.

He looked back at the hangar and down at the taser in his hand.

Don't be stupid, George.

He knew that the only real option he had was to get as far away as possible. Angelika would come back, he was sure of that. He had to hope that his dad had got away. He took one last look back at the hangar, and started to pick his way through the undergrowth.

As soon as he was far enough away from the fence-line, he broke into a run, following the snapped branches and torn up foliage that Sam had destroyed with the van.

The track can't be far.

But the path seemed to go on forever. He could feel a stitch eating at his side, and something stinging at his ankles, so he stopped to catch his breath. Bending down, he dug around inside his sock, trying to dislodge the glass dust, but as he lifted his head, he could hear something shuffling through the leaves behind him.

Dad?

His heart rate was already sky-high. He slowly turned; the taser held high, his hands shaking. Something moved in the undergrowth. He saw it. Red – bright red, it stood out like a blooming rose springing from dead wood.

Jin-é!

Without thinking twice, he turned and ran, crashing through the bushes like an elephant, trampling everything in his path. As he snatched a look over his shoulder, he could see her coming: her red bow, her bleached-white hair and the point of her needle. He ducked, stumbled and fell to his knees as it flew through the air and lodged itself in a branch above his head.

For a split moment, he sat dazed, staring up at it as it glinted in the dappled light. *Crunch!*

Get up, George!

He scrabbled on all fours, threw himself over a fallen tree trunk and slid to the ground. He waited, catching his breath, listening for any movement, but the woods had fallen silent.

She's out there.

Slowly, he poked his head over the trunk and searched the trees around him. *Crunch!* She was somewhere to his left. He held the taser up. *Crunch!* Again, the branches broke. The trees were too thick and he couldn't see her. But maybe that meant that she couldn't see him. He carefully rose to his feet, his heart pounding, and edged backwards, keeping the thickest part of the woods within his aim.

Ten, twenty paces back, he turned and made a run for it. Leaping over fallen obstacles, ducking between overgrown branches, he could feel the trees getting thinner, the path widening. The shadows seemed to lift and the air seemed to thin as he rounded a large tree and could see the shed and the track beyond.

Yes!

But then he saw her. Coming at him from his right flank, light on her feet, she almost flew at him, needle poised, like a wasp making for its victim. He held the taser high and went to squeeze the trigger, but she weaved between the trees.

You only get one shot.

His adrenalin took over. His feet were moving, he was running again, but she was coming around ahead of him. He raised the taser again but couldn't get a clear shot. He needed to make it to the track. If he could get her out in the open, he would at least have a chance at hitting his target.

He ducked off to the left and hurdled several patches of undergrowth, but as he glanced back, the needle was flying at him once more. He dived forwards, ploughed through a bush, tripping and stumbling, he lunged out onto the track and came face to face with an oncoming car. It slammed on its brakes, and he tumbled over the bonnet and came crashing to the ground.

He didn't see who was driving the car. All he thought, as he lost consciousness, was that Jin-é was wearing an awkwardly large pair of muddy boots.

Chapter 26: Hung out to Dry

George felt foggy. Something stung at his neck and his ribs throbbed.

Click! Click! Jin-é's camera was in his face.

"Poor boy – you so sweet," she said, smiling down at him. "Such a little fighter – I like this. You so fierce. Ra!"

George tried to lunge at her, but he was tied to one of the thick, metal posts that supported the gantry overhead.

Click! "Ha! Perfect picture. I call this one 'La Resistance'," she chuckled.

"Stop fooling around and get over here." Angelika's voice echoed around the hangar.

George tried to twist to see her, but all he could see were the billowing, white, plastic sheets that lined the hangar. They hung down from the rafters like sails, the plastic rustling and slapping as the air wheezed through the broken windows and under the hangar doors.

"Wake them up," Angelika ordered. "I'll be back."

"Oh, you so bossy," Jin-é said, as her tiny feet tip-tapped across the smooth concrete floor. "Wakey, wakey."

George could hear coughing. Someone was groaning.

"Get off me!"

Mum?

George strained his neck to see, but he needed to move, so he shifted his feet to the side and pushed against the floor. They slipped and slid, but he managed to swivel an inch, maybe two. He pushed again and could just make out two bodies, each tied to a chair, heads hanging.

Dad … Mum!

"Wake up!" Jin-é screeched, smacking Jay around the head.

Without warning, Jay's head snapped up and she lunged out at Jin-é with her teeth, almost taking a chunk out of her hand.

"Ha! Feisty!" Jin-é said. "Now I know why Mr Sokolov wants you alive."

She started laughing again, but Jay wasn't amused. She threw her weight backwards before rocking forwards, rising onto the balls of her feet, spinning a full 360 and smashing the back legs of the chair hard into Jin-e's shins, making her stagger backwards.

"That's enough!" Angelika snapped, as she slid from behind one of the plastic curtains and threw out her foot, sending Jay and the chair clattering to the floor.

Jay's head smacked against the concrete, and George saw her grimace in pain.

"Stop!" he shouted. "Leave her alone!"

Angelika looked over at him and raised an eyebrow.

"You should be thanking me," she said. "You don't need this piece of dirt in your life, boy. She's worthless, disloyal scum."

With that, she spat at Jay and kicked her in the stomach.

George strained at his restraints. They bit at his wrists. He looked to his dad, but he sat staring at the floor, his head swaying. He didn't even flinch when Angelika kicked out again at Jay.

"Victor trusted you," Angelika continued. "He thought he could turn you. But I knew you were nothing but a traitorous little–"

"Silence!"

George looked up. A shadow appeared behind Angelika, the curtains parted and George could feel the heat rise inside him. The voice, the stride, the sharp jaw, the hooked nose and the tattoo of the falcon emblazoned on his shaved head. George hated everything about him, and yet he felt a prickle of excitement run across his skin.

Victor!

"Pick her up," he said, as he sauntered out into the hangar.

Angelika dragged Jay's chair upright and stepped back.

"Load the crates, both of you," he said. "Be ready to leave. We won't have long."

Angelika nodded and disappeared through the side door with Jin-é in tow.

"Ah, what a day it has been," Victor said, turning to face George's parents. "I really wasn't sure if it would ever come to an end," he said, chuckling to himself. "But I do love it when a plan comes together."

"Tear gas?" Jay sneered. "I'm sure the weapon dealers of the world are lining up to be added to your long list of illustrious clients!"

"Ha! You think that's what this was about?" Victor said, smiling at Jay. "No, no, my dear Jay-Jay, this was about embarrassing *you*. You and everything that MI5 and the world's security services stand for – safety, surveillance, intelligence. How intelligent do you feel now, huh?"

Sam groaned. Victor grabbed him by the chin and forced his head upwards. George could see blood smeared across his dad's hairline.

"Huh, Sam, how intelligent do you feel now? You walked the detonator right into a room full of the world's top security officials. How clever of you!"

Sam grimaced and his chin dropped back to his chest. Jay glanced at him before turning back to Victor.

"Where's the weapon?" she asked.

Victor hesitated. "Why would I tell you that?"

"You don't have it, do you? I know you. You'd have used it given half the chance."

"I sold it."

"Really, for how much? To who? There's only one buyer I know of that would have taken it off your hands."

"You don't know anything."

Jay broke into a smile. "He double crossed you, didn't he? I knew he would."

"Shut up! You think a few years working with me and you know everything? You know nothing."

"I know enough to be sure that you wouldn't need to be sneaking around Paris stealing art if you'd been paid what he offered you for that weapon – so either you screwed up or he screwed you – either way, you're left with nothing – again. You're pathetic!"

"Really? Pathetic? I had you running all over Europe trying to work out where I'd strike. You think you're so brilliant, but I had you running in circles. Turkey, Spain, Paris. And then you let yourself get distracted. So desperate to play mummy. Couldn't resist saving your poor son, could you? And then Sam. I'm pretty sure that wasn't your training. Purpose before personal – isn't that what they drill into you?"

"I believe I managed both," Jay said. "And we still managed to find you – lurking in the dark like a coward, letting everyone else do the hard work."

"All good symphonies need a maestro," he smirked.

Jay hesitated, and George could see her smile for a second. Something had distracted her.

What's she up to?

"Your plan was feeble," she finally said. "You lost your mules, half your team and only succeeded by a stroke of chance. You're an amateur – a total laughing stock!"

"As feeble as your attempt to sabotage my deal in Turkey, huh? You think I don't know that you were behind that?"

Jay laughed. "That deal went south because the buyer knew a fool when he saw one."

Victor lashed out and slapped her hard across the face. George flinched.

"Who's the fool now?" Victor spat. "Two years of chasing me, trying to catch me out and look where you've ended up? Back where you started – my prisoner!"

He grabbed her, squeezing her cheeks between his fingers. "You'll regret the day you chose to leave. I trusted you. I gave you freedom, power, a chance to escape your pitiful job at MI5 and use your talents to make yourself a real career."

"I wanted none of it," Jay said, pulling her head away.

"That's a lie!" he snapped. "I saw the greed in you. You can't deny you enjoyed the rush. You wanted more. If it wasn't for your constant yearning," he said. "You're so soft, so easy to play."

"It was me that played you," Jay said. "It was me that made you trust me – and then I got away."

He turned his back on her. "You can believe that if you want, but I have you here now."

George shifted again, trying to edge further around the post. The wire at his wrists chinked against the metal, and Victor looked over.

"All three of you in fact," he said, wandering towards George. "A family reunion, no less – what an honour to be present at such an occasion." He clapped his hands together in fake joy. "Although, I'm so sad that I missed the look on your face, George, when you realised that your poor, dead, burnt mother was really just an over-zealous, deceitful crook."

George tried to push himself up as Victor came closer. He didn't want to be at Victor's feet. He wanted to stand eye to eye with him – man to man. He slowly slid up the post.

"Leave him!" Jay yelled. "He's done nothing. It's me you want."

"Oh, my Jay bird, but that's where you're wrong. I owe George a debt of gratitude, don't I, George? It was you after all that delivered the little package for me at La Défense."

George pushed himself onto his tip-toes. They were nose-to-nose.

"I must admit," Victor continued, "you had me a little worried for a while – outwitting Jose and Sabrina – you really do have your mother's spirit. Lucky for me, your parents came to the rescue, scooped you up and delivered you to the target for me." He leaned in and whispered to George. "Did I scare you, little boy? Did you think you'd killed all those people? And your poor friends? Oh, the tragedy of all those young lives!" Victor roared with laughter; his vile breath engulfing George's face.

"I hate you!" George screamed, pulling at his restraints again.

"Oh, George, of course you do. I wouldn't expect anything less, but your mother used to hate me too, you know," he said, wandering back towards Jay, "but then she realised how addicted she was to me and how much she loved the thrill of my world; the draw of my power. Didn't you my little Jay bird?" She stared at him as he came closer. "Jennifer Jenkins, the pride of MI5, the upstanding civil servant. Little Jay-Jay, with a thousand secrets. The lives she's ruined, the rules she's broken, the crimes she's committed."

"Shut up!" she spat.

"Oh, but doesn't your son deserve to know who his mother really is — the kind of woman she's become?"

"I'll kill you!"

"Oh, I don't doubt that. I know you're capable of it. I've seen it first hand."

"What do you want?" Sam suddenly groaned.

"Oh, you're awake. How nice of you to join the party," Victor chuckled. "I had assumed you didn't talk when your wife was present. A kind of … respect for your superiors." Sam slowly lifted his head. "I mean she was always so superior to you in every way, wasn't she?"

"I have nothing to say to either of you," Sam croaked. "You're a waste of my breath."

"Ha! That's gratitude for you, Jay. Your own husband hates you. Don't blame him though."

"What do you want?" Sam repeated. "You succeeded in putting on your little show and stole the Rothkos, so leave."

"Oh, but I came all this way to see you," Victor said, pouting. "I made a promise to Jennifer, you see. Didn't I Jay-Jay?"

"Your beef is with me," she said. "I double-crossed you, not them."

"How honourable. Protecting your precious family — even though they hate you. The thing is, Sam, I promised your wife that if she ever made contact with you or George again then I would kill you both. And I always keep my promises — unlike you."

The plastic billowed out as the doors flew open and Angelika re-entered. She marched over to Victor and whispered something in his ear.

George looked over at his parents. They were staring at each other, heads down. He looked closer. They were mouthing something to one another.

"It seems we will have to speed things up," Victor said.

Sam's chin fell back to his chest, and Jay sat bolt upright, her attention back on Victor.

"Your Spanish friend seems to have evaded capture – gone running off into the woods. Don't suppose he'll get far with a gunshot wound, but nevertheless, our time here is over."

Bang! Victor and Angelika spun around. Something had exploded outside. They both ran over to the hangar doors and peered through the small, misted windows.

"We've got company," Angelika said, cradling her rifle.

Crack! A bullet punctured through one of the windows, showering Angelika with glass. She ducked and scrambled for the cover of the concrete wall. Victor made for the opposite end, found a hole in the nearest window and fired several rapid shots back.

"How many?" he shouted at Angelika.

She stole a glance through the window closest to her while Victor continued to fire.

"Two – looks like two shooters."

George looked at his parents. Jay was mouthing something to him.

Hide?

He watched as they shuffled their chairs closer together.

"Hide behind the post," his mother mouthed at him again.

They had a plan. He had no idea what it was, but he spun back around the post and tried to conceal as much of his body behind it as he could.

The gunfire continued, crackling around the empty hangar.

"Get out there! I'll cover you!" Victor yelled, ducking out of the way as more bullets embedded themselves in the metal doors. "Get rid of them!"

Angelika rushed for the side door while Victor kept the attackers' attention by firing at them from the front. George watched her go, and as the door swung shut, he noticed the taser, dumped at the door, next to his mother's bag. He tried to stretch out his toe to pull it towards him, but it was just out of reach.

Damn!

He looked back over his shoulder.

What's the plan?

But his parents had vanished – chairs and all.

What?

He twisted, desperately searching the curtains of plastic for any sign of them, but they were gone.

George was alone. He'd been abandoned. He could hear gunfire and an engine – tyres screeching and the plastic sheets slapping as the wind whistled through the shattered windows. How long would it be before Victor realised that two of his hostages had escaped? He would only have George as his shield.

George pushed his back flat against the post and faced the side door. Someone was outside; shadows were moving behind the glass. Had Devant's team arrived? Were they surrounded? But to George's complete surprise, Mr Steckler's wrinkled face appeared at the window.

Yes!

He stuck his thumbs up at George and then ducked out of view.

What? No!

George tried to peer through the window, trying to see where Steckler had gone to, but without any warning, the gunfire stopped, and he was left balancing on his tiptoes in the silence.

"No!" Victor bellowed, as he spotted the empty space where his hostages had been.

George sucked in his shoulders, but he knew that his arms were visible behind the post and that Victor would be on him in seconds. He could hear the thud of his stride; the anger in his heavy breathing. But before he could come any closer, the plastic sheets flapped about wildly and someone stormed in from the back of the hangar.

"Don't move!" Jay screamed; her gun on Victor.

"Drop your weapons!" Sam said, coming up behind her.

"Well, well," Victor said, turning to face them, his rifles still in his hands. "Can't bear to stay away, can you, Jay?"

"Stand down," Sam said, moving around to Victor's right, drawing his attention away from George. "You're surrounded. You've got no way out."

"You've lost," Jay said, from his left. "It's over."

"It's far from over," Victor sneered. "You take another step and I'll kill you both, and poor George here will be an orphan."

Victor stepped backwards, inching his way closer to George. George peered past him and caught his mother's eye. She stared at him and then shifted her gaze to the door.

"Don't move or I'll shoot," she said, taking another step towards Victor.

Her eyes shifted again, and George turned to see Mr Steckler slipping in through the doorway.

"I won't hesitate!" Jay shouted loudly, masking the shuffle of Steckler's feet. "I've waited seven years!"

"And so have I," Victor said, sliding his foot another pace backwards. "Shoot me and you'll risk shooting your son."

Steckler worked fast. Even with one finger missing, he managed to squat in front of George, stretch around the post and untwist the wire that held George's wrists.

"We won't kill you," Sam said. "Surrender now and we'll take you back into custody. We'll get you out of Paris, and you'll be handled by British Intelligence."

"Is that supposed to be some kind of offer, Sam?" Victor laughed. "I think I'd prefer death."

"We need to know where that weapon has gone," Sam continued. "We may be able to get you a deal."

Steckler grabbed George by the arm, and they slid across the smooth concrete, towards the door.

"A deal?" Victor said. "Will that deal include handing me back to Russian Special Forces?"

Steckler gently pushed open the door and motioned to George to step outside. But George hesitated at the threshold. All he could see were Victor's arms, outstretched from behind the post, a gun pointed at each of his parents. Their handguns looked like toys compared to Victor's rifles. He knew that Victor would happily kill them both. He knew that Victor wouldn't stand down, and he knew that someone would have to take the first shot.

"We seem to have a standoff," Victor said. "So, I say we countdown from five and see who really has the courage to end this once and for all. Shall I get the ball rolling? Five…"

"You don't have to die," Sam said, his eyes shifting to Steckler.

Steckler grabbed at George's shoulder.

"Four," Victor chimed.

George looked at his mother. She was re-adjusting her aim.

"Three…"

Steckler was now yanking at George's arm.

"Two…"

Time was up. He didn't stop to think – he scooped up the taser, rounded the post, closed his eyes and squeezed the trigger. The taser darts tore from their barrel and hit their target – clean in the side of the chest.

Chapter 27: Flightless

With barely a split second's notice, Jay and Sam dived for cover, narrowly evading the spray of bullets that flew from Victor's rifles as he fell to the ground, convulsing.

George ducked back behind the post; the taser thrown aside, his hands clamped over his ears and the realisation of what he'd done sinking into the pit of his stomach. Not for one minute had he thought that the stun from the taser would do anything other than knock Victor out.

When the firing eventually stopped and the hangar fell silent, George slowly raised his head, fearful of what he'd see, but all he saw was Victor's body, spread-eagled on the floor.

Mr Steckler was crouched at his side.

"You OK?" he whispered, pulling George's hands from his ears.

But George just held his breath.

Where are they?

Suddenly, Victor flinched and Jay leapt out from behind a stack of crates, quickly followed by Sam. She slid across the floor, kicked one rifle aside and grabbed hold of the other. She flipped Victor over and pinned him to the floor with her knee, as Sam snatched up the wire that Steckler had cast aside and bound Victor's wrists.

"Dad … mum," George said, springing to his feet.

"You could have got us all killed!" Sam said.

"It was brilliant!" Jay said. "Victor wasn't going to back down. We had no way out."

Sam pulled the wire tighter around Victor's wrists. "The plan was for him to get out – to be out of the firing line."

"The plan was going to get at least one of us killed," she snapped back. "He thought on his feet and it paid off."

Sam stood up. "Only just."

"It paid off," Jay repeated, standing and facing Sam. "Sometimes you have to think quick and act fast. I think he saved our necks."

"I think you take too many risks!"

George could see his dad boiling up.

"I think you—"

"I'm sorry!" George shouted, and his parents both turned to look at him. "I … I didn't think at all. I just couldn't leave you both – I never would forgive myself if…"

"It's OK," Sam said, his shoulders sinking. He came over and grabbed George, pulling him into his chest. "I just wanted you out of harm's way, that's all. I just wanted you safe."

"I'm sorry, Dad. I didn't know—"

Victor groaned, and his legs thrashed about as he came to and struggled to right himself, but Jay was on him in an instant.

"Lie still!" she said, planting her foot on his shoulder and digging the nose of her rifle into his chest.

"Get off!" he snarled, thrashing out again.

"You're done," she said, leaning harder on the rifle and making him wince. "You're mine!"

"I should have shot you first," he spat.

"I'll shoot you if you don't keep still!" she said, slipping the rifle up to his throat. "I should kill you for everything you've done."

"Go ahead!" he croaked. "Add me to your list."

"Shut up!"

"Jay, leave it," Sam said. "It's not worth it."

"He deserves it!"

"Like the others deserved it?" Victor jibed. "Did the others deserve to die because of you?"

George watched his mother's eyes darken as she bore down on Victor, pressing the rifle deeper into the well of his windpipe.

"You're … no better … than me," Victor choked.

"Shut up!" she said, pushing harder still.

"Jay!" Sam warned. "Leave it be!"

"Mur-de-rer," Victor crackled between each rasping breath.

Sam lunged at her and tried to grab the rifle from her grip, but she swung her arms up and took aim. The next thing George heard was the shattering crunch of Victor's nose as she brought the butt of the rifle down hard.

"Jay!" Sam yelled. She raised her arms again but this time Sam had hold of the other end. "Leave it! It's over!"

"It's not over until I see him pay!" she screamed, trying to wrestle the rifle from Sam's grasp.

"Step back!" Sam said, turning the gun on her. "He's under arrest. You did it. You got what you wanted."

"He needs to pay for everything he's done!"

"I know! But not like this, Jay, please," Sam said. "It's not right."

She glared at Sam. George could see the frustration in her. He understood. There were things he'd done and things he'd wanted to do that were driven by anger and a thirst for revenge. He wasn't proud of it, but he felt it all the same.

"We'll get him back on UK soil, and he'll be dealt with," Sam said.

"He better be," Jay said, "or I'll deal with him myself, I swear it."

"Ha! You won't get near me," Victor said, spitting a mouthful of blood onto the floor. "I'll make a deal with your pathetic government. You'll never see me again."

"You've got nothing left to bargain with!" Jay said.

Victor laughed. "Oh, Jay-Jay, you should know by now, I've always got something left in my locker – some little surprise."

"You've got nothing they'd want."

"I've got you," he said, winking.

"Shut up or I'll smash the rest of your face in," she snarled.

"Jay, please," Sam said, stepping between them. "Let it go."

With that the side door flew open, and Elías and Dupont burst in, guns up.

"Tell me you've got him," Dupont panted.

"We've got him, alright," Jay said. "Did you get the other two?"

Dupont lowered her gun and bent over, trying to catch her breath. "No," she said, shaking her head.

"They split up," Elías said. "Angelika took the truck. We tried to stop it, but it was armoured. We even tried to shoot out the tyres, but it didn't help."

"And the other one?" Jay asked.

"The Chinese woman," Dupont said. "She fled. I chased her through the woods, but she was too fast for me … she won't get far on foot though."

Victor was chuckling. "You won't find them – either of them. They're too smart for you."

"As smart as you?" Jay sneered.

"What about the Rothkos?" Sam asked.

"We assume Angelika still has them in the truck – there's nothing on the jet but weapons," Dupont replied.

"She left you to fend for yourself – how'd you feel about that?" Jay asked Victor.

"She knows how to look after herself," he said.

"She's taken the Rothkos and left without looking back. Looks like she's done exactly that – looked after herself."

Victor didn't respond. George looked at him. For the first time, he could see a flicker of defeat in Victor's eyes. He sat crumpled on the floor, tangled in his own overcoat, blood trickling from his nose.

"What do we do with him?" Dupont asked.

But Jay didn't answer. She snatched the rifle back from Sam and made for the hangar doors.

"Are we sure there are no more hostiles?" she asked.

"We've done the rounds. It seems it was just the three of them," Elías replied.

"So, who's that then?" she asked, pointing out of the shattered window.

Dupont and Elías came to join her.

"What is it?" Sam asked.

"Three black cars. Looks like officials," Dupont said.

Jay backed away from the doors.

"It's probably Devant's team – French Intelligence," Sam said.

"You need to get rid of them," Jay said, checking the bullets in the rifle.

"Relax," Sam said. "They aren't the enemy."

"Deal with them," Jay bit back. "We don't need French Intelligence all over Victor. You need to get him back to the UK – we don't need all the hassle of extradition."

"Agreed."

"So, what are you waiting for?"

Victor chuckled. "Listen to your boss, Sam."

"Shut up or *I'll* smack you one," Sam said, before striding from the hangar.

Jay and the others huddled in the corner. George couldn't make out what was being said. He turned to Steckler who was still loitering by the side door.

"Where are my friends?"

"Safe," Steckler said. "We had to call the tour short and get all the kids back on the minibuses."

"Are they here, with you?"

"They're in the minibus – somewhere safe."

"Where do my teachers think I am?"

"Dupont came back with the others after you disappeared at the Louvre. She said you were back at Gare du Nord waiting for your dad – family emergency."

"They fell for that?"

"Mrs Stone did try to call your dad but Dupont had already briefed me. I stepped in and said that I'd spoken to you. But honestly, there wasn't much time to quibble. It wasn't long until we were all headed back to the station. And then it was just chaos, George."

"I know – I'm sorry."

"For what?"

"Leaving you – I mean, disappearing at the museum – I know I was supposed to be, you know…"

Steckler smiled and ruffled George's hair. "Curious mind, George. You can't help having a curious mind. It runs in your family."

With that, the door burst open, and Sam marched back in.

"Well?" Jay asked, coming over to meet him.

"I've sent them to track Angelika's truck and search the woods for Jin-é, but it won't be long until Devant is here. She's taken Austin in and is on her way."

"You need to get him out of here," Jay said, looking over towards Victor.

"I don't have a vehicle. I trashed Devant's van," Sam replied. "So, unless you want to ride pillion with him on your motorbike…"

"Steckler's got a minibus," George said.

"Yeah, we came straight from the station," Steckler said. "I can offload the kids. They can wait here for another ride."

"You've got kids in it? Where is it?" Sam asked, shocked.

"Back out on the main road. We came the rest of the way by foot."

"It'll have to do," Jay said. "Bring it here."

"Roger that!" Steckler beamed and then raced out of the door.

Sam rubbed at his temples. "How am I supposed to get him over the border?"

"Use your agency contacts," Jay said. "You're MI5, remember?"

"Barely, and anyway, I'd need clearance and currently have no idea where Chief is."

"Sam, I haven't been through all this to see him sit it out in a French prison, waiting for trial. A nice cosy bed, three meals a day…"

"OK, OK, I get it."

"Do you?"

Sam scowled. "It's not just your life he's affected – remember?"

"I know, I…" Jay glanced at George. He was rubbing at his side. "You OK?"

"Yeah, it's nothing," George mumbled. "Just a bruise."

Sam pulled up George's shirt. "My God, what happened there?"

George looked down. He had a huge, purple bruise spreading across his side.

"Um, I had a run in with a car bonnet," he said, grimacing.

"What?" Sam said.

"I was running from Jin-é, after *you* left me in the van."

"I was drawing Angelika's fire away from…"

"I know, Dad," George said, smiling.

"Who hit you?" Jay asked. "If Jin-é was on foot and Angelika was chasing your dad, who was in the car?"

"Um … I don't know."

"Was it coming towards the airfield?"

"Um … yeah, I think so, maybe … sorry."

"Victor's car didn't move from here, I'm sure of that," Jay said.

"You think there's someone else?" Sam asked.

"I don't know. Whoever it was, they never made it into the hangar. I'll get Dupont to do one more sweep."

"Sorry, Dad," George said, as Jay went to speak with Dupont. "I know you told me to stay in the van but–"

"Don't say sorry. You shouldn't have had to go through any of this: the catacombs, La Défense, being left in here alone."

"Yeah, thanks for that," George said.

"I didn't want to leave you, but your mother had a plan. Elías and Dupont had their hands full with Angelika and Jin-é, so we had to get out in order to get untied and armed before coming back in."

"I get it," George said, as Jay returned with her bag. "But how did you know that Dupont and Elías were outside?"

Jay tapped her ear. "Angelika didn't think to check for my earpiece."

"So, you knew they were coming?"

"It was just a matter of time. We just had to wait for them to attack the front before we could get out of the back. Steckler met us there and untied us, but we have Elías to thank. He managed to get away and get a message to Dupont."

George looked over at Elías; slumped on the floor, a makeshift, bloody bandage around his shoulder.

"Is he coming back with us?" Sam asked, but Jay didn't respond. She had retrieved her tablet and was obviously distracted by a message. "And what about Dupont?" Sam went on. "Isn't there still an arrest warrant for her in the UK?"

"Huh?"

"Jay, are you even listening?" Sam asked. "I'm assuming you'll be escorting Victor back with me?"

"I'll leave that to you," she mumbled, looking up over Sam's shoulder.

"What? This is your operation. I thought you wanted to take him in ... Jay?"

She still didn't answer.

George stared at her. She was miles away.

"You are coming back with us, aren't you?" George asked.

"I need to deal with something," she said, grabbing her bag from the floor.

"What?" Sam said. "How have you gone from being so desperate to take charge to—"

"I need to step outside for a minute," she said, turning and walking away.

"Great!" Sam threw his arms in the air. "Take your time!" he called after her.

George was left standing alone as his dad went back to deal with Victor. He turned and watched his mum leave, her head still buried in her tablet. Her saunter slowly became a stride, and by the time she had broken out of the door, she was running.

From: TDP
To: Anonymous
Cc: BETA
Re: Inbound {Encrypted}

They know where you are. They're coming for you.
Get out now!
Elías and I will meet you at the rendezvous.

End.

Chapter 28: Dearly Departed

The door swung shut, and George was left staring at the rusted metal. He looked for his dad. He was standing over Victor, a phone to his ear, his free hand massaging the back of his neck. George scanned the hangar.

Elías? Where's Elías?

Gone: Dupont, Elías and his mum – all gone.

What's going on?

George could hear the crunch of the minibus' tyres on the tarmac out front. He could hear the bus door fly open and the voices of his friends: Felix and Will, Josh and Francesca. He could hear his dad's footsteps making for the side door. The noises pulsed around the empty hangar – empty except for Victor. There he sat, smiling at George, a broad, sickly smile.

"She's left you," he smirked. George frowned. "She won't be coming back, you know. She can't. Didn't she tell you?"

"Shut up," George said.

"Ha! You think she's coming back to play mummy, do you? I told you, George – she's nothing but a deceitful crook – no better than me. In fact, she's worse!"

"Shut up! I'm not listening to you!"

"You don't need to listen to me. Go see for yourself – she's gone – long gone."

George tried to block Victor out. He closed his eyes and tried to think straight, but all he could hear was Lauren and Jess at the door, laughing. He opened his eyes and looked back at Victor.

"Gone," Victor mouthed.

George hated the thought of Victor being right and hated giving in to him but he needed to know, so before anyone had the chance to stop him, he slid between the plastic sheets and snuck out of the back door.

He could see her – making for the gap in the fence.

"Hey, stop!" he yelled, as he started racing across the broken tarmac. "Where are you going?"

But his words were lost in the space between them. He pushed harder and managed to gain on her.

"Mum, please … stop!"

This time, she heard. He watched her shoulders slump at the sound of his voice and she slowed.

"Why are you running?" he panted, as he approached the fenceline.

She turned and strode back towards him. "Go back, George, please."

"You're going – aren't you? Leaving!"

"Shh, please, keep your voice down."

"Why?" he asked.

"It's complicated, George," she said, looking back towards the hangar.

"Really? You've gone to all this effort – and now you're just leaving – again?"

She sighed and looked back down at her tablet.

"Follow me."

She led George into the woods – clambering over the fallen fence and ducking behind the cover of the trees. She pulled him down to his knees and squatted in front of him.

"I *have* to leave, George," she whispered.

"Why? I don't understand."

"People are after me. I've made enemies – even in my own country. There are things I've done, things I'm not proud of. Things I had to do to survive – to track Victor – to protect you."

"To protect me? If you cared about me, you wouldn't leave!"

"Shh! Please, George." She poked her head up over the undergrowth and looked back towards the hangar again. "I don't expect you to understand. I will be back though, I promise. I just need to clear my name and right some wrongs."

"But why can't you do that from home – from England?"

She rubbed her temples.

"I don't have time to explain, but I will, I–"

"No! You don't care," George said, standing up. "You've never cared. All you do is lie. You didn't do all this for me – you did it for yourself!"

"That's not true," she said, raising her voice. "I've done everything to get back to you. Every minute, of every day has been about getting back to you." She stared at him and shook her head. "Look!" She slung her bag off her shoulder, ripped open a side pocket, pulled out a crumpled, brown envelope and shoved it into his hand. "I've done everything I can to get close to you since I escaped from Victor."

George looked at the tattered envelope. "What's this?"

"It's you – my way of being close to you – open it."

He peeled open the envelope and over a dozen photographs cascaded out into the palm of his hand.

"What?" he said, glaring at them.

"I've carried them with me everywhere, George."

Blowing out his birthday candles, riding his bike, on the beach, playing with Marshall, wearing his new school uniform – a fistful of photos, dog-eared and torn, faded and creased.

"How?" he breathed.

"Gran – mostly," she said, biting the corner of her lip. "She found a way of getting them to me."

George sank to the floor. "What … I … I don't get it…"

"I've never stopped thinking about you, all this time, George. I've watched you grow up – through these. I've been as close as I dared without risking your life. That day, at Imperial College, when you ran right into me, I couldn't resist, just sitting and watching you."

George's eyes filled with tears. "But … you never said – never stopped to come home – to ask me how I was. You let me think you were gone – you let me believe you were dead!"

"I had to, George. I had to keep you at a distance for your own safety. Victor swore he would kill you if I ever made contact. I swear, George – so many times I just wanted to reach out – just be with you. Not a day passed when I didn't want to stop running and come home – to be next to you when you slept, to hold you when you cried, to pick you up when you fell, to laugh with you…" She grabbed his chin. "Look at me. I know I've failed you. I know I've made mistakes – unforgivable mistakes. But there is nothing that will stop me now from coming back home. I promise, George – let me right these wrongs – let me clear my name."

"We can help you, Mum. Dad and I, we can help you clear your name."

She shook her head. "No, they'll put me away – I can't spend any more time locked away. I will never go back to being trapped. I can't." She suddenly jumped backwards. "Get down!"

A procession of large black SUVs was racing across the airfield towards the hangar.

"Damn it!" she cursed. "I have to go. They're here."

"Who – who are here?" he asked, twisting to see the SUVs coming to a stop outside the hangar.

She grabbed him and kissed him on the forehead.

"Gran knows where the files are – the files that will help clear my name," she said, as she picked up her bag and stuffed the photos back into the pocket. "I have one thing to do. And I will be back, I promise." She leapt to her feet. "Tell your dad to get Victor back to the UK, whatever it takes."

George silently nodded.

She turned to leave and George couldn't help noticing the tears swelling in her eyes. "I love you," she said, before slinking off into the woods.

George sat alone in the undergrowth. He hugged his knees and stared at his feet. A part of him felt let down. After all those years, she'd burst back into his life and then disappeared again as quickly. Would she keep her promise? Would she come back? Victor's words ate at him. Was it all lies? He truly didn't know who to believe.

Bodies were piling out of the SUVs and swarming around the hangar. George just wanted to stay hidden in the woods. He wanted to close his eyes – forget it all, but he thought of his dad, alone with Victor, surrounded by – by who?

He lifted himself to his feet and trudged back towards the fence. He could see officers, armed and wearing body armour. They meant business. He skirted along the fenceline until he reached Devant's abandoned van. He crouched behind it and watched as the officers began spreading out, searching the littered airfield.

Who are they?

One was coming his way. He looked back the way that his mother had gone. The least he could do was give her some time – some time to get away.

"Hey!" he shouted, springing from behind the van.

The officer closest to him spun around.

"Stop right there!" he ordered, pointing his gun directly at George.

"Whoa!" George said, raising his hands up. "I'm just a kid."

The officer marched towards him.

"What you doing out here?"

"Toilet break," George grinned.

"You with the school party?"

"Yup," George replied.

The officer peered into the woods behind George.

"What's that?" he asked, pointing at Devant's van.

"Beaten up van," George said, shrugging.

"I can see that," the officer snorted at George. "I don't like your attitude."

"Er … my dad crashed it," George said, crumbling slightly under the officer's gaze. "While we were, you know, trying to stop Victor."

"What's your name?" the officer asked, looking at George quizzically.

"George."

"George Jenkins?"

"Er, yeah."

"Come with me. You're wanted inside."

With that, he was dragged off towards the hangar. As they approached the back door, he could hear his dad shouting at someone inside.

"George!" Felix was the first to spot him.

He was sat on the floor next to Steckler and the rest of his friends, an officer watching over them. They all turned to face him and smiles broke out across their faces.

"Guys!" George said.

They sprang to their feet.

"Stay right there!" the officer barked. "Get them loaded back onto the bus – all of them," he said to his colleague.

"Wait," George said. "Can't I at least–"

"You're coming with me!" he said, dragging George away.

He watched over his shoulder as his friends were all marched out of the building. Felix was the last to reach the door. "Good luck," he mouthed in George's direction.

As George turned back, Victor was being dragged past him, cuffed at the wrists and chained at the ankles. They locked eyes, and to George's surprise, Victor winked at him.

"He's my prisoner!" Sam was shouting. "I don't want him out of my sight!"

"He'll be safe in our custody, Sam," a woman's voice said.

George recognised it immediately. As they pushed through the plastic sheeting, he could see her standing in front of his dad, two armed officers at her side.

Cate Knowles!

"Officer Knowles," the officer at George's side said. "I found this one lurking outside."

Sam and Cate turned together.

"George!" Sam said. "Where have you been?"

"Fresh air," George said, glaring at Cate. "I went to get some fresh air. What's going on?"

"George, I'm sorry, but I'm here to arrest your mother," Cate said, barely looking at him.

"My mother's dead," he said, plainly. Sam stared at him. "She's been dead for seven years."

Cate frowned. "There's really no need for us to play games, Sam," she said, ignoring George completely. "Just tell me where she is."

"Seriously? All this time you've pretended to be my friend, and all you really wanted was to track her down!" Sam said.

"I know you want to protect her, but I've been on this case for two years and–"

"Two years – really? You've known for two years?" Sam said.

"Yes, I'm sorry, Sam, but it was classified – I was under strict instructions to–"

"To what? Cosy up to me? See if she'd make contact?"

"Well, yes, but that–"

"But what?"

She stood upright, her shoulders pushed back, her spine rigid. George watched her as she wrung her hands together, over and over.

Why? Why would she do this?

"You said you were helping us!" George blurted out.

Her shoulders rounded slightly. He didn't get it. She had seemed so nice.

Gran was right all along.

"I invited you into our home," Sam fumed. "God, I trusted you, I even thought…"

"Listen, Sam. I know you're angry, but I have to take her in. She was the one who gave Victor the intel."

"That wasn't her," George said. "It was Dad's chief."

"We have proof," Cate said, frowning at him. "Video evidence."

"Proof!" Sam said. "Why didn't I know this?"

"It was classified."

"Classified! You knew that my wife was alive and you felt that it was appropriate to keep that from me?"

"I'm sorry, but your chief insisted."

"Chief! Of course," Sam said, throwing his arms in the air. "Did it not occur to you that maybe he isn't so clean himself?"

"He was the one who called in MI6," Cate said. "He was sent the files; he called us in."

"What?"

"It doesn't matter, Sam. We just need to find her. She's wanted by several authorities. It will be better for her if we take her in. She's done things," she said, glancing at George. "Things that could get her serious time behind bars."

"It's not true," George said.

"She's not the woman you knew," Cate continued. "She's a traitor and she's lied…"

"No," George said.

"She's hurt innocent people, Sam. She's killed, murdered–"

"No!" George screamed. "It's not true! She was just trying to survive! She isn't guilty!"

"My orders are to take her in – at all costs," Cate said.

"You won't catch her! She's gone!" George blurted out.

Cate whipped around and looked straight at him.

"Gone where?"

"Don't say anything, George." Sam said, stepping between them.

"If he's withholding evidence…"

"You'll do what?"

One of Cate's officers scuttled back in. "She wasn't in the jet."

"So, keep looking," Cate snapped. "Widen the perimeter. She must have had warning – she's on the run and probably on foot. She can't have gone far."

"What makes you so sure she was here?" Sam asked.

"Let's just say, we weren't the only ones wanting her detained."

"Victor!" George said. "He did it, didn't he?"

Cate said nothing.

"Oh God," Sam said. "Please tell me you haven't cut him a deal?"

"Sam, I just need to find her. Once we have her in custody, we can sit down and talk."

Sam was pacing. "No, no, no – not after everything – for God's sake, Cate! Can't you see – he's set this up. He probably sent Chief the video files, he drew her in, he ratted on her – can't you see that?"

"She was here – at least confirm that. She was here with you."

Sam stopped and looked at George. George shook his head.

"Sam, come on – help me out here," Cate said. "What do you have to lose? You owe her nothing."

Sam kept his eyes on George. Cate waited. George shook his head again.

"Dad, you can't let him win. It'll all be worth nothing."

Sam nodded.

"OK, if that's the way you want it," Cate said. "Detain them both."

"What?" Sam shouted. "You have got to be kidding me!"

"If you won't comply, then I'm forced to take you in for questioning."

"Cate, get a grip, please!"

"Take them both to my vehicle," she ordered the officers at her side. "I'll escort them back to the UK myself."

With that she left the building. George watched her leave. Her shoulders had drooped, her spine had rounded and her head was hanging low.

Chapter 29: The Unknown Enemy

George could see his friends' faces pressed up against the windows of the minibus as he and Sam were marched out of the hangar and loaded into the back of one of the SUVs. He desperately wanted to speak to them. He could see the confusion in their frowns. He could even see Jess and Will arguing with the officer that was stopping them from getting back off the bus. How would he explain any of this to them? The last thing he saw, as the minibus pulled off, was Felix's smile – a sympathetic smile. Did he understand?

George sank down into the cool leather seat and fastened his belt as his dad slid in alongside him.

"Why is she doing this?" George asked.

"She's just doing her job," Sam replied.

"I don't understand. Isn't she supposed to be on our side?"

"So I thought, but she has her orders and she can't ignore them."

"But doesn't she care about us?"

"It's her job, George. I'd do the same – your mother would do the same."

George sighed and stared out of the window. He could see Cate securing Victor and delegating tasks to the gathering of officers.

"Are we in trouble?" he asked.

"That depends," Sam said.

"On what?"

"On whether you're really withholding information." George squashed his face up against the cool glass and said nothing. "Do you know where she went, George?"

He turned to face his dad. The doors were shut, but two officers were guarding their car, so he shuffled closer.

"She ran off into the woods," he said, keeping his voice down. "She said she had things to sort out."

"Hmm, I bet," Sam said, frowning.

"Seriously, Dad. She said she needed to clear her name."

"Running away from MI6 isn't going to help with that," Sam said, peering out of the window at Cate.

"Dad … there's something else."

"Yes?"

George hesitated. He knew that what he was about to say might not go down too well. "Um … she said that Gran knew. She's known all along."

"What?" Sam said, slowly turning his head back towards George. "She knew what?"

"About Mum … about her being alive."

Sam blinked. "You're joking?"

George shook his head. "No, I'm serious. Mum had all these photos of me that Gran had sent her."

Sam's eyes widened and he flopped back into his seat. "My God, that wiley old…"

"Dad!"

"Why on earth would she keep that from me?"

"Mum said that Victor had sworn to kill us both if she made contact."

"But she's my mother, for God's sake!"

"Listen, Dad, she said Gran knows about these files – the evidence that Cate has on Mum."

"Save it for later," Sam suddenly said, because Cate and two of her officers were coming back their way.

"Victor is secured," Cate said over her shoulder, as she slid into the front seat. "We'll be driving in convoy back to the UK."

"I hope you're prepared for anything," Sam said. "I wouldn't put it past him to have anticipated this."

"He won't try anything funny."

"Really? You may have made a deal with him, Cate, but that means nothing to him."

"I never said we'd made a deal," she said, as they pulled off. "I suggest you get some rest."

George was exhausted. He just wanted to sleep. He leaned his head against the window and peered into the woods as they trundled over the tarmac towards the track.

They had Victor in custody and his mum was free, and that was all that mattered to George. But however hard he tried to switch off, he couldn't help all the unanswered questions from buzzing around inside his brain. Where was she going? What had she done that was so bad? And where the hell had Elías and Dupont disappeared to?

With that, the SUV up front screeched to a halt, and George's head catapulted forwards as their driver slammed on the brakes.

Sam punched the release button on his belt. "Stay here!"

"What?"

"Don't move," Sam said, forcing open his door and leaping out.

"Wait! What's going on?" George asked, but Cate and her officers were already out on the track and racing towards the car in front.

George peered over the headrests. He could see someone on the road ahead, stumbling in and out of the headlights. He couldn't see much, but he was pretty sure that the figure was familiar.

Elías?

Some of Cate's officers were trying to wrestle him to the ground but several others had surrounded Victor's vehicle and were staring out into the woods. He sat upright and scanned the treeline. The light had faded, and the woods loomed dark on both sides, but something suddenly caught his eye. Something was moving off to his left. He tried to track it; to spot it again. He searched the darkness between each tree trunk until he had it back in his sights. Pale and ghost-like, something was weaving between the trees.

"Dad!" George screamed, slamming his fists against the glass. "There!"

Sam spun around just as the figure lurched out of the darkness, clutching at their chest.

"Dupont!" George gasped.

She stumbled onto the track and collapsed to her knees, blood running through her fingertips. George watched in horror as she teetered from side to side and then tumbled backwards. She had barely hit the ground before Cate's officers were on her like ants.

"No!" George roared as he threw open the door.

He had to fight his way through the sea of bodies but managed to reach her side. "Leave her! She's done nothing wrong!"

She was flat on her back, her chest heaving up and down. Blood had seeped across her pale blouse, turning it crimson. Her eyes looked up at him and she tried to speak.

"Step away!" one of the officers said, trying to grab George by the shoulder.

"No!" George said, swiping the man's arm aside. "She's trying to say something."

"George!" It was Sam. "Get back in the van!"

"No, Dad, listen!" George insisted. "She's trying to tell me something." But when he looked back, Dupont's eyes had fallen closed.

"She's not breathing," the officer said, and without hesitation, he started pumping her chest.

George stared at her lifeless face as her head lolled from side to side with every compression.

No!

Another officer had appeared at her side. He pulled something from inside a case and attached it to her chest.

"Clear!" he barked, pressing something in the case and sending a shockwave jolting through her torso.

Come on!

"Clear!"

This time her whole body seemed to leap from the ground, and as she thudded back to earth, her eyes sprang open.

Sam dropped to her side. "Therese, can you hear me?" She nodded, her breathing laboured. "We're going to get you to a hospital."

She mouthed something back – barely a whisper. George leaned in closer, and she grabbed him by the collar.

"Jay," she croaked, "find Jay!"

George felt a tremor race through him like he'd been shocked back to life himself.

"Where?" Sam said, clutching Dupont's outstretched hand.

"Bike," is all she could say, before she was surrounded again by officers as they pushed George and Sam aside and lifted her onto a stretcher.

"Wait!" George said, leaping to his feet. "What does she mean?"

"Bike – Elías' bike!" Sam said. "Come on!"

Sam dragged George around the back of the SUV and towards the darkness of the trees. They were moving fast, but George couldn't resist looking back. He could see Dupont and Elías being loaded into one of the SUVs, he could see Cate's officers standing guard around Victor's vehicle, and as they ducked off the road, he could see Cate turn and watch them leave.

"Dad," George panted, nervously glancing over his shoulder as they stormed through the undergrowth. "If Mum's heading for the bike, then we're leading Cate right to her."

"That's irrelevant now," Sam replied, not slowing down. "If someone got to the other two, then there's a chance they got to your mother too."

"You think she's…"

"I don't know – just keep up!"

The undergrowth grew thicker, and the dim light made it hard to recognise their surroundings, but it wasn't long before they broke out of the trees and onto the rutted track.

Sam stopped to catch his breath and get his bearings.

"There, look!" George said, pushing past him.

"Wait, George!" But George didn't stop. He sprinted down the track, towards the shed.

He was racing around the shed's perimeter by the time Sam caught up. "Where is it?"

"George, please, just stop for a second."

"It was here – the motorbike – right here!" he shouted from the far side of the building.

As George rounded the corner, Sam leapt into his path, making him jump, stumble sideways and career into one of the shed doors, which swung away leaving him tumbling into the darkness. Before he could brace himself against anything solid, he tripped over something soft at his feet and came crashing down to his knees.

"George!" Sam cried, as he wrestled with the half-collapsed door. "You OK?"

George was scrabbling around in the dark.

"Ahh!" he screamed in frustration. "Something's wrapped around my ankles. I can't see…"

With that, Sam yanked open the other door and the faint, dusk light filtered into the shed. "What the…"

George froze. The shed floor was littered with eyes – his eyes – all peering back up at him. Birthday candles, buckets, balloons, bikes – they were all there – every single photo that his mother had shown him barely an hour before.

He pushed himself up onto his knees and freed his ankles. It was her bag – his feet had got caught in its straps.

"These are the photos, Dad. The ones Gran sent to Mum."

Sam crouched down beside him and plucked them from the ground, one by one. "I don't believe it."

"She must have been here," George said, searching through her bag.

Empty!

Sam sat in silence, still staring at the collection of pictures in his hands.

"Dad, where is she?"

Sam snapped out of his daze. "She must have taken the bike and left."

"Without her bag?"

"She obviously needed to travel light."

"But…" George looked at the photos in his dad's hands.

Why would she leave them?

Crunch! Someone was coming. George leapt up and turned just in time to see Cate pulling at the shed door.

"Cate!" Sam said, quickly stuffing the handful of photos into his back pocket.

"What are you doing in here?" she asked, shining a torch in Sam's face.

"We weren't making a run for it, if that's what you're thinking."

"I didn't think you'd be that stupid," she said. "Elías told me that Jay was due to meet them here, but someone ambushed them before she arrived."

"Really?" George said, glancing up at his dad.

"What did you find in here?" Cate asked, gliding the torch beam around the shed.

"Not much, we…" Sam tried to say.

"Just an empty bag," George interrupted, pointing to the bundle at his feet. "We were looking for Elías' bike. We thought that whoever attacked them was after the bike – you know, to use it as a getaway."

Cate raised an eyebrow and turned the torch back on Sam.

"There's a chance she was here," Sam said.

"Dad! No!"

Sam looked down at him. "She could be in danger, George."

Cate nodded. "Your dad is right. Whoever attacked Elías and Dupont could be after your mother too."

Just then, one of Cate's officers appeared. "There's no sign of anyone. But we found the bike."

"Where?" George asked before Cate could respond.

"Not far from here. Looks like the tyres have been slashed."

"What?" George looked to his dad. "She might still be here – in the woods."

"She won't hang around," Sam said, "especially if she knows that her team have been compromised."

Cate sighed and scanned the shed again. "Well, we can't linger here. We need to get moving. Devant is on her way, and she'll want to lock down the whole area. We need to get you and Victor back to the UK."

"Wait! Where's Victor now?" Sam asked.

"I've sent him ahead."

"What?"

"We were like sitting ducks out there. I couldn't wait for you to come back."

"You do know how he escaped last time, don't you?"

"Yes, I'm completely aware. Don't panic, he's got a fully armed escort. We'll catch them up at the border." She stepped aside and ushered them out of the door. "We need to get moving."

"But what about Mum?" George said. "We can't just leave her."

"She chose to run, George. We can't help her if she insists on running," Sam said.

"My team will keep looking," Cate said. "She won't get far on foot. We'll find her."

George slunk past Cate and stepped outside. The daylight had all but disappeared, so Cate led the way with one of her officers up ahead and one trailing at the back.

George trudged behind his dad as they made their way back towards the road. He resigned himself to the fact that the day was over. Elías and Dupont were on their way to hospital, Victor was being transported back to the UK, and now he was being escorted home – leaving his mum to fend for herself.

He thought about the day and everything that had happened, and his heart felt heavy. He had been there – been responsible for taking Victor down, so why did he feel so deflated? Surely the day had been a success? But he couldn't help feeling like he had lost again.

Always the loser.

He lifted his chin and tried to focus on the positives. He had been reunited with his mother, he had helped her escape and he had to have confidence in her ability to make it back home.

She's survived this long. Surely, she can look after herself.

All he could hope was that it wouldn't be long until he saw her again.

The woods had fallen silent except for the shuffle of their footsteps. George watched his misty breath as it drifted up into the canopy overhead. In between the branches, he could see stars beginning to appear. He sighed and drew in a lungful of crisp air. He was still peering up to the heavens when a distant roar stopped them all in their tracks.

"What's that?" Sam asked.

The officer up front had his hand in the air.

The sound came again.

"An engine," Cate said, looking at Sam.

"Whose engine?" Sam asked. "Who did you leave back at the road?"

"No one. We're the last."

"So, whose engine is that?"

Cate and Sam said nothing more. They just started running.

"Fall back," the officer at George's heels barked, as he sprinted past him.

George raced to catch up with Cate and Sam, but the two officers up front were rapidly disappearing into the darkness. Cate's torch just managed to light enough of the path ahead for George to see that the road was only a few feet away.

Crack!

Gunfire. Cate stopped, and Sam pulled George down to the ground.

Crack! Crack!

"Who is it?" George panted.

Sam and Cate exchanged worried looks.

"I don't know," Cate said, "but my officers will deal with it."

"Shouldn't we help them?" George asked.

"It's their job; they know what they're doing."

George could hear shouting and more gunfire, but then there was silence. The three of them sat crouched on the path.

"Is it over?" George whispered.

Sam slowly stood up.

"Careful, Sam," Cate said. "We should wait for my officers to give us the all-clear."

But Sam edged forwards. "That's if they're still alive. Give me your gun."

Cate stood up and handed Sam a small handgun. "Please be careful."

"Wait there," he said, as he crept further towards the road.

"What can you see?" George whispered.

"Nothing – pass me the torch," Sam replied.

Cate tossed him the torch and he stepped out into the road. George watched him as he raised the gun and shouted, "Step out of the vehicle!"

But no one replied, and before Sam could ask again, the entire road seemed to set alight with the roar of an engine and the blare of headlights.

Sam fired. *Crack! Crack!* But the vehicle didn't stop, and he was forced to dive out of the way as the last remaining SUV tore past them. George lunged to his dad's side, and as he looked up, he swore he saw a silhouette in the back window – the silhouette of a woman – a woman with a ponytail.

Chapter 30: Revelations

They had to wait over twenty minutes for back-up to arrive. During that time, Cate and Sam had argued non-stop about whether it was Jay who had shot the two officers and taken the SUV or whether someone else was driving.

George had insisted that the silhouette he'd seen was in the back of the SUV, but Cate wouldn't listen. She had sent out a network wide alert to track the SUV and take it out, whatever the cost.

The drive home must have taken over four hours. Cate had somehow managed to clear Sam, George and Victor through customs, even without their passports.

George had struggled to sleep, but finally the exhaustion had overtaken him. He could recall snippets of the journey but barely remembered arriving home – just that feeling of warm familiarity when his head had hit his pillow.

When he finally opened his eyes the next morning, the hazy autumn sun filled his room. For a moment, he wondered whether the whole thing had been a bad dream, until he rolled onto his side and jolted at the pain in his ribs. His body felt beaten, but his stomach ached with hunger, so he dragged back his duvet. A shiver raced across his skin, reminding him that he'd stripped to his boxers before collapsing into bed.

His stomach rumbled again, and he could hear raised voices, so he crawled out of bed, threw on some clean clothes and lumbered downstairs.

He felt like the walking dead as he stumbled past Marshall in the corridor but was soon brought into the land of the living as he approached the kitchen door and heard three voices.

Dad, Gran and ... a Spanish voice.

He loitered outside the door, listening to the conversation.

"I just can't believe you've known all this time and not told me," Sam said.

Gran sighed. "Not so long, boy. I didn't believe it at first. It took quite some convincing here by Eddie."

Eddie?

"Jay warned me that she was stubborn," the Spanish voice said.

"How long?" Sam asked. "How long have you known?"

"A year, maybe more," Gran replied. "But to begin with, I was sceptical. She sent me letters through Eddie. She begged me not to tell you. She said that MI6 and Victor would be watching."

"You still could have told me."

"There was nothing to tell, boy. I knew nothing of where she was or what she was doing. She just wanted letters back. News of how you were and photos of George. So, I obliged," Gran said. "She said that if everything went to plan, she'd be home ... but she didn't know..."

"When?" George said, pushing open the door. "When will she be home?"

His dad and Gran stood wrapped in their dressing gowns around the breakfast bar, talking to the postman!

"My boy!" Gran said, trotting towards him and smothering him in a hug.

Sam rubbed his eyes and collapsed onto one of the bar stools.

"What's *he* doing here?" George asked, once Gran had let go.

"Georgie, don't be so rude," Gran tutted. "This is Eduardo Correa – a friend of your mother's."

"Oh, right," George mumbled.

"You can call me Eddie," Eduardo said, holding out his hand to George.

"I was just explaining to your father that Eddie here has been acting as a go-between, communicating between your mother and I."

"Have you heard from her?" George asked, looking hopefully at Eddie.

"No, I'm sorry," he replied, "not since yesterday morning."

George felt dazed. He swayed a little and had to grab hold of the door frame.

"Come and sit down, my boy," Gran said, fussing over him. "Have something to eat – there's toast and jam."

George plonked himself on the empty stool next to his dad, while his Gran poured him a tea.

"When did you last see her?" Sam asked.

"She keeps her distance," Eddie said. "I last saw her that night."

"What night?"

"The night your mother was kidnapped. She'd been watching from a distance. I didn't know that she'd come so close. She was in the woods, after the fire at the school. She saw Angelika leave and tried to follow her. Then, somehow, she got wind of Victor's plan to break in here and she called me – made me drive her here. But we were too late."

"It was her!" George said. "I saw her running down the street just before we got home; just after the post van nearly ran us off the road."

Eddie smiled apologetically. "That may have been me. She sent me to help pick up Victor's tail."

Sam shook his head. "So, what was the last thing she said to you? Do we have anything to go on?"

"She asked us to locate the files," Gran said.

"What files?"

"The files that Victor had edited and sent to MI5. The videos of her supposedly trading information for her freedom."

"Supposedly?" Sam asked.

"When she escaped, Victor desperately wanted to stop her from coming back to UK," Eddie said. "She knew so much about him and his network. He had to discredit her; to make her go underground. He sent the recorded footage of her direct to MI5, to your chief, who then put her status up to 'most wanted' with immediate effect and called in MI6 to try to track her down."

"So, she sent us looking for the originals – the ones that prove her innocence," Gran added.

"Wouldn't Victor have destroyed them?" George asked.

"He thought he had," Gran grinned.

"But Mr Jefferson had got his hands on them and taken copies," Eddie added. "Maybe he thought he could use them as bribery or to make a deal."

"Jennifer discovered that Jefferson had given them to his son," Gran said.

"What?" Sam said.

"Jefferson has a son, Peter MacGuire."

"Yes, I know. Jay sent me looking for him," Sam said.

"Well, then you'll know that he's a student at Royal Holloway. And that's where he's been holding the memory stick with the files on this whole time."

"And how exactly did *you* get your hands on them?" Sam asked, raising an eyebrow.

"I'm not without my contacts," Gran smiled. "It so happens that an old friend of mine is the Dean."

"Really?" George said.

"Really," Gran said. "So, yesterday, Eddie and I paid him a visit and found out where Peter lives."

Gran stood leaning against the sink with a broad grin on her face. Sam and George just glared at her.

"Oh, God," Sam said. "What did you do? Please tell me you didn't break into his digs?"

George actually smiled. The thought of Gran as a criminal was vaguely amusing.

"No!" she replied, "I used my womanly charm and–"

"There was an urgent pest problem," Eddie said.

"What?" Sam asked, puzzled.

"Rats," Eddie said. "The neighbour had reported rats."

Sam shook his head. "Pretending to be pest exterminators is the same as breaking in."

Eddie shrugged. "We did them a favour. The place stank. I bug-bombed it when I left. It smelt much better."

George laughed.

"I don't think this is funny," Sam said, curtly.

"We have the files," Gran said. "That's all that matters. Once your chief sees them–"

"What? You haven't given them to anyone, have you?" Sam asked.

"No," Gran said. "I tried to call you first, but you didn't answer."

With that, the doorbell rang, making them all jump.

"Who's calling at this time?" Gran grumbled, shuffling towards the kitchen door.

"I'll go," George said.

"Check who it is!" Sam called after him.

George went into the lounge and peered through the net curtains.

"It's Cate," he whispered back towards the kitchen.

"I'll get it," Sam groaned, dragging himself towards the door.

"Wait!" Eddie called after him. "I can't break my cover. I'm your wife's only contact point. Cate will wonder what the hell I'm doing in here!"

They all stood in the corridor.

"Let me handle it," Gran said, pushing past.

"Call me the minute you hear from her," Sam said to Eddie.

Eddie nodded, pulled on his Post Office cap and picked up his delivery bag.

Gran threw open the door and shoved a handful of toast into Eddie's hands. "There you go, young man. That will keep you going on your rounds. Must keep your strength up."

"Er, thanks," Eddie said, stepping past a baffled looking Cate.

"Remember to call again next time!" Gran shouted after him. "I'm baking banana bread tomorrow!"

Cate stood squashed up against the hedge that bordered the path.

"Oh, it's you," Gran snorted. "What do you want?"

Sam stood on the doorstep behind Gran. "You come to put cuffs on us?"

"No," Cate said, looking down at her hands. "I've come to apologise."

"Huh! I should think so too," Gran huffed.

"Can I come in?"

Sam led her through to the kitchen. Gran hovered by the sink while George stood at the kitchen door; his arms folded.

Cate looked around at the gathered faces. George could see her running her tongue over her teeth and struggling to swallow.

"Is there any chance of a glass of water?" she asked, putting down her bag. "I've been working all night."

Gran didn't move, and Sam had to lean over her to grab a glass from the draining board and fill it from the tap.

Cate glugged half the pint down and then rested it on the counter.

"I've got some good news," she said, focusing on Sam. "Therese Dupont just came out of surgery and is stable. She and Elías will be on their way back here as soon as we can get through the extradition paperwork."

"Good," Sam said, re-tying his dressing gown cord.

"Devant's team are still looking for Angelika and the Chinese woman."

"Jin-é," George said.

"Yes."

"And Mum?" George asked. "Are you still looking for her?"

Cate took another swig of water. "Well – yes, but not quite in the same way."

"What's that supposed to mean?" Sam asked.

"A lot's happened overnight. The situation has … changed."

"How exactly?"

"Firstly, the reason that Officer Devant took so long to get to the airfield was that she apprehended someone on her approach."

"Go on," Sam said.

"She stopped a car that was speeding away from the area with a rather large dent in the bonnet."

George clutched at his side and locked eyes with his dad.

"And?" Sam pressed.

"It's just, we were a little surprised to discover who was driving it…"

"Spit it out, Cate!" Sam said, losing his patience.

"It was your partner – Freddie Crane."

Sam stood dumbstruck, his mouth hanging open.

"He wasn't supposed to be in Paris," George said. "He was back here leading the case of…"

George had a sudden flashback: tyres screeching, his ribs cracking, his head hitting the ground and a large pair of mud-clad boots, and then: tip-tap, tip tap across the hangar's concrete floor.

"Jin-é's feet!" he blurted out.

"What's that, boy?' Gran asked.

"Jin-é's feet are tiny. I mean, it wasn't her that picked me up and took me to the hangar after I was hit by the car. It was a man – a man with boots – large boots. It must have been Freddie! He must have been there, with Jin-é – with Victor! It must have been him in the car!"

"Not Freddie," Sam said, shaking his head. "That can't be right."

"It makes sense, Dad," George insisted. "Think about it. You said it: a mole inside MI5, someone who had knowledge of the case, where we lived…" Sam was still shaking his head. "Dad, it was probably him. That night, outside the village hall – and – wait! It was probably him that came here – and took Gran!"

"No, no, I don't believe it," Sam said, struggling to swallow. "I know Freddie, he's been my partner for–"

"Sam, I'm sorry, but there's more," Cate interrupted.

"What?" Sam said, snatching George's tea and glugging a mouthful.

"He had your chief – in the boot."

Sam actually snorted tea out of his nose.

"He what?"

"He had him bound and gagged. It looks like he accosted him at La Défense and brought him to the hangar, but when he saw that you'd arrived and that everything wasn't going to plan, he fled."

"Why? Why would he take the chief?"

"We're not completely sure, he's not saying much and your chief is still a bit woozy, but we think he got wind of the forensics report from the fire in the woods."

"The fire Felix saw?" George asked.

"Yes," Cate said. "It took a while to piece together the burnt fragments, but it was mainly classified documents with the MI5 seal: maps, building blueprints but also photographs."

"Photographs of what?" George asked.

"Photographs of Freddie meeting with Philippe Bernard and another unknown person."

"Bribery?" Sam asked.

"Most likely. It looks like Victor had something on Freddie – something that he leveraged to force him to give over the information about the hub and the vault. When Victor got the weapon and his team out, he must have promised to leave all the evidence in the woods for Freddie to burn. But I imagine that as soon as Freddie realised that your chief had received the forensic report, he panicked and made his way to Paris to take him out."

"My God!" Sam said, slumping back down onto the bar stool. "Freddie – a mole and right under my nose."

"So, if Freddie's the mole, then Mum's definitely off the hook," George said, excitedly. "It wasn't her that gave Victor the intel. You can't arrest her now."

"Um, I..." Cate seemed reluctant to respond. She tried to catch Sam's eye but his head was in his hands.

"We've got the tapes – the real ones – we can prove she's innocent!" George went on.

"We need to find a way of contacting her," Gran said.

But Cate still said nothing.

"We need to let her know that she can come home!" George added.

Cate looked at Sam again. "Sam, I ... maybe I could have a moment with you ... alone."

Sam sighed and lifted his head. "What more could there possibly be to say?"

"It's sensitive and I..."

"There's nothing you can't say in front of Mum and George. I think they've been through enough to earn the right to be included."

She glanced nervously at George and then back at Sam. "Have you heard from her?"

"No," Sam said, cautiously.

"I'm not trying to catch you out, Sam. I need your help. I genuinely need to know if she's tried to make contact."

"No," Sam repeated. "I take it you lost all trace of her then."

Cate took a deep breath. "The team kept looking all night." She glanced again at George. "We didn't find her – but we did find the SUV."

"And?" George asked.

"Well, the reason for my apology is that I think you may have been right. I don't think it was her that stole the SUV. I think that she was taken – probably by the same person that ambushed Elías and Dupont."

"I told you!" George said. "I told you she wouldn't have done that – I told you she was in the back – she wasn't driving!"

"Wait," Sam said, looking at Cate. "What exactly made you come to that conclusion?"

George's fleeting glee at being right was suddenly dampened by the concern he could see in his dad's eyes.

"Her weapons and comms – they were all still inside the vehicle," Cate replied.

"She could have dumped them on purpose," Sam said. "What else?"

"I'm really sorry," Cate said, looking at them each in turn. "But there were signs of a … struggle."

"What kind of signs?" Sam said, standing up from his stool.

She swallowed hard again. "Um … blood … traces of blood."

"Her blood?" Sam asked.

George could feel his knees going weak. Gran came closer and wrapped her arms around him.

"We ran DNA," Cate said. "Her blood was all over the back seats."

"No!" George said. "You're lying!"

"I'm sorry, I really am – but if she hadn't had run…"

"No! This is your fault!" George screamed at Cate. "If you'd believed in her, she wouldn't have needed to run! She'd be right here now – here, at home with us, where she belongs!"

"George!" Gran said, trying to hold him tighter.

But George had heard enough. He tore from his gran's arms, burst out of the kitchen, flew up the stairs and threw himself onto his bed; slamming his door closed behind him.

Chapter 31: Dancing Moths

George spent most of the day shut up in his room with his head buried in the TV. Sam went into the office to help Cate, and although Gran tried to console George, he just wanted to be left alone. He ignored phone calls from his friends, he ignored his growling stomach and he tried to ignore the draw of the tattered, brown envelope that sat abandoned on his desk.

It was dusk by the time he turned the TV off and collapsed back onto his bed. His eyes drifted to the pile of filthy clothes on his bedroom floor – more ruined uniform and his mother's jacket.

His heart sank. He rolled onto his back and lay staring at the photo of her on his windowsill. Her cheeks were fuller then. Her wavy, chestnut hair softly curled around her shoulders and a light fringe skimmed her dark eyes. It was difficult to see her as the same woman. She looked so different now: the ever-changing hair colour, the freckles, the dark eye-liner or the coloured lenses, but most of all her thin frame and drawn-in cheeks. Years in captivity and on the run had changed her – as it would anyone.

He closed his eyes and tried to picture her in the woods in Paris, and he realised one thing: however much her appearance had changed, it was something about her eyes that made him feel safe. It was the first thing he'd noticed when he bumped into her at the science fair and the last thing he'd seen when she left his side in the woods. Her eyes held something – he couldn't quite put his finger on it, but it was what had made him trust her.

He sat up and grabbed the framed photo. He held it up and stared at it. The light bounced off his face, and he caught a glimpse of his own reflection in the glass. Then it hit him. Looking into his mum's eyes was like looking into his own. He saw everything about him in her eyes: his fears, his frustrations, his determination. They were so similar and yet he barely knew her.

He glanced over at the desk, and the brown envelope stared back at him. He finally gave in to temptation, plucked it off the desk and emptied the photographs onto his mattress.

Birthday candles, riding his bike, on the beach … he flicked through them, and with every turn, his vision grew more blurred as he tried to hold back the tears. He could feel the anger and the anguish swelling inside him.

Where is she?

He hurled the photos towards the bedroom door, and they fluttered through the air in a cascade of colour before scattering across the carpet. He screwed his eyes shut and tried to suppress the scream that was fighting to erupt from within him.

Who did this?

He had no idea if he'd ever see her again or whether she was even still alive, but when he opened his eyes again, he saw something glaring up at him from beneath the mosaic of glossy paper – his face – close up – the picture of him – the one from the hangar.

Jin-é!

He tumbled out of bed and snatched it up. It was blurry and out of focus, but it was unmistakably the photo that Jin-é had taken. He flipped it over, expecting nothing, but there, scrawled in black ink, clear as day, was her message to him.

'La Resistance'

The warrior who seeks revenge should first dig two graves.
Be careful of what you seek, fierce boy x

He sank into his pillow and cried. He cried the kind of
tears that come in a tidal wave, flushing away the anger,
draining out the anxiety and leaving only exhaustion.

That night he dreamt. He dreamt of a room: blood-red
walls, black silk hanging at the windows, billowing in the
breeze and a single red lantern hanging from the rafters.
Golden light filtered through its patterned sides, sending
an array of shapes dancing across the walls – dancing
moths – dancing, golden moths.

EPILOGUE:

Sabrina Fraulove was plucked from the Seine by French Police and taken into custody. MI5 have requested her extradition to the UK to face trial for her part in the murder of MI5 officials, attack on Oakfield Manor and theft of MI5 property. She also faces charges in France for her part in the attack on Paris.

Jose Gonzalez was found stumbling out of the catacombs with serious concussion after his run in with Felix's Eiffel Tower. Jennifer Jenkins' Alpha team held him for several hours, pressing him for information and then dumped him outside the Police Headquarters in Paris. He was taken to a high security hospital where he also awaits extradition and trial for the attacks in London and Paris.

Alex Allaman's body was pulled out of the catacombs and returned to Switzerland.

Austin Van der Berg was caught by French authorities trying to flee the city in an armoured security truck – he sustained several injuries during the arrest. He claims to have had nothing to do with the attack or the theft of several highly valuable Rothkos from the Louvre.

JP's body was never found. However, a person by his description was treated for a punctured lung in a nearby hospital before discharging himself. MI5 still want to speak to him. His father, **Marcel Perron**, was tracked down by MI5 and offered asylum and a safe house in the UK if he continued to share what he knew of Victor's network with them.

Angelika Volkov was not found. MI5 believe that, as soon as Victor had been apprehended, she fled the city with the Rothkos. She remains on their 'Most Wanted' list.

Jin-é was not found. However, thanks to George's evidence, MI5 believe that she fled Paris with **Jennifer Jenkins** (Jay), potentially as a hostage. She is now on their 'Most Wanted' list, and a special task force has been set up to track her and Jennifer down.

Cate Knowles had been sent by MI6 to shadow **Sam Jenkins** with the specific orders to do whatever it takes to locate and intercept his wife. After the events in Paris, she reported back to MI6 that, due to new evidence, Jennifer's status should be reduced from 'Most Wanted' to 'Person of Interest'. MI6 still want to question **Jennifer Jenkins** about her involvement in several overseas incidents and are keen to work alongside MI5 to track her down and find out the truth behind her seven years of absence.

Chief eventually regained consciousness and reported that Freddie Crane had indeed abducted him at gun point at La Défense, smuggled him out of the building using the chief's pass, knocked him out and stowed him in the boot of his car. Chief was also able to clarify that he had sent Sam to Paris on Freddie's suggestion.

Freddie Crane is waiting to face an internal investigation and possible trial for treason, espionage and aiding the attacks on London and Paris.

Peter MacGuire (Mr Jefferson's son) went on the run after realising that someone had broken into his digs and stolen the memory stick that his father had given him. MI5 would like to speak to him.

Most of Jennifer's mysterious associates (Team ALPHA) vanished back into thin air, except **Therese Dupont (TDP), Elías García** and **Eduardo (Eddie the Postman) Correa** who have agreed to work alongside MI5 to help track down the whereabouts of Jennifer Jenkins.

Victor Sokolov was smuggled out of Paris by MI6 immediately after he was captured. He is being held in a top security isolation cell and awaits questioning and trial.

Sam Jenkins is heading up the task force that aims to find Angelika Volkov, the stolen Rothkos, the Russian weapon, Jin-é and Jennifer Jenkins.

George Jenkins intends to do everything he can to help!

Thank you for reading **The Undergrounders and the Deception of the Dead**.

If you enjoyed this adventure, please head over to Amazon to find book three in the trilogy, **The Undergrounders & the Malice of the Moth.**

In the meantime, I would love to hear your feedback, so please leave a review on Amazon and follow me on:
Website: ctfrankcom.com
Twitter: @ctfrankcom
Facebook: CT Frankcom
Instagram: CT Frankcom

Printed in Great Britain
by Amazon